Sarah Vern began writing fiction as a hobby, which she continued after giving up her job to become a full-time mother. She went to Strathclyde University as a mature student and gained a BA in English and Psychology, followed by a postgraduate Diploma in Education to qualify as an English teacher. After teaching for several years, branching into pastoral care, a creative urge during the school holidays produced *The Witching Woman* and its sequel, *The Woman Outside*. She lives in Lanarkshire, Scotland.

THE WOMAN OUTSIDE

Alexander McNair is a changed man since visiting the island of Tora. He is now heir to the Strathcairn estate, and the discovery of his son has precipitated his marriage to Victoria Liversidge, whom he met and seduced on Tora. As the couple vanishes abroad on honeymoon, Alexander hopes to forget Mhairi-Anne Graham — the Witching Woman — who claimed his heart during his island visit. But when they both learn that James McNair has become engaged to Mhairi-Anne, Alexander is consumed with jealousy — whilst Victoria is terrified her husband may discover that he has married the wrong woman.

Books by Sarah Vern
Published by The House of Ulverscroft:

THE WITCHING WOMAN

SARAH VERN

THE WOMAN OUTSIDE

Complete and Unabridged

ULVERSCROFT
Leicester

First published in Great Britain in 2006 by
Robert Hale Limited
London

First Large Print Edition
published 2006
by arrangement with
Robert Hale Limited
London

The moral right of the author has been asserted

British Library Cataloguing in Publication Data

Vern, Sarah
    The woman outside.—Large print ed.—
Ulverscroft large print series: romance
    1. Inheritance and succession—Fiction
    2. Islands—Scotland—Fiction 3. Love stories
    4. Large type books
    I. Title
    823.9′2 [F]

    ISBN 1–84617–560–7

Published by
F. A. Thorpe (Publishing)
Anstey, Leicestershire

Set by Words & Graphics Ltd.
Anstey, Leicestershire
Printed and bound in Great Britain by
T. J. International Ltd., Padstow, Cornwall

This book is printed on acid-free paper

1

Although the couple had now vanished abroad on an extended honeymoon, the scandal surrounding the marriage of Alexander McNair to Victoria Liversidge, during August 1897, continued to reverberate over the vast Strathcairn estate and the surrounding district for many weeks after the quiet ceremony had taken place.

'It was only to be expected,' said Lady McNair consolingly to her husband the day after the wedding, when belated messages of 'congratulations' began to roll in accusingly from many of the local gentry, who considered they had been deprived of an invitation. After all, their son had been one of the most eligible bachelors in Scotland — handsome heir to the Strathcairn estate and the vast McNair fortune, since the death of his elder brother, Eric. Even without the titillating element of his sudden acquisition of a seven-month old son, his unceremonious departure from the marriage market was bound to have caused a banquet of gossip among the ranks of young women and their families, whose personal designs upon him had now been thwarted.

'By the time they return, all the minutiae will be forgotten and no one will have the nerve to comment on our grandchild's age,' resumed Lady McNair, one manicured hand patting a soft satin cushion, before she sat down to pour afternoon tea in her elegant drawing-room. Now in her fifties, Rowena was still a beautiful woman, slim in figure, with only traces of grey in her thick, light brown hair and every graceful movement highlighted her aristocratic breeding.

As she turned her startling, mink-coloured eyes on her husband, Sir David muttered sardonically, 'Ever the optimist, Rowena!' The waspish edge to his tone suggested, however, that his wife had still some way to go to convince him of her theory.

'I thought Victoria looked wonderful,' commented Isobel, the wistfulness of her tone drawing her mother-in-law's eyes.

'As you did, my dear,' responded Rowena gently, noting the pallor of the younger woman's complexion, as she recalled the lavish celebration which had taken place when her older son had married. Isobel was now missing Alexander, of course, as she had come to depend so heavily upon him, since Eric's death the year before. 'I'm sure you and Victoria will become great friends on their return.'

'At least, she's of our class,' conceded Sir David, grudgingly, as he took the cup of tea, proffered by his wife. 'I suppose that's something — although I dare say some of our acquaintances will be only too delighted to remind us that her father chose to shoot himself into the hereafter.'

'Oh, David, you're impossible! That was ages ago!' retorted Rowena, after passing a cup to Isobel, but she decided not to remonstrate any further on this point, as she was well aware that her husband still needed a degree of humouring, to recover fully from the shock of Alexander's belated discovery that he had fathered a child during his visit to the island of Tora the year before. The product of a military background, Sir David had the decided tendency to view most situations in black and white, until his wife pointed out other tonal possibilities. At heart, a kind man and loving husband, he could, nevertheless, do an excellent imitation of an autocrat, who would brook no argument. He presided as laird over the Strathcairn Estate with all the aplomb of a general, complete with a mane of iron-grey hair and whiskers to match. Only Rowena knew that he had a soft core and had cried like an infant on the night Alexander had announced the existence of their grandson.

Of course, the child would be their salvation, thought Rowena now, as she sipped her tea thoughtfully. Once all the gossip had died down and they returned from abroad, David would be a devoted grandfather — of that she had no doubt. He had doted on both Eric and Alexander, as children, and they would have had more offspring, but for two painful miscarriages she had suffered. Only as the boys had grown into men, had David's relationship with Alexander become strained. Understandably, she thought, Eric, as the older son and heir, had become closer to his father, while Alexander, secretly her favourite, had gone through a rebellious, extravagant phase, which had tested David's temper on numerous occasions. Although they had grown closer again after Alexander's return from Tora and in the months before Eric's death, they had, in fact, barely been on speaking terms, she recalled now, when David had insisted that Alexander, as heir to his uncle's infamous island, pay a visit to see James on Tora, in the spring of 1896.

She, herself, had only visited Tora once many years before, when Elizabeth, James's wife had died — and once had been enough. Consequently, she had not blamed Alexander

4

for his reluctance to comply, as his inheritance of this remote island had long been something of a joke in the family. James's castle was a medieval, draughty warren of a place, in her opinion, and she had taken an instant aversion to being so visibly surrounded on all sides by the choking grey of the cold Atlantic Ocean, as well as sweeping hills and moorland, bereft of any woodland or the flowers she loved so much at Strathcairn. David disliked it, too, for the very different reason that the island was not and never would be, in his view, a money-making piece of property and he was still set on Alexander selling it immediately, when it came into his hands, and particularly now he was also heir to Strathcairn. Not that Alexander agreed with his father on this issue, since his enforced visit, Rowena suspected. Like James, it seemed that he had, ironically, developed a bond with the island, although she wondered now whether this view had been influenced by the recently discovered fact that he had met Victoria there and evidently fathered Alex, his child.

'Pity, James and Calum had to leave this morning,' said Sir David presently, interrupting his wife's reveries, while he helped himself to another delicious scone, which was still slightly warm from the oven. 'But I think

Calum had some urgent business in Perth.'

'I was surprised they came to the wedding at all,' responded Rowena. 'It seems to me the older your brother gets, the more besotted he is with that island of his, but I suppose Alexander is the nearest he'll ever have to a son of his own.' She paused to glare at the swiftly vanishing scone on her husband's plate. 'Do be careful with those crumbs, David! You know how Robbie hates a mess in the drawing-room.'

Well aware that it was his wife, not their housekeeper, Mrs Robertson, who objected to the mess, Sir David cast her a disdainful glance, before defiantly brushing his hand down his front, so that an avalanche of crumbs snowed on to the floor.

'I must say I like Calum,' Isobel intervened tactfully. 'He seems like a wise old soul.'

Distracted, as intended, from her husband and her drawing-room carpet, Rowena responded, 'Yes — I noticed Alexander spent quite some time talking to him.'

'He may look like Santa Claus, Isobel, but he's a wily *old soul*,' rejoined Sir David, a trifle sarcastically, having wiped his mouth with his napkin and calculated that Calum, at ten years older than James, was nearer his own age than he would have liked. 'Tough as old boots, I'd say, if his exploits in Nova

Scotia are to be believed. Made a fortune there, according to Alexander.'

'Which he's spending on your brother's island,' resumed Rowena silkily, before adding with a smile at Isobel, 'I think he's certainly been a Santa Claus to James.'

Sir David's bushy grey eyebrows twitched his concession. 'That, I'll grant you,' he admitted gruffly. 'I'd always wondered how James managed to keep his head above water on that island of his. Now we know.'

'Your brother never had a head for figures,' observed Rowena, laying down her fine china cup carefully on the saucer.

'Not the profit-making kind, at any rate!' muttered her husband wryly, before catching his wife's warning look, which told him there was no need to lower the tone of the discussion by commenting on his younger brother's womanizing exploits in front of Isobel.

Rowena stood up then and tugged a gentle summons to the servants' quarters on the thick tasselled cord, which hung adjacent to the fireplace. 'I think I'll go up for my nap now.'

Isobel rose, too, from her chair. 'Do you think Alexander and Victoria will be in England, by now?'

Rowena glanced at the grandmother clock,

which adorned one wall. 'I should think so. They will probably be exhausted by the time they cross the Channel.'

'But it will be so romantic — travelling all over Europe,' sighed Isobel enviously, as she followed her mother-in-law from the room.

Sir David waited for the soft click of the door after the two women departed, before he reached for another scone and sat back to demolish it in messy comfort, before the servants came to clear everything away. It was all very well for women to be carried away by romantic notions, he thought cynically, but men had to keep a level head. Certainly, Alexander had developed better than he had ever expected, in the wake of Eric's death, but his irresponsible behaviour on Tora had landed them with this scandal to weather and his determination to marry this girl had been a bitter potion for Sir David to swallow, considering he could probably have bought his way out of the mess. Still, the child was certainly his and that was a huge bonus, he concluded with some satisfaction, as he licked the crumbs from his fingers. Nobody would be able to say young Alex was a cuckoo in the nest, as he was already Alexander's double: not a bit like his mother, ironically, but that did not matter.

As the servants arrived to clear away all the

paraphernalia of afternoon tea, Sir David rose to go to his study, little realizing that his grandson's lack of resemblance to Victoria Liversidge was significant in a way he could never have guessed — a fact which Calum MacRitchie was about to discover in Perth.

2

Of those present at the McNairs' wedding, none was entitled to be more surprised than Calum that Alexander had evidently had an intimate relationship with Victoria on Tora — for the very good reason that Calum, alone, was uncomfortably aware, it was Mhairi-Anne Graham with whom he had fallen in love — not Victoria. Indeed, not only had he enjoyed a brief affair with *her*, during James's absence, he had departed from Tora in a desperate frame of mind, after she had vanished from his life.

Alexander had apparently felt the embarrassment of Calum's knowledge the day before, because he had sought some time alone with him, to express his self-disgust. But Calum had always liked Alexander and he was not in the business of judging anyone. Besides, he knew only too well that James had been pushing Alexander and Victoria together for his own very selfish reason: Mhairi-Anne had been *his* mistress for almost nine years before his nephew's arrival.

Long accustomed to relying on plain, unvarnished truth, Calum had not liked lying to Alexander on his wedding day, to the effect that he had heard nothing of Mhairi-Anne since her disappearance, and he was even less comfortable the following day, when he felt the need to lie again — this time to James — in order to explain away his intention to remain in Perth and not return immediately to Tora with him.

'Don't be staying away too long,' said James affably, when their coach stopped in Perth to set Calum down.

'I'll see how he is,' Calum mumbled, as he swung open the door, referring to the ailing imaginary friend from his Nova Scotia days, whom he had manufactured as the reason for his stay. 'All being well, I'll be back in a few days.'

James nodded, while Calum closed the door. 'Hope he's on the mend! See you soon then.'

Calum waved guiltily, as the coach rattled away and he turned to pick up his case, before entering The Swan Hotel which seemed to be the obvious place to stay, considering it had been mentioned in the strange letter he had received. Not that he intended to ask any questions there, at this juncture. He had a much more important task in mind and, as soon as he was settled with his luggage in his room, he ordered a coach to take him to St Magdalene's Convent Hospital. On the way there, he rested his head back on the padded seat, as he reflected on the fact that James would be utterly furious with him if he learned that his decision to remain in Perth had anything to do with his former mistress. Only last week, he had stood gazing morosely out of a window in the castle on to a bleak, rainy day and muttered involuntarily, 'Do you ever wonder where she is?'

Calum had looked up reluctantly from his newspaper. The problem was that James had never learned of her affair with Alexander and still cherished the unlikely notion she might return to him. Consequently, he was cruelly unsympathetic, only to be kind. 'Aye, but there's no good wonderin'. You had your chance with her and never took it.'

In fact, James had had more than one chance to make Mhairi-Anne his wife, but had chosen otherwise for rather selfish reasons, Calum thought. Born the only child of crofters, Mhairi-Anne, who was six months younger than Alexander, had been like a daughter to the late Elizabeth McNair, who had sponsored her education on the mainland. At eighteen years of age, she had returned to the island, but had regularly been forced to seek refuge at the castle, during her widowed father's drunken rages. By this time, however, Elizabeth had died and one night, James, then in his early forties, had seduced her. This was James's first opportunity, but — as he told Calum one night — he 'took cold feet' and stood by while she sought her own escape in marrying someone else.

Her marriage to a young crofter had been brief and calamitous, before James had finally taken a level of responsibility for her, in the wake of her husband's death. Their ensuing affair had been an open secret on the island, with Mhairi-Anne reviled as a slut, because they still remained unmarried, while James, as proprietor of Tora, was considered entitled to his weakness. Nevertheless, he had installed her as the island's school teacher and given her a home at the castle — a situation which had prevailed until Alexander's visit.

Unfortunately, James had insisted then that his private life remain private and the peculiar tight-knit intimacy of island life was his ready-made insurance policy against any outsider like Alexander, being included in gossip. A mere whisper from the castle had been enough to ensure there were no misunderstandings. The master wanted no blabbing! Thus, Alexander had all too readily swallowed James's explanation that the alluring young widow had been like a daughter to his late wife and he had only finally learned the truth from her own lips, when it was already too late.

The last time Calum had seen Mhairi-Anne had been more than a year before, when she had secretly fled from Tora, believing that prolonging her affair with Alexander could only ruin his life, and ending her relationship with James. But on the day after his brief conversation with James on the subject of her whereabouts, Calum had received an intriguing letter, which had necessitated this journey. Presently, he extracted it from his pocket, to reread this strange epistle, while the coach rattled along a cobbled Perthshire street.

Dear Sir
You will, no doubt, be surprised to receive this communication from a perfect stranger, but I believe that you may be acquainted with a young woman who is currently a patient in my ward at St Magdalene's.

She was brought here more than two weeks ago in tragic circumstances, having been found washed up on the banks of the River Tay and initially presumed drowned. Indeed, she was nearer death than life for several days thereafter, as she remained unconscious to all our attempts to revive

14

her. During that time, police enquiries ascertained that she was, in all likelihood, a Mrs Graham, who had recently been reported missing from The Swan Hotel in Perth and, indeed she was subsequently identified as this person by the hotel manager, while she remained comatose.

How she ended up in the river is uncertain, although the police are satisfied that there are no suspicious circumstances to suggest anything other than an accident — or a deliberate attempt to end her own life. Events since she recovered consciousness appear more consistent with the latter, as, unfortunately, although she is physically gaining strength, her mental state continues to cause serious concern. While she is polite and appreciative of our care, essentially she talks little to anyone, which is particularly worrying, as we are convinced that she carries the psychological burden of some catastrophe which has befallen her and that she needs to share this load, if she is to recover from her trauma.

It is for this reason that I am contacting you and as you may immediately wonder how I came to believe you may be interested, let me explain at once that when Mrs Graham's belongings were brought to us from *The Swan Hotel* while she was yet unconscious, we found among them a letter addressed to you, which had never been posted. This, I am taking the liberty of passing on to you, although I have to confess that I do so without the writer's permission, as I fear this may be withheld, because she has repeatedly insisted that she has no friends or relations who may wish to visit her.

Soon, I fear, she will have to be released from St Magdalene's. There is already talk that she may be transferred to an institution in Aberdeen — with, or without, her permission, given the absence of next-of-kin and our concern that she may come to some further harm. If you are her friend, as I hope, she desperately needs your support if this course is to be avoided.

Yours sincerely
Sister Mary Theresa
St Magdalene's Convent Hospital

Calum turned now to read once more the letter in Mhairi-Anne's familiar hand, which had been attached, as indicated, and which had been written on Swan Hotel crested notepaper.

16

My Dear Calum

It is so very long since I saw you and I write now with no good news. I am in a desperate situation and do not know where to turn or what to do. Unfortunately, I cannot leave this hotel, where I am currently residing, as I await news, which I fear may never come. Would it be possible for you to visit me here as soon as possible — without telling James? I know this is a lot to ask, but you are the only person from whom I might seek advice, which I urgently need. Please come quickly if you can.

Love, Mhairi-Anne

As Calum carefully folded the letter, before returning it to the envelope, he wondered once more what vital 'news' had held her restrained in The Swan Hotel and led her to such desperation. He could only speculate, of course, but felt instinctively that it must somehow be connected to the wedding he had attended the day before. Had possibly learning of this so crushed her that she had attempted to take her own life, as the nun had suggested? Somehow, he doubted it, although he fully appreciated the strength of feeling which had existed between her and Alexander, and which — from Alexander's

17

clumsy question the day before — he suspected still haunted him, at any rate. But it seemed altogether uncharacteristic of Mhairi-Anne that she should write to him, if her desperation had been instigated solely by the marriage. She had always been a proud creature, more likely to hide her personal feelings than display them, but people change, he reminded himself, and he was basing his assessment more on her relationship with James, than with Alexander. The fact, too, that she had never actually posted the letter might indicate she had decided that she did not wish his interference and he could only hope that his arrival now would be welcome.

As the coach drew up at the iron gates of St Magdalene's, Calum promptly climbed down and, having told the driver to wait, he lifted the rusty latch to push open the heavy gate, which protected a driveway beyond. His feet crunched on the gravel beneath his feet, as he wound his way through thick, swaying trees for more than a hundred yards, before he reached the locked front door of the hospital. After giving the brass bell a solitary tug, he glanced around, noting that the dark, grey stone building was attached to a chapel and other living-quarters, where he presumed the nuns resided. A strange place for Mhairi-Anne to end up, he thought, as the door creaked open fractionally.

'Can I help you?' An elderly nun peered rather timidly out at him.

He immediately explained his business and was relieved to find himself promptly ushered inside.

'I'm so pleased you've come,' said the nun, walking at a leisurely pace beside him, although her voice clearly betrayed some excitement.

'I take it, you're Sister Mary Theresa?' queried Calum quietly, as they proceeded along a broad arched corridor, in which their voices echoed around them.

'Oh no — I'm Sister Bernadette, but we've all been praying for Mrs Graham — such a sad case.' She glanced up at Calum, her small eyes twinkling. 'God does listen, you know.'

Calum nodded respectfully, although the idea that he was being classified as something approaching a miracle was daunting.

'Here we are,' she indicated, then pushed open the swing doors on her right. 'This is Sister Mary Theresa's ward.'

As if the mention of her name had been a summons, another nun promptly emerged from a room on the left. A much younger woman, with unflinching pale-blue eyes, she, nevertheless, had an aura of wisdom about her expression, as she openly scrutinized her bearded visitor, who, having already removed his cap to reveal the rebellious frizz of his white hair, was presented to her with a conspiratorial air of triumph by Sister Bernadette.

'He's come, Sister! Mr MacRitchie — all the way from the island of Tora.'

'How do you do, sir,' said the younger nun, inclining her head politely.

'Sister Mary Theresa, I presume?' responded Calum, nodding back, as he realized there would not be the usual introductory handshake.

'I wrote the letter, which brought you here,' the nun admitted.

'I'm glad you did, Sister.'

'You are, indeed, a friend — or a relation — of our Mrs Graham, then?'

'A good friend, I hope.'

Sister Mary Theresa allowed a small smile of satisfaction, before turning to the older nun. 'Perhaps, you could advise the Mother Superior of our visitor, Sister.' She turned then to Calum to explain. 'Our Mother Superior may wish to speak to you before you leave, Mr MacRitchie, as she agreed to the idea of my writing to you, in the first place.'

The elderly nun obediently left them alone, after another twinkling glance at Calum.

'Come, we'll talk in my office, Mr

20

MacRitchie, before you see our patient, if you don't mind,' said Sister Mary Theresa, immediately ushering Calum towards the small chamber from which she had emerged. Having invited him to sit in a comfortable seat in front of her desk, while she sat down in a leather chair behind it, she then resumed.

'You may well wonder why Mrs Graham ended up in this religious establishment, as opposed to an ordinary hospital, Mr MacRitchie. The fact is that we are frequently the recipient of patients, where death is imminent or presumed, or when a victim cannot be identified, as was initially so, in Mrs Graham's case.' She smiled briefly. 'Religion, ironically perhaps, is generally assumed to be Catholic, in these cases, until proven otherwise.'

Calum smiled with her. 'I presume you know that Mrs Graham isn't Catholic.'

'We had gathered that, but need is the governing factor with regard to our patients. Besides, we are all God's children, are we not?'

'I wouldn't argue with that, Sister.'

'Regarding our patient — Sister Bernadette suggested that it was my idea to write to you and she was correct in that, but I did so with the approval of the Mother Superior, of course, and with the encouragement of our

21

doctor, who believes that Mrs Graham needs to unburden herself, if she is to make further progress. Unfortunately, it has been very clear that — whatever provoked her tragedy — it is too personal to reveal to any strangers, however kind or willing they may be.'

'I'm certainly ready to listen, Sister, if that's what she needs.'

'On the other hand, of course, as she did not actually post her letter to you and has denied all knowledge of friends who might visit her, I have to warn you that we are a little concerned that we have brought about this meeting, without her consent, although I hope you will appreciate that we have done so entirely in her interests. Her reaction, however, might be quite the opposite from what we hope and the doctor has indicated that you should be advised not to press her.'

Calum nodded. 'I've known Mhairi-Anne a long time, Sister, so I know to go canny.'

'Mhairi-Anne . . . a lovely name! We know so very little about her.'

Briefly, Calum responded to the unspoken question expressed in the woman's eyes, by giving a censored account of Mhairi-Anne's history on Tora.

'I'm not surprised to learn she is a teacher,' responded the nun, after listening attentively. 'Despite the brevity of our conversations, it has been clear that she is an intelligent woman. But you did not say why she left Tora?'

'To see something of the world beyond the island,' Calum answered evasively.

'I see,' came the short retort, her expression telling Calum immediately that his invention had not gone unnoticed.

He decided to pose a question of his own, to obviate any further demands on his creativity. 'Has she explained how she came to be in the river?'

The nun shrugged uncertainly. 'Either she genuinely does not remember the event very clearly, or she is avoiding the issue. Apparently, she went for a walk along the riverbank and *slipped* — yes, I think that was the word she used. Of course, it's possible that this is exactly what happened, Mr MacRitchie, but my feeling is that in walking so very close to a dangerous river that one could *slip* in, she may have been contriving to have an accident, at the very least, don't you think?'

Remembering Mhairi-Anne's sure-footedness and agility over the rocky landscape of Tora, Calum inwardly agreed, but he was non-committal. 'Who knows, Sister? If she was worried about something, she may not have been alert to any danger.'

The Sister nodded thoughtfully. 'There's no doubt that she is deeply troubled. Sadness hangs over her like a veil. There's also the possibility that we are the very last people to whom she might admit such folly.'

'I take it, you mean because of your religious beliefs?' queried Calum.

'I'm sure she is aware that we regard suicide as a mortal sin, but, luckily, she has the chance to repent it. Our worry is that, at the moment, she regrets only that she did not succeed.'

Knowing that religious consequences were unlikely to be figuring in Mhairi-Anne's thoughts, Calum remained tactfully silent at this point.

Nevertheless, she appeared satisfied at last that he should be allowed to see her patient. 'Come, then! Let me take you to Mrs Graham. She's sitting in the garden, I believe.'

As they emerged from the back of the building into the sunlight, Calum immediately saw Mhairi-Anne seated on a chair, some distance across the lawn, but she did not look their way. It was a beautiful summer's afternoon and the sun was beaming from an unblemished sky through a haze of shimmering mist, which added a dreamlike quality to the scene. She was so

24

still, she might have been a statue.

'I'll leave you to your conversation, Mr MacRitchie,' said Sister Mary Theresa quietly. 'God go with you.'

Calum thanked the woman, before setting off over the grass towards the motionless figure, who sat, face in profile, apparently staring at a rosebed in front of her. The sun glinted on her corn-coloured hair, which was hanging in a thick plait over one shoulder, while her eyes remained unblinking, as if she were totally absorbed in her thoughts. As he came nearer, she still made no sign that she had heard his approach and he slowed his steps, not wishing to startle her. Only when he stood beside her chair, did she glance up. For a moment, she simply stared at him. Then her mouth moved incredulously.

'Calum . . . how . . . I can't believe it's you.' Her voice was a husky whisper, as her eyes filled.

He leaned over her chair and gently kissed her cheek. 'Don't you be goin' upsettin' yourself now, lassie,' he murmured, reverting automatically to the homely dialect of his island tongue, which he had suppressed in his more formal conversation with the Sister.

'Are you up to takin' me for a stroll round this lovely garden?' he suggested, when words still failed her.

With the encouragement of his arm, she rose and, as he had hoped, she gradually gained composure. They strolled for a time along the meandering paths through waving flowers and shrubbery, while insects droned with lazy indifference and birds chirruped to their passing. He had noticed that she had lost a considerable amount of weight and she looked frail — her striking green eyes larger in her face than he remembered — but she walked without faltering. Eventually, he explained how he had been summoned. To his relief, she showed no signs of displeasure at the presumption of her benefactors — instead murmuring, 'They've been very kind to me.'

'They seem to think you need my help,' he encouraged gently.

She sighed deeply, as she glanced up at him with a glimmer of her old smile. 'If anyone could fix things for me, it would be you, Calum, but I realized after I'd written that letter that not even you can work the miracle I want. I can only burden you.'

He smiled back at her. 'Oh, I don't know about that. The old nun who let me in here seemed to think I was a miracle incarnate?'

'I suppose you are — in the sense that you're the only person I feel I could confide in.'

'You'll not be wantin' James to know anythin' of this, then?'

Briefly, she shook her head. 'In fact, that's why I never got in touch, Calum. I know how close you are to James and I know how you hate deception.'

'As I recall, you didn't care much for it yourself, lassie, when you were on the island.'

'No, I've hated all the lies. I thought when I left Tora, at least I would have left all that behind. But they're like a disease. One leads on to another and so on. Now, I'm part of a lie . . . ' Her voice tailed to a halt, emotion evidently again threatening to engulf her.

They walked on for a time in silence, before he said, 'God knows, lassie, I don't want to be party to any deception, but it seems to me that I'm here now for the purpose of helpin' you an' if that means sharin' the load that's nearly killed you, then it must be meant to be.'

She pressed the arm through which her own was linked. 'You're a good man, Calum. It would be such a relief to talk . . . '

'Well then . . . ?' he intervened encouragingly.

'I need to tell someone, don't I?' she murmured, almost as if to herself.

His response was to pat her hand and they walked on in silence, until she was able to begin.

'That night — before I left Tora — I arranged to stay with Victoria at her hunting lodge in Perth.'

'She never let on before she went.'

'No, well, that was the way I wanted it. But, of course, I didn't realize at the time that she had her own reasons for wanting it that way, too.'

Calum nodded, although his eyes were puzzled. He wondered apprehensively where this was leading.

'She arrived about a week later, as planned, and we settled in. Then . . . '

As her voice broke and she stopped, Calum patted her hand, before he prompted intuitively, 'You found out about her and Alexander, when she discovered she was expectin'?'

'No . . . No!' she muttered, shaking her head. 'I didn't find out about her and Alexander until recently.'

Calum stopped on the path, forcing her to face him. 'I don't understand,' he murmured earnestly. 'Did you leave her there alone — or what?'

Again she shook her head, before she blurted out words which shook Calum to the core. 'She was not pregnant — I was!'

Calum's face was comical in shock, as every aspect of his expression seemed to inflate.

A sound like a laugh escaped her lips, before she said bitterly, 'Yes, it's unbelievable, isn't it? But it's true — it's true — Alex is mine. I'm his mother — not her!'

Calum shook his head dazedly. 'How did it happen?'

Mhairi-Anne shrugged and they walked on. 'Alexander arrived at the hunting lodge one day I was in Perth and assumed the child was hers because of what had happened between them on Tora.'

'And she let him?'

She nodded. 'When I arrived that night, they were gone. She'd left a note sticking in the door telling me to await news at The Swan Hotel.'

'That's when you wrote to me?'

'Yes. I went through five days of hell, not knowing what had happened, before she eventually appeared.'

'But why didn't you claim him?' demanded Calum, his mind reeling with the knowledge of the wedding he had attended only the day before.

'God knows I wanted to!' she exclaimed bitterly. 'But she gave me a choice. She had opened up the possibility of Alex having his father, his birthright and her as a mother. He could have that — or me, a penniless single woman — and all the scandal I'd drop on his head, if I appeared at Strathcairn.'

'Oh Mhairi-Anne!' he muttered, his voice like a moan. 'So you left him there.'

She nodded — her eyes bright with tears — and he put his arms around her, while she wept her anguish against his shoulder.

From an upstairs window, Sister Mary Theresa watched their progress around the extensive gardens, her hands clasped in a silent prayer of thanksgiving. Their walk lasted all of half an hour and by the time they returned to the lawn, Calum noticed that another chair had miraculously appeared alongside the one that Mhairi-Anne had occupied. They both sat down, Calum now stunned by her revelations and wishing fervently he had known about this dreadful secret in time to tell Alexander, before his marriage had taken place. While he understood perfectly why she had kept silent and admired her for the terrible sacrifice she had apparently made, he had learned bitterly in life, that no level of wealth or position was worth the price of love and inner peace of mind. He suspected that it was a lesson that Alexander had already learned. Now, however, it was too late for all of them.

'They're married, aren't they?' Mhairi-Anne's voice rose softly out of the silence, which had grown between them.

He glanced assessingly at her, before he responded simply, 'Aye.' There was no point now in demeaning her decision, by expressing any of his belated regrets. The belief that she had done the right thing for her son must be all that she had left.

'That was why I went to the river,' she resumed quietly, after a long pause. 'I didn't trust myself to see it through. But now it's done, I wake every morning with the same question: how am I to live with it, Calum?'

He sighed deeply, as he patted her hand gently. 'I once felt I couldn't go on . . . that I didn't want to go on. I've never told James — anybody, in fact — but I was married in Nova Scotia. Had a fine wife and . . . and a son, who was the pride of my life.'

She glanced round at him, as he stopped, sitting forward, elbows resting on his knees, so that she could no longer see his expression, but there was no need: pain constricted his voice.

'They were killed — both of them — went over a ravine, when a wheel came off the cart.' He paused, clearing his throat, before he resumed bitterly, 'Y'see, I was too busy makin' money in those days, to check what they were up to. Everybody said it was a terrible accident, but I've never forgiven myself. That's why I came back to Tora to

31

spend my money. I suppose it's been a kind of penance.' He sat back again, evidently more sure of his emotions, but still embarrassed, as he looked at her. 'Don't know why I'm tellin' you all this now, except that I wanted you to see that — well, I've been there. You're not alone.'

She smiled her thanks, too moved by his revelation to trust her voice.

'And if it's any comfort to you now,' he added, after a pause, 'sittin' here, I'd give anythin' just to know my laddie was alive and thrivin' somewhere in this world, as he should be.'

'What age was he, Calum?' she asked softly.

'Fifteen — almost the man I'd hoped he'd be.'

Silence again gathered between them, before she murmured, 'You're right. I'll always have that, won't I?'

At this point, Sister Mary Theresa, still watching them from the building, signalled to one of her Sisters that tea should be served to the couple on the lawn, during which time, Calum had the opportunity to consider how to proceed. The obvious course of action was to encourage her to return to Tora, but he was all too aware of the possible future complications. As they drank their tea, he broached the subject tentatively.

'Have you done much paintin', since you left Tora?'

She shook her head. 'I was all set to begin, when all of this happened,' she revealed. 'Now . . . ' She sighed. 'Well, everything seems pointless.' A cynical smile touched her lips. 'Truth is, I've missed the island more than I ever expected and I haven't felt the urge to paint, since I left.'

'Would you consider comin' back?' he asked now.

She thought for several moments. 'I think I'd like to come back for numerous reasons — all selfish, I'm afraid. The main one, of course, is that I might hear news of Alex from time to time. But there's James to consider. Even if he still wanted me, I couldn't go back to the way things were. And there's you, too, Calum. Telling you has been a great relief, but I know I've done you a disservice and if I returned to Tora, you'd never be able to forget about it.'

'Whether you're there or not, lassie, there'll be no forgettin' this. And as for James — chances are he might welcome you back. We had a teacher at the school for a while after you went, but it didn't work out. He was a young lad and he didn't settle. You could maybe have your old job back and you wouldn't even need to live at the castle, if you didn't want to. We had rooms built on to the schoolhouse for the laddie.'

'You're making it sound so simple,' she mused.

'Simple? Well, as far as those things go, it could be, but I'm more worried about what you said earlier. I mean — about gettin' news of the bairn and such like. Will that not just keep the wound open? Are you up to that?'

'At this point, I think the idea of never knowing anything is worse,' she responded pensively. 'But it's also true that I'm not sure how I'd cope with any news of him.'

'And then, of course, there's always the chance of a visit.'

She glanced at him sharply and their eyes held, while an array of possibilities flashed through both of their minds. Alexander might appear . . . he could bring Victoria and Alex . . . How could she tolerate seeing them together — a happy family — *her* child and pretend otherwise? Her gaze fell away from his, as a nauseous lump gathered in her throat and she muttered thickly, 'It . . . it would be very . . . difficult.'

'Aye,' agreed Calum on a sigh. 'But what's the alternative? Do you think you could put this behind you, make a new life on the mainland somewhere, paint for a livin'?'

She looked down at her hands. 'The idea of

being alone — really alone — terrifies me,' she admitted. 'Sometimes, I wish . . . ' Her voiced faltered to a halt, as memories of that gloomy night in Perth welled up in her unbidden; trees whispering around her, promising concealment; the icy waters caressing her feet . . . her knees; the surging force lifting her body, carrying her away; the utter loss of control. She had thought it would be so easy to give up her life. The water had appeared darkly inviting. Had it been gentle with her, she might have drifted unresistingly into oblivion. But the river, low from a relatively dry summer, had been in a vicious, grasping mood, dragging her mercilessly over exposed boulders and spinning her in its dizzying currents. Pain awakened in her the rebellious beast of survival. As a child on Tora, she had learned to swim early and instinctive skills came to her rescue, as she fought against the sucking force of the currents and the deadly sodden weight of her clothes. But she remembered the ghastly feeling of being dragged under by invisible forces; her terrified gasping for breath; material and flesh being ripped from her body — until an inky blackness enveloped her. Later, she had been told that she had struck her head and she had no memory of reaching the bank.

The pressure of Calum's hand on her arm startled her from the vivid intensity of these images and sensations and she became aware that he was gazing at her in concern. Patently, she was still far from well, he realized anew, and it was suddenly clear to him that there was no alternative. He would never know a moment's peace of mind if she did not return to Tora, for a time, at any rate. There, she could recuperate and begin to come to terms with her experiences, where he could keep an eye on her. Besides, hadn't he been told that Alexander was to be out of the country for many months and he had all of Strathcairn, as well as a wife and a family to keep him busy on his return? With any luck, she would be strong again before any difficulty arose. Driven by these thoughts, he now set out more positively to persuade her.

'Och, the more I think on it, I'm of a mind that the island's the only place for you to be now, lassie,' he resumed, with as much enthusiasm as he could muster, while the unsteadiness of her expressive green eyes continued to reflect the lingering malaise of her thoughts. 'I'm sure I can sort things out with James an' you can have your rooms at the school, if you want an' — I forgot to tell you another piece of good news.'

She looked up, her attention finally caught.

'William Morrison won't be gettin' under your skin any more. He's moved on to bigger an' better things on Lewis, no less, and we've got ourselves a brand new minister with two youngsters an' a nice wife as well.'

As she remained silent and unresponsive still, he rattled on, 'My, his sermons on a Sunday mornin' are a thing to see. He's actually had folk laughin' in kirk, would you believe?'

A weak smile flirted with her mouth. 'Did Morrison manage to get his statue of Elizabeth up, before he left?'

'No. You'll be glad to hear as well, I suppose, that James cancelled that project?'

'Did he?' she echoed in surprise, recalling how this had caused an unholy row between them, although it all seemed so trivial now.

'Aye — used the money that had been collected to add the rooms to the schoolhouse. An' another piece of news you'll want to hear — sad in a way, but then again he was never a friend of yours. Neil Graham died two months back with a heart attack.' Neil had been Mhairi-Anne's father-in-law from her brief, calamitous marriage and along with William Morrison had instigated and nurtured much of the ill-feeling against her.

'I'd not have wished for that,' she responded soberly, however. 'I always thought that in other circumstances, I might have liked the man.'

'Anyway, what I'm sayin' is that you can have the chance of a fresh start.'

'I'm not so sure of James's reaction.'

'You leave him to me. I think you should stay on here for another week or so, while I go back to Tora and prepare the way. How's that?'

'What will you tell him?'

He shrugged uncertainly. 'That I met you — you've been ill — an' that you want to come back to your job — *as an old friend.*'

She smiled at him, for the first time a gleam in her striking eyes. 'Not too old!'

'Far from old,' he corrected, nudging her chin. 'With any luck, I can be back to collect you next week some time.'

'You don't need to come back, Calum, I could — '

'I'll be back,' he intervened determinedly. 'That way, I'll be able to reassure you of your welcome. In the meantime, all you have to do is concentrate on gettin' well.'

It was late afternoon — the falling sun now misted by a veil of cloud and a breeze whispering through the shrubbery — before he rose to leave. Sister Mary Theresa, timing as immaculate as ever, promptly met them on the lawn, as they strolled back towards the hospital.

'Remember to pay my bill at The Swan,' Mhairi-Anne murmured, as they hugged each other in farewell. 'I'll pay you back.'

'Aye, so you will. Till next week then,' he called, waving as he again followed the Sister to her office, where he promptly explained their plans. The nun was clearly delighted with the outcome, as was the Mother Superior, whom he met briefly before finally leaving the building with God's blessings raining upon him.

I might need them, he thought, as he climbed aboard the waiting coach, after ejecting the dozing driver from his seat. Despite all his assurances to Mhairi-Anne about James's reaction to her return, in reality, he was certain that James would have serious difficulty in taking the step from lover to friend. Furthermore, James had changed since Mhairi-Anne's departure. His attitude of appeasement to people like William Morrison, for example, who had come between him and Mhairi-Anne, had vanished — a row between the two men actually precipitating Morrison's departure — a fact which he had concealed from her.

Calum knew only too well that James bitterly regretted not marrying her at the outset of their relationship and he could only hope now that he could persuade him otherwise.

3

For the first time in their relationship and as expected, James was utterly furious with Calum on his return, when he learned of his duplicity.

'You had no bloody right to go visiting her without telling me she was ill!' he raged, 'Good God, man! Are you daft or something? What will she be thinking now? That I don't want to see her! I was there in Perth with you.'

'If you'd calm down a minute, I'll tell you what she's thinkin' and it's not that you don't want to see her. She didn't even know I was comin' an' from the letter I got from the nun, I didn't know what I was goin' to find, or even that the lassie would want to see *either* of us. An' besides, it was my name on the letter that Mhairi-Anne wrote — not yours!'

'And why was that, I wonder?' fumed James. 'She's ill and she writes for your help — not mine.'

'Aye, an' she ended up not postin' it!' retorted Calum. 'You've got to see things from her point of view, James. She left here at odds with you. The lassie's proud. How was she to know you'd still be interested in how she was farin' after she took off like that?'

They were in the morning-room of the castle during this exchange and James was disconsolately pacing the floor. Four years younger than his brother and almost as tall as Alexander, he was still a vigorous, well-built man, whom time had yet to rob of his appeal to women or his desire for the one he had so carelessly lost. Clean-shaven, unlike David, his skin was a healthy bronze from his outdoor activities and he turned arresting blue eyes on Calum, when finally he sat down in one of the armchairs by the fire, as his anger cooled.

'Now, if you'll just let me explain how things are,' said Calum, sitting down on the chair opposite him, 'maybe we can have a sensible conversation, eh?'

Keeping his revelations as brief as possible, Calum was able to comfort himself that his story involved significant omissions more than serious lies. Necessarily censored was the real reason why she had ended up in hospital and, thankfully, James did not question the edited version that she had been suffering from a debilitating fever, had taken ill outside, had ended up in a convent hospital and had since fallen prey to a deep depression, which had caused the nun to get in touch with him.

'She wants to come back here, James,' he continued carefully. 'Things haven't worked out for her on the mainland, but she's concerned about you.'

'Me? Well, didn't you tell her I'd want her back tomorrow?' retorted James, still irritated that he had been denied the opportunity to see her and speak for himself.

'I told her that her old job was vacant and that I thought you'd welcome her,' said Calum warily. 'I couldn't say more than that now, could I?'

James ran one hand distractedly through his thick greying hair, before muttering, 'I would have thought it was obvious. Christ, man, you know I'm not one for wearing my heart on my sleeve!'

Calum's blue eyes narrowed shrewdly. 'So, you're still in love with her?'

Taken aback by the older man's boldness, James rose restlessly to his feet and wandered to the window to gaze out on the panorama of ocean, while Calum sat brooding in the armchair. It was as he had thought, he concluded worriedly. More complications!

Back still to him, hands stuffed in his pockets, James eventually responded reflectively. 'I suppose I was always in love with her, but I was always holding something back,

43

too. She knew it: I knew it. She aroused feelings in me that Elizabeth had never touched, but I stamped on them; treated her in ways I'd never have treated Elizabeth.' Briefly, he glanced round at Calum, as if to ensure his interest. 'But when she left, I finally took a good look at myself. Fact is, it was Elizabeth I never loved.' He turned round fully now to gaze at Calum across the space which separated them. 'Does that shock you?'

Calum shrugged helplessly. 'I'm too old to be shocked any more, but it begs the question — why did you marry her?'

James's expression was cynical. 'Tora, of course. The first time she brought me here I fell for the place. Besides, big brother David, was all set up at Strathcairn by this time and capturing an island for the family collection got my father's attention for a bit.' He perched himself on the edge of a sturdy writing table by the window. 'Of course, it gradually dawned that Tora was not a commercial venture and, fortunately, by that time my avaricious tendencies had given way to genuine feelings for the life here. But regardless of how it all turned out, Elizabeth was a means to an end, although I'd never have admitted it back then.'

'But you were happy enough?' prompted Calum.

'Oh, I suppose we were — in a way. Superficially, I treated her like a queen, which salved my conscience, particularly when I couldn't even give her the children she wanted.' He sighed regretfully. 'You never knew her, Calum, but she was a paragon of virtue and I don't mean that in any sarcastic sense. Goodness shone out of her and she deserved much better than me. She always made me feel inadequate somehow.' He gazed evasively out of the window once more. 'All through our marriage, I was never faithful to her, always making excuses to go to the mainland.' He looked back, shaking his head. 'And she never questioned me once.'

Calum stood up to tap his pipe on the fireplace, before filling it with tobacco. 'I'm not sure what all this has got to do with Mhairi-Anne.' He might have added that he was not sure he wanted to hear any more of this either, but now the dam was open, there was no stopping him.

'The main point is that I was always faithful to Mhairi-Anne, but my guilt over Elizabeth kept a distance between us. Before she died, she found out about my shenanigans, y'see.'

Having lit his pipe, Calum glanced over at

45

him through a haze of smoke.

'Her father told her after someone on the mainland let slip about me and — silly old bugger that he was — he thought he'd pass on the information, while she was dying of cancer.'

Calum puffed hard on his pipe, as James's eyes quite suddenly glazed over and his chin dropped.

'The worst of it was — she knew, but even then she never gave me any inkling that she thought less of me — never mentioned it. I . . . I only found out after her . . . her funeral.'

'Perhaps, she didn't believe it,' Calum muttered, endeavouring to sound very matter-of-fact.

James stared at him, evidently taking control of himself. 'Still, I'd have felt better, if I'd been horse-whipped.'

'Probably, you weren't meant to feel better,' suggested Calum ambiguously. He had heard tales of Elizabeth McNair all over the island and had a healthy suspicion that this 'paragon of virtue' had faults, like everyone else, including a penchant for commandeering the high moral ground at the expense of others. But the last thing he wanted now was a debate on Elizabeth's qualities and he was glad when his involuntary insinuation went unnoticed by James,

46

who was again staring out of the window morosely, as he resumed.

'All those years with Mhairi-Anne — I never told her any of this, even although I knew she always felt second-best to Elizabeth. I fooled myself into thinking that telling her the truth about my marriage would have been the ultimate betrayal of a dead woman, but I realized after Mhairi-Anne disappeared, that all I'd been doing was protecting my *own* image and soothing my *own* guilt.' He roused himself suddenly from his seat on the desk. 'But things will be different when she gets back,' he ended determinedly.

'What do you mean by that?'

'I'm going to marry her, of course — what I should have done in the very beginning?'

Stomach churning, Calum retorted, 'Doesn't she have any say in this at all?'

James's blue eyes yawned in surprise at the sarcasm in Calum's tone. 'What are you talking about, man?'

'She doesn't want to come back here to the way things were.'

'They won't be the way they were . . . I told you — '

'She wants to live at the schoolhouse!' interrupted Calum, unable to bear any further dubiety.

'You discussed our relationship?' queried

47

James, anger beginning to colour his face.

'Not in the way you mean. I'm only the messenger in this, but she made it very clear that it's friendship she wants — nothin' else.'

For a moment, Calum thought an explosion of anger was imminent, but instead a rumble of laughter escaped James's lips.

'You had me going there for a minute, Calum. But, of course, that's what she'd say after taking off like that. She's proud — you said it yourself — not sure if I'll want her back. Women play these games all the time.'

It was Calum's turn to feel anger and frustration boiling up inside him. 'It's no game she's playin'. She meant what she said!'

James's face sobered, but he clearly did not believe him, as he responded complacently, 'When I talk to her, you'll see.'

Calum stood glaring at him, shaking with impotent rage, as he suddenly remembered Mhairi-Anne's words. One lie leads on to another. Here he was being faced with the consequences of concealing her affair with Alexander. The truth bubbled up in him, clamouring for escape, and it was only with an immense effort that he restrained himself from blurting it all out. James could only gape, when Calum hurled his pipe into the hearth, where it snapped in two halves, before he stalked from the room.

Over dinner that evening, they conversed like polite strangers — Calum still simmering with a confused concoction of annoyance at James's blinkered attitude, sorrow at the prospect of his being hurt, and guilt over his own complicity in deceiving him. James, never having seen Calum in this intransigent and rebellious mood, was wary and increasingly worried. Was it possible her feelings had changed? The age difference between them had always niggled at him. Had she, perhaps, met someone else on the mainland? Pride, however, held him silent, until Calum made to rise from the table.

'Sit down, Calum,' he muttered. 'We need to talk, don't we?'

Calum frowned down at him. 'Aye, I suppose we do, but I don't like bein' treated, as if I'm in my dotage. I heard what the lassie said and I know what she meant.'

James nodded reluctantly, before Calum resumed his seat across from him. 'It's just so damned hard to deal with something like this through a go-between.'

'Aye, well, let's get it clear from the start. Mhairi-Anne's not well enough to be playin' any games and she's not well enough to be up to you pressuring her either. The idea is that she'll be comin' here to get her strength back.'

'Of course — of course,' agreed James. 'But maybe that's it, don't you think? When she's fully recovered — ?'

'She'll change her mind an' marry you?' interjected Calum, already shaking his head. 'Don't bank on it!' As James's expression tightened, however, he added more tactfully, 'Not that I'll be speakin' for her then. It'll be up to you an' her, but what I'm sayin' is — let her get back an' settled without any upset, eh?'

'All right, all right!' agreed James tersely. 'I'll not say a word.'

'I have your promise on that now, do I?' persisted Calum, still not convinced that James was totally sincere.

'Christ, Calum!' he exclaimed. 'You'll be asking me to swear on the Bible next. She can have her old job back, live at the school-house and I'll give her all of three months — how's that? Definite enough?'

Calum liked the certainty of numbers and he promptly stuck out his hand across the table. 'I'll shake on that.'

James clasped the outstretched hand with a wry grin. 'You're a determined old bugger, when you dig your heels in.'

Calum smiled back, relieved to have

negotiated a means of ensuring her recovery at least.

Beyond that, he could only fear and guess, he realized, as he lay sleepless in bed that night. Perhaps, James was not so very far wrong in what he was clearly hoping. With Alexander married and her child forever beyond her reach, it was possible, he supposed, that she might find a marriage proposal from him increasingly attractive. Such a contract could ensure continued news of her son over the years ahead and wouldn't it be very tempting for another very different reason? In all his discussion with Mhairi-Anne, she had not once referred to her feelings about Victoria — this woman who had not only stolen her child, but also the man she loved. What a sweet and fitting revenge it would be to install herself permanently in the McNair family — not only a constant reminder to Victoria of the wrong she had done, but a relentless threat to her security.

Calum turned over restlessly, plumping his pillow in annoyance, as these thoughts came to him, as well as awareness of the fact that he could again find himself an unwitting accomplice in deceiving James. But surely Mhairi-Anne would not use him in this way? He thought not, but he was uncomfortably aware of the fact that Victoria, Alexander and James had all used her in different ways and who could really blame her if she decided to become Mrs James McNair and thereby get her own back on all of them?

4

Victoria and Alexander's honeymoon might have been idyllic and, on a superficial level, it was.

The glories of Venice, the sunshine of Naples, the historic splendour of Rome, the romance of Capri, the excitement of Monte Carlo, the awe-inspiring Alps of Switzerland — all were on their itinerary and much more. As Alexander had already travelled extensively, he was an excellent guide and companion to Victoria, who had never before been beyond the English Channel and she was entranced by all they saw.

Everywhere they went, too, she was aware of the envious eyes of other women, although Alexander seemed largely oblivious to the interested glances which came his way, or, perhaps, was so accustomed to such attention that it no longer affected him. But his careless disregard for the way he looked was very much part of his charm. He had no time for foppery; his thick blue-black hair frequently looked as if it had never seen a comb; and, in their excursions, he liked nothing better than to return home dirty and dishevelled, before a relaxing bath. Yet, it all seemed to be a natural part of his cavalier nature, which leant potency to the masculinity of his appeal. One casual smile could cause Victoria's heart to somersault; one glance from his sultry grey eyes seemed to melt her very bones. She both loved and hated the effect he had upon her, this wonderful weakness.

The fact that they had engaged a nanny, before they left Scotland, to accompany them on their travels, allowed them considerably more freedom than they might have had to explore and enjoy themselves. Mrs MacMillan was a middle-aged widow, who doted on Alex, and they could leave her looking after him without worry, although, whenever possible, Alexander always contrived to have his son with him. Furthermore, embarrassment which might have arisen, had they revealed their newly married status was easily avoided by pretending that the trip was to celebrate their second wedding anniversary.

Although Alexander was well aware that Victoria would not have been averse to extending him his marital rights on their very first night together, feeling as he did about Mhairi-Anne, to make love to Victoria seemed rather like repeating his offence on Tora. Consequently, while he was affectionate in his behaviour, he constantly manufactured excuses to postpone their physical union. She was tired after a journey; he was tired after a journey; Alex was restless; they had a long day ahead of them. He always engaged a suite of rooms to accommodate them, so that they did not even sleep in the same bed — an arrangement he would not have considered under normal circumstances, although it was not unusual among their class. When excuses began to wear thin, he started to disappear after late dinners — spending time in casinos or bars, where he brooded over his guilty heart and inevitably drank too much. It was not that he found her unattractive. On the contrary, she had blossomed since their marriage, her figure fuller, more sensual. In some respects, she was a more obvious and conventional beauty than was Mhairi-Anne, so that he often told himself he was a fool for depriving himself, but his feelings for Victoria remained stubbornly platonic in nature and he was at a loss to alter them.

At first, Victoria was touched by his reticence and restraint and felt that he might be trying to impress her, after the ferocity of his lovemaking on Tora. However, her memory of the swift, intense passion that had engulfed them and the continuing force of her attraction to him soon made her restless and indecently eager, she considered, to savour the intimate side of their marriage. As the days passed into weeks, inevitably, she became increasingly vexed and fearful. Tormented daily, as she was, with guilt over what she had done, alone in bed at nights, she often wondered miserably, if this was to be her punishment: to be with him every day, increasingly tortured by her growing conviction that he found her utterly unappealing and her lonely awareness that their marriage was a sham.

They were residing in a palatial villa in sun-drenched Naples, when she first dared to broach the subject with him. Having been served breakfast at a table on the bougainvillaea-shaded terrace, overlooking a breathtaking expanse of silky turquoise ocean, she could not conceal a sigh at the seeming waste of the beauty around them. Her head ached from another restless night and she had no appetite, despite the extensive range of tempting crusty bread, luscious fruit, fish and meat displayed before her.

He glanced at her over the newspaper he was reading. 'You look tired. Alex didn't wake you, did he? Perhaps, we should postpone our trip to Pompeii.'

'No, he slept through, but I am a little tired — maybe we could go tomorrow,' she murmured tightly.

Realizing suddenly she was close to tears, he put his newspaper aside and gave her his full attention, although he said nothing.

'Mrs MacMillan is becoming . . . er . . . suspicious, I fear,' she murmured hesitantly, after an awkward pause.

'What do you mean?' he queried, although he understood perfectly what she was insinuating.

'About us!' she retorted, colour rising from a mixture of annoyance and embarrassment.

'It's none of the woman's damned business!' he exclaimed, feigning an anger he did not feel, in preference to dealing with the real issue. 'How we choose to live our lives is our concern.'

'Choose?' she echoed softly. 'You went out again last night.'

He looked away from her pleading gaze, eyes simmering on the ocean, as he wondered how to voice his feelings without hurting her further.

'I'm beginning to think our marriage was a mistake,' she muttered wretchedly.

'We need time,' he murmured, still avoiding her eyes.

'Is that all it is? If I could believe that we would be happy one day . . . '

As her voice trailed off wistfully, he cursed himself as a selfish bastard and forced himself to look directly at her. 'We are happy,' he insisted, leaning forward to clasp her hands. 'We have Alex and we have each other. It's just that everything happened so suddenly — we need time to adjust.' He kissed her fingers lightly. 'I don't want things to be the way they were on Tora.'

'I'd be happy with that,' she whispered eagerly.

'We've never had a courtship,' he insisted gently. 'We've done everything the wrong way round.' He paused, before adding softly, 'I want to be able to love you — not simply make love.' This was very true, but, ironically, it was also a fact that, hitherto, he had never experienced the need to be in love with any woman before going to bed with her and, as he was already convinced that he would never love Victoria, he wondered repeatedly why he felt the constant urge to delay the inevitable. The only credible reason he could find was that he genuinely *cared* for her in a way that he had, perhaps, not cared for other conquests. But herein was possibly the crux of the problem: she was all too much like a sister to him — not a wife, whom he could desire.

Caught in his charismatic gaze, however, and ignorant of the confusion of his thoughts, Victoria's fears temporarily evaporated and for the time being his words were enough to satisfy her.

This situation had not altered substantially by the time they took up residence in Capri for six weeks — an island adored by decadent Roman emperors and a favourite haunt of Alexander's in previous times. However, he had tried very hard to ensure that his lack of lustful interest was less obvious, by kissing her regularly and keeping his solo outings to a minimum. He had leased another beautiful villa for their sojourn, with servants at their beck and call, and magnificent views over the sublime Bay of Naples, as well as lush mountain greenery. While she could not yet get through a day without being haunted, at some point, by what she had done, because of his efforts, she was feeling altogether more positive about their future and had convinced herself that the romantic aura of the place would surely lead to consummation of their marriage, before they moved on elsewhere.

One morning, a few weeks into their stay, a letter arrived from Lady McNair. Recognizing the copperplate handwriting on the envelope, Alexander tossed it to Victoria, who sat at the breakfast-table on the terrace.

'It's from Mother. Have a read while I shave and then we'll have breakfast,' he suggested.

Victoria immediately opened the envelope and began reading eagerly. She had grown to love Lady McNair's epistles — full of news, as they always were — and always addressed to both of them, so that they made her feel like one of the family. The first few paragraphs contained few surprises, but made lively and enjoyable reading. Then came a paralysing shock, which turned her complexion to the colour of fresh snow:

No doubt, you will be interested to know that David and I have been flabbergasted by the latest news from Tora. It seems that your Uncle James is engaged to be married to a woman you both probably met during your stay there. She is a widow, I understand, and a teacher in the local school. David insists that Alexander mentioned her in one of his letters, but I cannot recall hearing the name of Mhairi-Anne Graham before. Do write and tell me what she is like, as I am dying of curiosity about my new sister-in-law to be! Teachers are usually such ancient, dull and dusty creatures, I simply cannot imagine what has taken James's fancy. And at their age, too! Of course, James has always led a rather Bohemian life, one way and another, and I can only hope that she has some of the social graces, as we will, no doubt, have to meet her, sooner or later.

Having turned rigid with terror, Victoria was visibly startled when Alexander breezed on to the balcony, only to stop short when he saw her.

'What's wrong? You're white as a sheet!'

As she struggled to respond, he noticed the letter lying open on the table. Fearing bad news about one of his parents, he slowly lifted it up.

'The . . . the top of page two,' muttered Victoria, trying desperately to pull herself together, while her mind raced. There was no immediate danger, she told herself feverishly. Plenty of time to think! But she must not give herself away by panicking now. She had to remember that she was supposed to know nothing of her long-term affair with James McNair. Astonishment had to be the key-note. And what a surprise was in store for Lady McNair, when they met. She had clearly assumed that Mhairi-Anne was of an age with James — *'ancient, dull and dusty'*! An hysterical laugh bubbled to her lips, stifled only by her clenched jaws. She had to calm down, she concluded again. Obviously, Mhairi-Anne had done this to gain access to her son, while punishing both of them for their duplicity! Was he still in love with her? She glanced up fearfully, only now becoming aware that he had moved to stand leaning his hands on the wall of the terrace, his back to her. The offending paragraph had evidently been digested, the letter dropped carelessly at the other side of the table, while the taut breadth of his shoulders told her nothing about his emotions.

For several minutes, utterly consumed with jealous fury, Alexander was beyond words. How could she go back to him? If she was on Tora again, she must have learned of his marriage . . . his child . . . his deceitful behaviour. But to become engaged to James . . . his uncle . . . out of spite or for revenge? Or had their affair been a mere diversion from her first and only love? He gripped a trailing branch of bougainvillaea, his knuckles turning white, as he fought an insane urge to rip it from the ground. Suddenly, he heard Victoria's voice above the pounding in his eardrums.

'Your mother . . . will . . . will be amazed, no doubt, if she ever meets Mhairi-Anne. I can scarcely believe it myself, considering the age difference between them. Of course, I always knew they were fond of one another,' she prattled on, warming to her theme, 'and it will give her a security she has never had.'

What must she be thinking, he wondered wretchedly, as these words penetrated the fog of his rage? Married to a man, who was no husband to her, and now learning that her arch rival was to become a fixture in their family — she must be inwardly devastated, he concluded — an accurate deduction, albeit that his reasoning was flawed. He turned to face her, resolutely taking a grip of himself.

'It seems she has recovered from her trauma over Seorus Dhu,' he remarked tersely, referring to the accidental death of a simple Torean man, whose dramatic fall from the schoolhouse roof had seemed to precipitate the crisis of conscience, which had led to her departure. 'But I fear my uncle must be losing his mind.'

'It's most surprising, I confess,' she murmured, her bewildered expression almost genuine. 'But . . . but she's intelligent, beautiful . . . ' She allowed her voice to hang questioningly in the air, while her large brown eyes tried anxiously to read his expression.

'I used to think so,' he muttered carelessly. 'But she's also a very complex woman — young enough to be his daughter.' The words stuck venomously in his throat, feeding a ruthless smile. 'You'll remember I was rather taken with her myself, at one time, but it would seem I had a lucky escape. Evidently, however, she's determined to become a McNair at any price.'

'I was fond of her, too,' Victoria rejoined, following his line. 'Although I must admit the way she vanished without a word made me wonder if I'd ever really known her at all.'

'Perhaps, neither of us did,' he concluded, finally sitting down across from her at the breakfast table. 'But let's talk of more pleasant subjects. What do you want to do today?'

Thus, Mhairi-Anne's name was dropped from their conversation, never to be raised again during their honeymoon — both of them glad for very different reasons. Meanwhile, Lady McNair's letter continued to lie noxiously between them on the table that morning — like some rotting monstrosity that had dropped from the sky — both acutely aware of it, but determinedly ignoring its stench. Only as they rose from their breakfast, did Alexander lift the letter again and stuff it into his dressing-gown pocket with the casual words, 'I take it you've finished reading this?'

She hadn't — and badly wanted to pore over Lady McNair's words again in private, but deeming it unwise to exhibit any further interest, she confirmed his assumption.

Thus, while she took even longer than

usual to dress, struggling as she was to assimilate the dire news, it was Alexander who read and re-read the damning paragraph, until the pain of it seeped into his heart, hardening his feelings to a cold resolve. She was going to marry James; he was already married: there was no more to it. Now, he really was free, he told himself bitterly.

Never more dangerous, unpredictable or contrary, than when he was hurt, that day and night began an exhibition of an aspect of his character, which Victoria did not really begin to understand. Expecting him to be, at the very least, annoyed and strained in his efforts to maintain a façade of normality, instead she was treated to a masterful display of his considerable charm and wit, and she was inexorably captivated. Worrying about Mhairi-Anne could wait, she thought, as he repeatedly whispered intimacies in her ears, his lips tantalizingly caressing her skin.

They had decided that instead of going out they would have a relaxing time in the secluded garden of the villa, along with Alex, who was now making strenuous efforts to take his first steps unaided. For Victoria, it became a divine day — full of memories she would always cherish. Although now early in December, the mildness of climate ensured that the garden was still sprayed with flowers, scented by the fragrance of lemon groves and illuminated by the golden light peculiar to Capri. With three enormous parasols strategically placed on the lawn and rugs laid out, they established a shady base for a family picnic, which was constantly replenished with food and wine from the kitchen. Watching Alexander romping on the rugs with his son gave her endless pleasure and there was a particular joy, when the infant finally managed, after numerous plummets on to his well-padded bottom, to take a few teetering steps, unsupported by his father's two index fingers. While Alexander whooped in triumph and swung Alex in the air, she clapped delightedly and determinedly suppressed the guilty, stabbing thought, that Mhairi-Anne had missed yet another milestone in her child's development.

Early in the afternoon, Mrs MacMillan took Alex indoors for his afternoon nap, while they stretched out on the rugs, in the shelter of the parasols. Drowsy with wine, they fell asleep in each other's arms for a time, her head resting comfortably on his chest. She awoke with the touch of his lips on hers and looked up into eyes dark with intent. His fingers trailed tantalizingly down the side of her face, until his thumb lightly massaged the corner of her mouth. She had a beautiful face, he thought, with dark-lashed, expressive brown eyes, which were currently inviting seduction, and fresh, silky lips, which he enjoyed kissing. Mhairi-Anne had captured the mercurial nature of her appeal in her portrait, he remembered suddenly, this memory instantly squashed, as his fingers locked in Victoria's hair and he plundered her mouth until they were both breathless.

'Let's go in,' he murmured urgently.

'In the middle of the day?' Her voice was an earthy whisper.

'That didn't stop us last time.'

'What about Mrs MacMillan?'

He raised himself from the rug, catching her hand and pulling her up with him. 'Doors have locks!'

The house was shuttered and silent with siesta when they slipped in through the terrace and tiptoed softly to Alexander's room, which was nearest. Inside, the key turned, he pressed her back against the door, to ravage her lips once more, before he swung her easily into his arms and carried her to the bed, where he laid her on the satin coverlet. Her muslin dress having ridden up, exposing her bare limbs, his fingers tracked immediately up to her thigh, as he descended on her. She moaned softly, as his moist lips explored the sensitive crevices of her neck and found the firm swell of her breasts, while his hand discovered the warm secrets of her under-wear.

'Wait,' she murmured reluctantly.

They sat up, and he opened his shirt while she undid the small buttons on the front of her dress, to allow him to slide it from her shoulders. Her lacy camisole followed in a whisper to her waist and his eyes devoured her, as she released the thick length of her long brown hair over one shoulder. He wound one hand possessively in the silky tresses, as he gathered her nakedness against his chest and bore her down once more. The soft curves of her body melted into him, while his lips tasted the sweetness of her dark nipples and the soft swell of her abdomen.

All of their clothes were gradually dis-carded in mounting abandonment. They knelt, naked, touching, kissing and moaning, before they subsided into the satin, and his hardness finally parted her thighs, filling her repeatedly, while he stifled her cries of pleasure with his mouth. Outside the door, *en route* to the kitchen with Alex, who had awakened thirsty for a drink, Mrs MacMillan paused long enough to smile and blush, before she proceeded quickly down the corridor.

Like thunder rumbling into the distance,

the room gradually quietened then, until even their exhausted breathing slowed to a drowsy hiss and she fell asleep once more, cradled in the crook of his arm and curled into his body, listening to the steady drumming of his heart, while he lay awake staring at the ceiling.

He had enjoyed her more than he had ever expected, but in his satisfaction there was a strange, familiar perversity, which reminded him of an experience in his youth, when he had presented to his father a sparkling school report card, which far outshone Eric's grades.

'The exams must be getting easier,' had been Eric's biting comment, while his father had laughed, as he had handed back his report, after only a cursory glance.

Within a few short weeks, he had managed to behave so badly, he had been expelled from his school and sent home in disgrace in mid-term — a fact which had so enraged his father, he had not spoken to him for a month. And every day, he had congratulated himself on his achievement in so annoying him; every day, he had felt as he did now — justified and complacent. The only difference here was that his smugness was tainted with a self-awareness that he had not possessed in his youth and he recognized the unpalatable truth that he had exorcized his demons — not in self-destructive behaviour, but in his lustful use of the woman who lay so happily next to him. But, perhaps, this was what most marriages were like, he mused cynically — people using one another. In his relationship with Mhairi-Anne, he had deluded himself into thinking that they had enjoyed a rare physical and spiritual compatibility. It had felt like love. But all it had brought him was misery and disillusionment. Most of his friends had married for practical reasons, although they had tried to pretend otherwise. Even his mother and father, he supposed, would never have married, had their union not been 'suitable' and they seemed to have grown into a kind of love. Already that seemed to be happening between him and Victoria. He glanced at her sleeping head, her thick hair tousled enticingly over his chest. She would never be like a 'sister' to him again, he thought, now he had removed the self-inflicted blinkers from his eyes, and he drew her closer, feeling again the sensual hunger he had too long denied.

She awakened dreamily. 'We should get up,' she murmured, even as she arched her neck to savour his lips. 'Mrs MacMillan will be wondering where we are.'

He rolled on to his side, pulling her naked body against his, so that she was in no doubt as to his intentions. 'By now, Mrs MacMillan and the entire household will know where we are,' he retorted with a low laugh.

'You think they will have heard us?'

'I should think so — unless they're stone deaf'

'Good God, how will we face them?' she giggled.

'A few weeks ago, you were worried about us not going to bed.'

'Yes, well, now we have, there's a limit . . . ' she said, with mock severity.

He rolled her on to her back. 'Is there?'

'I feel like a slut,' she whispered against his lips.

'I'm very fond of sluts.'

Her face sobered, as her hands slipped around his neck to touch his thick dark hair. 'I think I would sell my soul for you. Perhaps, I already have.'

Ignorant of any darker meaning to her words, he moved sensuously against her and retorted mischievously, 'You haven't been nearly naughty enough yet.'

'You're wicked! What would you have me do?'

'Well — you could . . . ' He whispered suggestively in her left ear.

'I won't!' she gasped. 'You're outrageous!'

'Or, I could . . . ' This time, her right ear tingled to his words.

'I won't let you!' she shrieked, wriggling underneath him.

'Won't you?' he muttered, as his hands threaded through her hair, so that her head was held at his mercy, as he plundered her lips, until she was moaning incoherently once more. From the hollow of her neck, his mouth then left a slow trail of throbbing sensations down between her breasts . . . down to her navel . . . and beyond. Experiencing feelings she had never dreamed existed, her body opened invitingly to him, while he took his time in proving just how wicked he could be.

Later, they shared a candlelit meal in the dining-room, with the villa quiet around them.

'I thought my cheeks were going to burst!' exclaimed Victoria, laughing as she recalled how he had brazenly joked with Mrs MacMillan, when they had emerged from his bedroom, now ravenous for food.

He popped one of his strawberries into her mouth, shrugging carelessly. 'She's been married — she knows what it's all about.'

'We're supposed to be celebrating our second wedding anniversary,' she hissed, glancing at the door, which was slightly ajar.

'Yes,' he murmured, rising and rounding the table to kiss the juice from her lips. 'And I believe you owe me.'

They were in Monte Carlo, almost eight months after their wedding, when they learned that Victoria was pregnant — news which brought both delight and consternation, as they realized that they could delay no longer their return to Scotland and reality. Despite her joy that she was to bear him a child, she was filled with foreboding. Abroad, she had grown adept at pretending for long periods of time that Mhairi-Anne did not exist and that Alex was her natural child: going back was a return to guilt and fear. He, too, for very different reasons, could have happily prolonged their absence. No further information about the residents of Tora had been received, but it would be just their unfortunate luck, he thought, that they might return to news of a wedding invitation. While he had grown confident in the closeness he now shared with Victoria, some obstinate part of him still hurt like the toothache, whenever Mhairi-Anne entered his mind. And he could not fool himself that watching her marry his uncle would be anything other than the most sickening ordeal.

News of Victoria's condition having been communicated quickly to his parents, however, Lady McNair wrote urging them earnestly to return immediately, in order that they might avoid the ignominy of having to announce two grandchildren within an indecent space of time. Thus, they left the blue skies of Monte Carlo the following day, a distance growing again between them with every mile they travelled.

5

The late afternoon spring sunshine glinted on Mhairi-Anne's corn-coloured hair, turning it gold, as she worked with every delicate brushstroke to bring the child to life on her canvas. Her model — an 8-year-old girl in her class — played happily in the sand pit behind Tora school, building a castle, decorated with a myriad of shells collected from the beach.

In the eight months since her return to the island, painting children had become a new, bittersweet passion, punctuated with sadness, as she wondered how her own child must now be changing beyond her recognition, while there was a perverse enjoyment in trying to capture the elusive, innocent qualities of their faces. The fact that some parents had granted their permission for this activity was a sign of her increased acceptance, particularly by those who recognized the value of education and the difficulty in securing any teacher for this remote post. Without William Morrison and Neil Graham to stir and lead opinion against her, although her reappearance had caused an initial feast of gossip and older residents still regarded her with dour hostility and suspicion, there was certainly now the potential for her old reputation to be overlooked. The fact, too, that she was living at the schoolhouse and not constantly provoking comment by brazenly residing with James McNair in his castle, was another significant step towards her possible redemption. Above all, however, their popular new minister, the Reverend Robert Wallace — a great advocate of the virtues of love and forgiveness — was the principal cause of the change in attitudes towards her, as far as Mhairi-Anne was concerned. His elder daughter, Margaret, had led the way in her class by volunteering to model for a painting, and Mhairi-Anne had taken such a liking to him and his family that recently she had even accepted his invitation to join the congregation for worship on a Sunday — much to the amazement of everyone in the kirk.

While Morrison diehards still muttered darkly around the fires in their crofts, about the roasting flames and bondage certain to be awaiting all those who were straying from the narrow paths of righteousness and dogma, many of the younger generation were beginning to emerge from the shackles of religious oppression, superstition and fear, to embrace a new culture of optimism and self-awareness. How much easier it was to admit to one's own faults and tolerate the sins of others, when remorse and forgiveness were guaranteed as the keys to Heaven, instead of punishment and torture as the consequences in Hell.

'There's Mr MacRitchie comin', miss!' the child suddenly cried, pointing to the moorland slope behind her teacher.

She glanced round to see Calum striding towards them, before she said, 'I think we've done enough for today, Fiona. Tell your mum and dad that your picture is almost finished, but ask if you can stay behind again tomorrow.'

The girl rose to her feet obediently, dusting the clinging sand from her dress. 'Bye, miss! See you tomorrow,' she called, bounding off like a young deer over the moorland, in the opposite direction from Calum, while Mhairi-Anne cleaned her brush and wiped her hands on a cloth.

'I didn't chase her off, did I?' queried Calum on joining her.

'No, it was time to finish,' she reassured him.

'That's fairly comin' on!' He nodded at the painting on her easel. 'Will you be sellin' this one?'

'There's no need, when the old ones are going so well. I sent another three off to

Grant McPherson yesterday,' she ended, referring to her agent in Perth.

'You'll be makin' quite a name for yourself, I expect.'

She shrugged. 'It's nice to have the security of some extra income. Who knows when I might be needing it! But I like doing these as presents for the children.'

As she gathered up her equipment, Calum helped and followed her indoors to her small but comfortable sitting-room, furnished with two armchairs, a sideboard, table and stools, all surplus, rustic pieces of furniture, which had formerly been stored in the attics of the castle, like everything else in her accommodation.

'James sent me with an invite to dinner the night.'

She closed her box of brushes and glanced up. 'Will anyone else be there?'

'No, just you an' me. He has a surprise, so he says.'

'A pleasant one, I hope?' Her expression was wary.

'He had a letter from Strathcairn this mornin', but don't ask me what was in it. All I know is he looked pleased with himself and that all will be revealed when you appear.'

'I wish he wouldn't dramatize things,' she murmured uncertainly.

'Aye, well, he seems to think he's entitled to keepin' secrets, nowadays. Do you want me to send John over for you on the cart?'

She shook her head. 'It's going to be a fine night. I'll enjoy the walk.'

Calum nodded, before turning to leave. 'See you about eight, then!'

Mhairi-Anne's appetite for surprises had vanished since her traumatic experiences in Perth, and during the intervening hours before dinner, she wondered apprehensively what news James had to impart. Following her return to the island, it had very shortly become apparent, that she and Calum could not keep her secret from James if they wished to continue living harmoniously on Tora. They knew each other too well for the tensions of secrecy to go unnoticed and, eventually, two months or so after her return, she had raised her concerns with Calum, when he visited her one afternoon after school.

'I'm sure James is suspicious about what happened to me,' she suggested tentatively, as they sat across from each other in her sitting-room, drinking cups of tea.

'He keeps makin' barbed comments to me, as well,' Calum revealed. 'In fact, I've been wonderin' when to speak to you about him, because there's another problem comin' up.'

79

Only then, had he thought it necessary to alert her to the fact that James was still set on asking her to marry him within a matter of weeks.

Mhairi-Anne laid her cup down with a telltale clatter, her face reflecting her alarm. 'He told you this?'

'Aye, but I made him promise to wait until you were well settled. That was the best I could do.' He gazed at her over the rim of his cup, before adding carefully, 'I've been thinkin' lately that the lies have gone on long enough, that he needs to know the truth — all of it.'

She stared back at him, her mind racing and her voice reflected the turmoil in her mind. 'I . . . I can't imagine what he would do if he finds out about Alexander's part in all of this. Heavens, he might go to Strathcairn and create havoc.'

'Oh, he might feel like that initially, but Alexander's out of the country, remember, and James's secret about you an' him was how this all started.' He paused thoughtfully, before continuing, 'I've a feelin' he'll not go off at tangents, when the fate of Tora is all tied up in this as well. And what's the alternative? We go on lyin' and makin' up more lies, as things transpire. He already knows somethin' is amiss . . . '

As his voice tailed off, she realized suddenly how badly this was affecting him. 'I'm sorry, Calum. It must be awful for you, living at the castle. You've always had such a good relationship with James.'

'Aye, well, it's not been easy right enough, but I'll not go tellin' him anythin' until you're ready. Just think it over, will you?'

For several days after this conversation, Mhairi-Anne had thought of little else; and eventually she concluded that she really had no alternative, but to go along with Calum's view. To continue lying was to keep placing an utterly unfair burden on the relationship between the two men and, although James was bound to feel angry and betrayed, she gradually became more convinced that he would not do anything rash. Besides, telling him would obviate the embarrassment of a marriage proposal she could not accept and, given that the future of Tora was linked to his relationship with both Calum and Alexander, it seemed increasingly likely that he might ultimately forgive them, at least.

The decision made to end the secrecy, Calum had not only volunteered to be the bearer of the news, but felt that it was imperative.

'It's all down to a question of salvagin' his

pride, lassie. Believe me, he'll take it better from me.'

'But it's so unfair, Calum,' she murmured anxiously. 'None of this has been your fault.'

He smiled with a shrug of his shoulders. 'Life's no' fair, as you've found out. Besides, I'll be glad to get this off my chest, once and for all.'

And so, the following morning after breakfast, Calum had insisted on pouring both of them a stiff drink of whisky, before he revealed everything — from Mhairi-Anne's affair with Alexander to the loss of her son. Like a storm gradually passing over, James's anger erupted in thunderous bursts at various points, until eventually he sat grim, pale-faced and deadly silent, while Calum concluded the tale. His silence was infinitely worse than his outrage, as far as Calum was concerned, as he knew from experience that James was never more hurt, than when he was speechless. To make matters worse, after a few minutes, he simply stood up and left him, denying him the opportunity to impart any of the ill-formed apologies, which were scrambling for coherence in his brain.

At four o'clock that afternoon, Calum had arrived at the schoolhouse.

'Is he here?' he asked worriedly, as soon as Mhairi-Anne opened the door.

She shook her head. 'What happened?'

Briefly Calum explained, as he followed her into her sitting-room. 'I haven't seen him since,' he ended worriedly.

She subsided into one of her armchairs by the fire, her eyes large with fear. 'You don't think he would do anything . . . I mean . . .' Her voice halted, as memories of the River Tay bubbled up in her mind: the dark inviting water; the enticing promise of release . . .

He remained on his feet, fidgeting in his agitation, although he said reassuringly, 'He's probably off lickin' his wounds somewhere, that's all. But I'd better get back. There's no point in lookin' any further for him. He took one of the horses an' he could be anywhere.'

She stood up. 'I'm coming with you.'

She and Calum had subsequently endured many frantic hours of worry at the castle, as night cast its black quilt over the island, without any sign of James. While Calum bemoaned over and over again the fickleness of his conscience, which had instigated the revelation in the first place, she became increasingly convinced that they would never see James again. Ending one's life on Tora required only a necessary degree of courage, or wretchedness. All around the coast were sheer rocky cliffs which led to certain death. Had she been on Tora when she had made her own bid for oblivion, there would have been no time for second thoughts.

Listening for every sound, when the door of the castle had finally clicked open around midnight, they both started simultaneously to their feet and rushed into the hallway. Evidently, it had begun to rain and James stood shaking the wet from his hair and his jacket, blue eyes glancing defiantly at their frightened faces. Words were superfluous. He had come back . . . alive! As he marched past them and up the stairs, Mhairi-Anne gripped Calum's hand. 'Thank God!'

For the first time, since her return to the island, she had stayed at the castle that night, sleeping fitfully in her old room and dreading what daylight might bring. Calum evidently slept no better, as she discovered when they met at the breakfast-table. To their amazement, however, when James joined them five minutes later, he looked well rested, utterly calm and resolute.

'I don't want any apologies or recriminations,' he said brusquely and as if he had rehearsed every word he was about to say to them across the table. 'I was mad as hell at both of you . . . and Alexander, but I know there was no personal malice in it; and I've been a bloody fool, myself.' He stopped, looking steadily from one to the other. 'The question now is: where do we go from here?'

'I'm not sure what you mean,' Mhairi-Anne murmured cautiously.

'You realized that I needed to know the truth. So does Alexander!'

'You can't go blurtin' this all out now, James,' Calum intervened.

'I'm not going to blurt anything out,' James retorted decisively. 'Victoria needs to admit what she did and how she got away with it. Then it will be up to Alexander to decide what he wants to do about it — if anything. At the very least, I should think that he'll recognize that you're entitled to see your child occasionally.' For the first time, his eyes dwelled on Mhairi-Anne's face, before he added softly, 'You made a noble sacrifice, but I think you were wrong and it doesn't need to be a life sentence.'

'My sacrifice, as you put it, will be for nothing, if my son ends up the subject of ridicule — a bastard with the wrong mother! I kept quiet to safeguard a future I can never give him. Please, James, don't do anything that will make me wish I'd . . . '

Her voice ground to a halt and there was an awkward silence, before James resumed, 'But you want to see your son, don't you?'

'Of course.'

'And if Victoria admits her guilt now, how

will that damage him? If she has a conscience, she might confess at any moment, without help from us, and that doesn't mean that Alexander will stop caring about his son or his future. All I'm proposing is that we help her to see the error of her ways and Alexander will then be able to manage the situation, as he thinks fit.' He shrugged, as he spread his hands expressively. 'Of course, he might choose to keep things as quiet as possible, not tell his parents and continue with his marriage as if nothing has happened. Who knows? The point is he'll need to acknowledge that you have rights.' As her expression remained doubtful, he added persuasively, 'He might even bring Alex here to see you from time to time.'

This possibility made her heart ache, but she remained wary. 'You seem to be very sure of how Alexander will react. You forget, we both have cause to mistrust him.' Her cheeks coloured at this assertion, but James continued to gaze at her steadily.

'I trust he will do right by his son. After all, he married a woman he didn't love because of him.'

'You can't know that!'

'I was at his wedding, remember? And I was responsible for pushing them together, despite the fact that he indicated repeatedly that he wasn't interested in her. But I ignored that, just as I ignored the fact that he was drawn to you.'

Mhairi-Anne's cheeks flushed again, as she retorted, 'He was evidently interested enough to seduce her, so that she could claim my child!'

'One thing I realized last night,' James said slowly, 'is that we're all to blame for this mess. Otherwise, I wouldn't be trying to put things right now.'

Calum, who had remained silent during this exchange, cleared his throat. 'I think we'd all like to see things put right, James, but while I know what you're gettin' at as far as Alexander is concerned, I don't see how we can get Victoria to admit what she did — even if she does regret it. After all, she's got all the more reason to keep quiet, now she's married him. It's a bit late for confessions, don't you think?'

'You're probably right, if she thinks she's got away with it and Mhairi-Anne has vanished into the blue. But what do you think might happen if we send a very clear message that Mhairi-Anne hasn't gone away?'

Calum shrugged, his face puzzled. 'And how do you propose to do that?'

'I'll write a letter, telling them we're engaged!'

Initially, both Mhairi-Anne and Calum had been staggered and suspicious of the idea, but James was determined and persuasive that his 'brainwave' would work. Within a few days, their objections and reservations were worn down relentlessly. Desperate to see her child, Mhairi-Anne was essentially easier to win over to the idea than Calum, who remained concerned that James was harbouring some alternative plan to transform a fake engagement into the real thing, at some time in the future.

A couple of days later, over dinner, he had tackled James directly on the subject.

'So what happens, if the plan works, eh?' he asked bluntly. 'The last I heard, you were *really* set on marrying her.'

James glanced across the table at him, eyes narrowing. 'I haven't stopped loving her, if that's what you mean. And if I thought she'd say 'Yes' tomorrow, I'd have her. But that's not going to happen, is it?'

'No, I don't think it will.'

'So, I'll have to get used to the fact that I missed my chance years ago. It's like facing up to old age, isn't it? I can't put the clock back, but I can look to the future — her future and the future of Tora. Do you realize *her* son will inherit this place one day?'

'That thought had occurred to me.'

'In a funny way, it's as if he's part of me as well, and I don't want him growing up, never knowing that she's his mother and that he belongs here. I can't see Victoria wanting him associated with this place ever, if things stay as they are. She'll see Tora as a threat, just as Mhairi-Anne is.'

'I don't want things to stay as they are either,' Calum admitted. 'So long as you're sure you can handle this pretence.'

The following day, James had written a letter to his brother.

★ ★ ★

All of that, of course, had been six months ago and, as Mhairi-Anne made her way over the moorland in the gathering twilight of spring, to find out the nature of the surprise, which James now had in store, she wondered anxiously if he had finally received word from Strathcairn, that her child was on his way home. That alone would be cause for celebration: just to know exactly where he was and that the miles between them were far less numerous. Since imparting the news of their 'engagement', they had only received one very short letter of congratulation, in which Lady McNair had not even revealed whether she had passed on the information to the honeymoon couple. Consequently, all the initial drama and debate surrounding this decision had lost its significance and she had frequently wondered since, if it had been a pointless gesture.

When she arrived at the castle, however, she shortly discovered it had been far from pointless, as James dramatically handed her an embossed invitation.

'They're coming home and we're all going to a ball at Strathcairn!' he announced grandly.

As she stared incredulously at the cream card, her lips trembled with a shudder of anticipation which raced through her body, while Calum sank into an adjacent armchair, to tap his pipe worriedly on the hearth and wonder where this was all going to end. James could dream all he liked, he thought worriedly, and she could hope, but Alexander McNair was not the man Calum thought he was, if he meekly accepted his son being uprooted from his home — regardless of whether his wife confessed to the crime or not.

6

Late in the spring of 1898, Victoria and Alexander arrived back in Scotland to a fond family reunion and it was as if the scandal which had surrounded their marriage had never existed. People on the estate turned out to welcome them and there was a pile of cards inviting them to call at various houses, as soon as they were settled. Obviously, as his mother said, the local gentry still wanted to see the new bride, to give her the final stamp of approval, but the arms of forgiveness and forgetfulness were being outstretched, despite the denial of a wedding invitation, and they must build on that. Realizing she was right, as usual, Alexander gave her a long hug.

Alex was now walking and the proud grandparents were amazed by his development from a chubby baby into a toddler with his very own personality, summed up as 'daring' at this juncture. Everyone agreed that he bore a strong resemblance to Alexander, while nobody could decide whose green eyes he had inherited. Isobel, who had taken an instant liking to Victoria, eventually vouchsafed that they must come from her side of the family — a comment which earned her a thankful smile from her sister-in-law.

As Mrs MacMillan had decided to retire after their sojourn abroad, Victoria and Alexander soon approved of the 40-year-old widow, Mrs Davidson, the nanny, whom Lady McNair had engaged to start on their return, but agreed privately that they would need to take a firm line on certain aspects of Alex's upbringing, if the child were not to become altogether spoiled by the adults, including the servants, who were clearly set to dote on him.

By dinner that evening, Alexander had been brought up to date on a range of matters appertaining to business and the estate, and the conversation turned to the forthcoming May ball, which was to be held at Strathcairn in two weeks' time.

'We had to cancel last year's event, of course,' Lady McNair explained to Victoria, 'but it's a long established tradition, which everyone has come to expect.'

'It must take a lot of organization,' said Victoria. 'I hope I can be of some help, although I don't know much about the details relating to such occasions.'

'You'll be invaluable,' assured her mother-in-law. 'I was wishing you were here, when the invitations had to go out.'

'All those stamps!' exclaimed Isobel.

'But handwriting as beautiful as always, my dear,' said Lady McNair.

'We sent an invitation to your Uncle James, his new fiancée and that fellow Calum,' Sir David informed casually. 'I must say I rather liked him. Totally eccentric, of course, like James, but quite a character.'

While Alexander and Victoria inwardly reeled at this news, Lady McNair added, 'It turns out that his fiancée is rather more than a teacher. Did you know she was also an artist?' she enquired, glancing from one to the other.

Alexander cleared his throat. 'Yes . . . she did some painting, I believe,' he managed, keeping his eyes focused firmly on his food, while Victoria, too, trained her eyes on her plate and steeled herself to stifle the panic threatening to overwhelm her.

'But she's actually extremely good, darling!' enthused his mother, as yet unaware of the inner trauma she was causing. 'In fact, I bought one of her paintings in Perth a couple of weeks ago, when I saw it displayed in a window. You know, that little art shop near the river! Mr Peters couldn't praise her work highly enough. I've hung it in the corridor upstairs. Do have a look.'

Finally forced to glance up, a smile frozen

on his face, Alexander merely nodded and it was only then that Lady McNair's instincts began to be intrigued.

'You never did tell us a thing about her, after I wrote to you,' she murmured casually.

'Because there's nothing to tell, Mother,' he retorted, his tone belligerent. 'I doubt if they will come all the way from Tora for a ball, in any case. What made you decide to send an invitation this year?'

'At your wedding, James and I got talking about how we really should keep in touch and visit more regularly,' intervened his father. 'Neither of us is getting any younger, you know, and when you lose someone . . . Well, we'll see if he meant what he said.'

'Hasn't he replied yet?'

'Oh yes,' rejoined his mother. 'One of the first responses we got.'

'But you know James, Rowena! I'll believe it when I see it,' said Sir David lightly.

'Of course,' murmured his wife, still eyeing her son and her daughter-in-law curiously. 'But I've a feeling, he'll want to show off his new fiancée. I must say I'm more interested than ever to see what she's like.'

Having noted, however, that Victoria, in particular, was looking extremely uncomfortable and had fallen utterly silent, Lady McNair decided to drop the subject of the mysterious Mrs Graham for the time being and turned to a more congenial topic. 'You've brought Victoria home just in time for her to have a new gown made for the ball, Alexander.'

'I . . . I think I feel . . . sick!' Victoria stood up so suddenly, her chair clattered over backwards, as she fled from the room.

Alexander made to follow her, but Isobel rose quickly, too. 'Let me!' She gestured to Alexander to remain at the table, before following in Victoria's wake.

Alexander sat down slowly, annoyed at his mother for raising Mhairi-Anne's name and for harping on about this damned ball, although he knew he had no right to be.

'Maybe we should send for the doctor,' said Sir David. 'How far along is she?'

'About five months,' responded Alexander, glancing at the open door to the dining-room. 'I think I'd better see what's happening.'

'Isobel will be an angel with her,' assured his mother, manufacturing a weak smile, as she wondered guiltily whether Victoria's condition, or her talk of Mhairi-Anne Graham had caused this upset. 'I'm sure she'll be fine. Heavens, I was sick constantly when you were on the way, Alexander.'

'So she was,' agreed her husband.

'Still, I think I've lost my appetite, in any

case,' said Alexander, rising and dropping his napkin on the table.

As her son left the room, Lady McNair whispered discreetly to her husband. 'I was hoping to keep their little secret quiet until after the ball, but it may not be possible.'

'Most people can count up to nine, Rowena!' retorted Sir David caustically. 'Besides, at least this one is legal, so we don't need to make another conspiracy out of it!'

★ ★ ★

On his way up to their suite of rooms, Alexander spotted Mhairi-Anne's painting in the upper corridor, but he forced himself to walk past it with only a glance. Victoria was lying on the bed, with Isobel at her side. She was pale and tearful.

'I . . . I feel terrible . . . spoiling the evening for everyone.'

Isobel rose as Alexander came forward. 'Tell her not to be a goose, Alexander! It's wonderful to have you both home. The house was so empty without you.'

Alexander took Isobel's place on the edge of the bed and clasped one of Victoria's hands. 'You need a long rest after all the travelling and you must stop worrying about . . . anything.'

'I expect you're both exhausted,' said Isobel, moving towards the door. 'I'll see you tomorrow. We'll get started looking at patterns for your ball gown, if you feel up to it.'

Victoria smiled feebly before she left, her eyes then returning to search Alexander's face, wondering if all the magic of their love-making since Capri had eradicated Mhairi-Anne from his heart. During past months, she had felt loved, but he had never once actually uttered those precious words. Abroad, it had hardly seemed to matter. Now, it was as if all the magic had vanished with their return to reality and he was again holding himself at a distance, his expression inscrutable, as he bent over to kiss her softly on the cheek.

'I'll sleep next door tonight,' he murmured. 'You'll rest more soundly.'

She clung to him, until he gently removed her arms from his neck.

'Sleep!' he ordered, rising to leave the room by an adjoining door to an adjacent smaller chamber, which generally served as a dressing-room, but which also housed a single bed.

As she listened to the sounds of his movements, while he undressed next door, she wondered fearfully how she would be able to endure the coming weeks. If only he *really* loved her, she thought wildly, she might consider relieving her mind of its terrible secret, the secret that was eating away at her soul. For all she knew, Mhairi-Anne was now set on coming here to announce her claim. Wouldn't it be better if she told him herself? Now she was going to bear his child, surely he would not consider ending their marriage because of what she had done. If only he *really* loved her . . .

But if he didn't — how could she compete with *her* and a child whom he already adored? Surely, she would have spoken up long ago, if she were determined to have Alex back. And there was her engagement to James McNair to consider. It was impossible that she could be thinking of claiming Alex, when she was set on marrying him. This consideration calmed her somewhat. It was much, much more likely that she simply wanted to see her son, she concluded, and, providing she did not give herself away by panicking, all might be well. After the ball, they would go back to Tora and they might never see them again for months and months. She had to cling to that belief!

Next door, Alexander, too, lay sleepless, gazing into the twilight darkness of the room, haunted by the face of the woman he could not expunge from his heart. How he would tolerate seeing her again — engaged to his uncle — he could not imagine. Jealousy burned like acid within him. Yet he knew — somehow — he had to prepare himself.

Around midnight, he arose quietly, put on his dressing-gown and crept into the corridor, where lamps still burned low, while the house was silent with sleep. The painting was of Tora harbour — the scene, he immediately recalled, that she had been sketching on that carefree Sunday, not long after his arrival on Tora, when he had sat with her, while the haunting singing of the church congregation wafted over them. In the afternoon, they had skipped over the rocks on the shore, laughed and collected crabs for their evening meal. For several minutes, he was back there, feeling her nearness so acutely, the scene before him gradually blurred. His chin dropped to his chest, as he took several deep breaths, before he finally returned to his room, unaware that some distance along the corridor, the door to his mother's chamber quietly closed on a worried sigh.

7

During the following two weeks, Alexander threw himself into matters concerning the estate and tried to ignore as much as possible the relentless preparations, which were proceeding all around the house and gardens for the May ball. The new line of management, which had been installed prior to his honeymoon, appeared to be working well and the decrease in daily paperwork was a welcome bonus. Regular weekly meetings and a small team of able administrators meant that he and his father knew as much as ever about what was going on, without being embroiled in the time-consuming minutiae of every transaction. Thus, he had much more free time to ride over the estate and become involved at grass-roots level — a role he preferred — and this ensured his growing popularity with tenants and labourers alike. At least one McNair was not afraid to get his hands dirty, so it was said, and the physical activity suited him. In the evenings, he could come home claiming truthfully, he was exhausted, and if Victoria's condition did not warrant an excuse from lovemaking, this did.

Since their return to Strathcairn, his interest in this sphere of their marriage had evaporated and they were again sleeping apart most nights, ostensibly to ensure her comfort. In his lighter moments, he told himself that this was merely a passing phase, allied to a fear of hurting her: in the moods of gloom, which frequently claimed him late at night, he faced the unpalatable truth that he was still as obsessed as ever with Mhairi-Anne and the prospect of seeing her again was consuming him, like some incurable disease.

Time and again he visited the picture in the corridor in the anonymity of night, for the vicarious pleasure of being close to an item she had touched and for the addictive rush of memories it invariably evoked. Yet, far from raising his spirits, he always returned to his room feeling more depressed and trapped than ever, due to the infidelity in his mind, while his pregnant wife lay alone next door.

These days for Victoria were no less tormented and emotionally exhausting, particularly as she was expected to take pleasure in all the preparations, like Isobel and Lady McNair, and the constant demand upon her ability to act her role was draining. As planned, patterns for a beautiful new gown were soon being perused and discussed,

101

before one was chosen which all agreed would conceal her condition from even the most discerning eye. A trip to Dundee ensued, in order to choose materials, as well as numerous fittings with the dressmaker, who was promptly summoned to the house, to become almost a permanent fixture, as she was also making gowns for Isobel and Lady McNair.

It might all have been so enjoyable, she often thought — this fact only intensifying her inward misery, especially, as she had very quickly decided that her best line of defence against Mhairi-Anne must be to eliminate herself from all the proceedings, shortly before she was due to arrive. Because of her condition, this could easily be achieved and, even though she realized that she would, no doubt, spend the time of her 'indisposition' suffering the tortures of the unknown, she had recognized that in this situation, giving herself away was probably the greatest risk she faced. By not being available she would minimize this danger. Lady McNair would protect her privacy and, with any luck, any ideas that Mhairi-Anne might have of confronting her, causing a scene, provoking her conscience, or otherwise initiating alarm, would be frustrated. Furthermore, by remaining closeted in her room, she would avoid

Mhairi-Anne's likely visit to see Alex in the nursery. The thought of having to witness the reunion terrified her conscience and she guessed shrewdly that Mhairi-Anne was much more likely to remain composed if there was no one there to recognize the traumatic significance of the meeting. Of course, she was well aware that the whole situation remained fraught with danger of discovery, intentional or otherwise, and her absence might invite other risks; but, all things considered, avoidance continued to seem the best strategy, as the event approached.

On the day that the party from Tora was due to arrive, therefore, while Alexander left the stables early on his black stallion, determined to stay away until late afternoon, after a late breakfast, Victoria returned to her bed, complaining of niggling pains, which caused Lady McNair to send immediately for their physician.

'Definitely no bleeding, my dear?' queried Dr Morgan, gently prodding her abdomen, as he examined her early that afternoon.

Victoria shook her head on her pillow, face tear-stained. Ill with nervous anticipation in any case, it was not difficult to play her part.

'Had you any episodes like this last time?' he asked.

'No — never,' she responded, gazing over to where her mother-in-law stood, back discreetly turned on the proceedings, while she gazed out of the window. 'Is that a carriage, I hear?'

Lady McNair glanced over her shoulder. 'Yes, someone's coming up the drive.'

'Several days of complete bed rest for you, young lady, I'm afraid,' pronounced the doctor, who had been physician to the McNair family for several decades and, as a young doctor, had delivered both Eric and Alexander.

Tears came easily once more to Victoria's eyes, as her mother-in-law approached him. 'We'll certainly see to that, Peter. I suppose you'll call again tomorrow?'

'Of course, although I don't think there's any cause for alarm. There are no signs of premature labour, but we must err on the safe side.'

She turned her attention to Victoria. 'I know it must be terribly disappointing, my dear, with the ball and everything going on, but we'll keep things as calm as possible for you. It may be just the time to let it be known that you're to have another child.'

Victoria nodded mutely.

'I'll see you out, Peter. It seems I have visitors to attend to, as well.' The sounds of the carriage now arriving in the courtyard below drew her again to glance out of the window. 'Good Heavens, it's James!' she exclaimed. 'I didn't think he would be here for hours yet.' She paused, as she continued to survey the scene below, while Victoria closed her eyes in anticipation. 'But who on earth is that?'

Victoria opened her eyes again slowly, to find Lady McNair's perplexed gaze upon her. 'There's a young woman with them, but no sign of Mrs Graham.'

'What does she look like?' asked Victoria needlessly.

Again her mother-in-law peered down, just as Mhairi-Anne lifted the veil on her bonnet and gazed upwards at the array of windows above her. Lady McNair immediately drew back, not wishing to be caught peering. She turned and approached the bed, as she said, 'A most striking face, I must say — tall for a woman and fair hair plaited over her shoulder.'

'Sounds . . . like . . . like Mhairi-Anne,' Victoria responded with a jerky smile.

Lady's McNair's expression was a study of incredulity. 'But she's young enough to be James's daughter, my dear!'

Victoria pressed her lips together to conceal their trembling and made no further comment, while her mother-in-law's look became almost accusing. 'I knew there was something odd about this engagement,' she declared eventually, a hint of anger rising in her tone, as she swept from the room, followed by the doctor.

Downstairs, she discovered her guests had already been shown into the palatial drawing-room to be welcomed by her husband and she hurriedly bid the doctor farewell, in order to join them. She entered the room in time to see Sir David clutching one of Mhairi-Anne's hands, as he beamed at her.

'I must say, we never had any teachers like you in my school.'

At that moment, Lady McNair could cheerfully have throttled her drooling husband, but, drawing on every ounce of her good breeding, she planted a gracious smile on her face, as she came forward and said, 'That would have been rather difficult, darling, in an all male establishment.'

All heads turned at the sound of her voice, Sir David's trained eyes instantly receiving the telepathic gleam, which told him to close his mouth and stop gawping like a schoolboy. She went first to her brother-in-law.

'How nice to see you again, James,' she murmured, accepting his light kiss on her left cheek. 'And you too, Calum,' she continued, extending her right hand. Now at her husband's side, she prepared her most welcoming smile. 'And you must be Mhairi-Anne.'

The striking green eyes which turned directly upon her were benign, but a shock of recognition hit her brain with dizzying force. As his wife's face suddenly blanched, Sir David caught her elbow.

'Are you all right, Rowena?'

Her hand to her throat, she struggled for words. 'I . . . I feel a little faint . . . I think.'

Helped immediately to an adjacent chair, she rapidly endeavoured to regain her composure. 'Do forgive me . . . I . . . I expect it's all the excitement . . . with Victoria.' She managed to look up with a shaky reassuring smile at the startled group. 'Some tea, David, I think.'

Her husband immediately pulled the thick cord adjacent to the fireplace, in order to summon the servants.

'Please sit down everyone,' insisted Lady McNair, gesturing around the room. 'I'm sorry to upset your arrival. I can't imagine what came over me.'

'You mentioned some excitement with Victoria?' prompted James, settling himself on a long sofa next to Mhairi-Anne, while Calum occupied one of the adjacent armchairs.

'Yes, we've just had a doctor's visit. She's unwell, I'm afraid, and she'll have to miss the ball, which is a great pity, but he has ordered complete bed rest.'

At that moment, one of the servants appeared and afternoon tea was promptly wheeled in on a wagon-train of trolleys, while James, Calum and Mhairi-Anne exchanged surreptitious glances. During their journey, they had speculated endlessly on how Victoria might be feeling about their visit — James maintaining that the prospect of facing her victim in these circumstances would surely be her undoing, while Calum had been far from confident about the outcome.

'If she'd been going to confess, she'd have done it before now,' he had opined.

'Maybe she already has,' James had suggested obstinately. 'I simply can't believe that the timorous girl I knew on Tora is capable of keeping up this charade, with the child's mother set to arrive on her doorstep.'

'I don't think you knew Victoria as well as you think you did,' Calum had retorted. 'None of us did.' His eyes had then signalled the fact that Mhairi-Anne, who was seated in the carriage beside James and in the corner diagonally opposite him, was staring out of the window thoughtfully, saying nothing.

As the two men had fallen silent, however,

Mhairi-Anne's head had turned.

'I don't think she will ever confess now,' she had murmured, her tone resigned. 'Calum's right. The longer it has gone on, the more she has to lose.'

'But if she thinks you are come to claim your son . . . ' James had intervened, his voice tailing to a halt, as Mhairi-Anne shook her head.

'Why would I do that now I am supposed to be engaged to you?'

'That's an impression we can easily correct. Alexander has to know the truth whether it comes from her or us.'

'I thought the idea of this visit was that it came from her,' Calum had rejoined.

'Preferably, of course,' James had responded. 'But if the worst comes to the worst, we can give her an ultimatum.'

'We?' Calum had echoed. 'She doesn't even know that Mhairi-Anne has told us.'

'Then maybe it's time that she did.'

'Please!' Both men's heads had turned as Mhairi-Anne's voice rose between them. 'I'm here because I want to see Alex and you must promise not to do or say anything during this visit, before we consider the consequences for him.' She had looked particularly at James. 'I know you're determined that Alexander must be told, come what may, and, believe me, I want that, too, but not at the expense of my son, and not if it means he will be damaged. He's not a baby any more — he won't even remember me . . . '

As her voice had ground to a halt, James murmured, 'Of course, we'll wait and see how thing go. I'm just anxious for the matter to be settled, that's all, but we'll talk again, depending on what we find.' Now that he had been forced to accept the fact that Mhairi-Anne would never be his wife, it was as if the recovery of her son had given him a whole new purpose in life. Alex might have been his son or grandson — the new heir apparent to Tora — and his dreams were now fired with the joy he might experience in seeing him grow up there. Catching Calum's eye at this moment, he had shrugged his shoulders benignly, as if to reassure the older man, but Calum had not been fooled. He was uncomfortably aware of James's new aspirations and had concluded that, despite all he had learned, James, unfortunately, still tended to be led by a streak of selfish single-mindedness, which blinkered his view of the consequences for other people.

Meanwhile, over tea in the drawing-room at Strathcairn, Lady Rowena, evidently fully recovered from her dizzy spell, announced her purchase of one of Mhairi-Anne's

110

paintings and proceeded to find out as much as she could about the artist, using delicate interrogation techniques, masked in the fine art of polite conversation and honed to perfection over innumerable sessions of afternoon tea in her circles. Eventually, she said, 'You know my son, of course?'

'Yes, we met during his visit,' responded Mhairi-Anne, returning the deceptively direct gaze of the older woman, with as steady a look as she could muster.

'And Victoria?'

'We became friends. I'm sorry to hear that she's ill.'

'Yes, indeed,' agreed James. 'Nothing serious, I hope?'

Lady McNair smiled conspiratorially and lowered her voice. 'You may as well be the first to know, we are to be grandparents again.'

Mhairi-Anne's hand trembled as she laid her cup down, but aware that the older woman's scrutiny of her was unrelenting, she summoned an answering smile. 'How wonderful! You must be delighted.'

'Yes!' echoed James, glancing at his brother, who was beaming with pride.

'Makes quite a difference having a toddler in the house,' Sir David remarked, in response to the look. 'After Eric died, I

111

thought we'd never recover, but young Alex has certainly lifted the gloom.'

Mhairi-Anne swallowed on the nervous lump in her throat. Not for the first time, it was borne home to her that her secret had dreadful implications, which went beyond Victoria and Alexander.

'I'm sure Mhairi-Anne would like to see him,' responded James. 'We all would.'

'Not right now, I'm afraid.' Lady McNair quickly intervened, her smile belying the decisiveness of her tone. 'He'll be having his afternoon nap.' She rose to her feet to take full charge of the situation. 'And I'm sure all of you will want to rest after your long journey.'

James's hackles rose, as they always did, at the way his sister-in-law could steer proceedings with all the aplomb of a general disguised in lace. 'Oh, none of us is too exhausted,' he demurred. 'We made the crossing yesterday, you see, and stayed over in Perth last night. Mhairi-Anne wanted to see her agent and do some shopping.'

'I must let you see where I've hung your painting, my dear,' resumed Rowena, none daunted, as she took Mhairi-Anne's elbow and proceeded to lead the party from the room.

Upstairs, the location of the painting was

approved, before the party from Tora was conducted to the guests' rooms, which were all located in the east wing of the house.

'Well?' said Lady McNair, as she and her husband departed back along the corridor to their own quarters in the west wing. 'Your brother is certainly full of surprises, isn't he?'

Sir David's answering chuckle was quenched by the stern look cast by his wife.

'It's no laughing matter, David! How on earth are we to explain this relationship to everyone?'

'Don't be such a prude, Rowena!' retorted her husband. 'There won't be a man at the ball tomorrow night who doesn't envy him.'

'You included, I suppose!' snapped his wife, before she suddenly accelerated ahead of him along the corridor to her own bed chamber, apparently with a view to slamming the door shut in his face.

The gesture served no other purpose than the venting of her irritation, as her husband very shortly entered her room through the adjoining door from his own bedroom — a manoeuvre, which had evidently had many precursors.

'One of these days, you'll unhinge that door!' he commented drily. 'I'm beginning to think this damned ball was a bad idea,' he continued, subsiding on to the edge of her bed, while she continued to ignore him, as she gazed out of her window. 'Victoria's confined to bed; you're taking dizzy turns; and now you're in one of your moods — for God only knows what reason.'

She whirled round, her elegant face pinched with her agitation. 'I would have thought you might also have some concern for your brother's sanity. That diamond ring she's wearing belonged to your mother and it's worth a small fortune — never mind everything else. She's obviously a fortune hunter! Doesn't that bother you?'

'She's going to be rather disappointed, if she is,' he retorted. 'All of James's money is sunk in that damned island of his and she must know all of that will come to Alexander. If it's a fortune she's after, I'm quite sure she could have aimed a lot higher than James.'

'Nonsense! She's the daughter of a crofter, and her first husband was evidently of that ilk.'

'I noticed it didn't take you long to worm out all the grizzly details,' responded Sir David sarcastically.

'Normally, you would be as concerned as I am. Look at the fuss you made about Victoria's history and she is, at least, of our class.'

'Yes, and I hope I've learned from that

— not to be so hasty in my judgements. Besides, it's not as if things like that matter on Tora and she can't do us any harm.'

'Can't she?' echoed his wife, a shiver traversing her spine, as she recalled those memorable green eyes. But how could she voice the terrible suspicion that had taken root in her mind? If only it were a simple matter of jealousy, as he thought.

'She looks every inch a lady and I, for one, will be delighted to count her as a sister-in-law,' Sir David resumed dismissively, as he rose from her bed. 'Jealous tantrums are never attractive, Rowena,' he rebuked mildly. 'The point is that she's my brother's fiancée and a guest in this house: I trust you will treat her accordingly.'

Lady McNair smiled grimly. 'I won't forget that I *am* a lady, if that's what you mean.'

He nodded brusquely, before leaving her to stare once more out of her window. About to exit by the adjoining door, he was stopped, however, by a final question. 'Did you notice her eyes?'

'Eyes? What do you mean?'

She glanced round at him. 'Quite remark-able, I thought.'

'I think you need to lie down, Rowena. You're clearly overwrought!'

And you're blind — blind, as usual, she

thought fearfully, as he closed his door behind him. But if he had noticed nothing amiss, perhaps, her imagination was playing tricks, she mused. Perhaps, she was jealous of her brother-in-law securing such an unusual beauty at his age. If not . . . she could only hope that everyone else was as blind as her husband.

8

In her room, Mhairi-Anne paced the floor disconsolately. Victoria pregnant! Of all the possible complications she had considered, this eventuality had somehow not entered her mind. Now he would have a child to both of them. It was as if fate were constantly conspiring against her, she thought vexedly, not daring to dwell on the fleeting consideration that jealousy was adding bitterness to her feelings of terrible disquiet. If only she had not visited Perth that dreadful day when Alexander had appeared in the glen, things might have been so different. If only she had thought the whole situation through more rationally that day Victoria had come to the Swan Hotel, she might have stopped their marriage. If only she had died in the River Tay . . .

Her pacing of her bedroom was a rhythmic accompaniment to the remorseless nature of her thoughts and took her frequently towards the window, where she eventually paused to look out over the sweeping panorama of shrubbery, lawn and trees, which fronted the house and separated it from the River Cairn.

Now, at the zenith of spring and the promised dawn of summer, cherry trees and blooming shrubbery punctuated the greenery with a myriad of pink and white. A light wind blew stray petals over the grass in flurries of freak snow, and the sun, peering from a sky painted with fluffy white clouds, glinted on the distant turbulence of the river.

Longing to walk off her uneasiness, she opened the window on the fresh perfumed air of spring in these parts — very different from the ocean and peat-scented air of Tora. Despite the beauty of the scene and her aching proximity to her son, for whom she had longed day and night — a wave of homesickness washed over her. Now with Neil Graham and William Morrison gone from the island, and the income she derived from her painting, she had discovered in her schoolhouse home a sense of security and feeling of belonging that she had never really known before in her life. If she could have had Alex there, she would have been content, she had often thought. Here, she was in an alien environment, where all she most loved and feared awaited her.

Her train of thought was halted abruptly by the sounds of movement below and her heart began to thud wildly, as she saw a woman, carrying a child, emerge into view. Although she could only see the top of his dark head, there was no doubt. It was Alex! The woman, wearing a dark-navy straw-brimmed bonnet and uniform dark-blue dress was presumably his nanny.

The opportunity was irresistible. Without pausing for thought, she fled from the room, her gown rustling with her agitation. In the corridor, she stopped fleetingly to consider her exit route. The last thing she wanted now was to run into any of the family. Instinctively, therefore, she turned right — in the opposite direction from the main stairway. There had to be a servants' staircase in a house like this, she thought hopefully.

She passed numerous doors, before she finally reached the end of the corridor, where a broad leaded glass window arched high over her head. Here, a narrower door was inset to her right — a bathroom, perhaps, or . . . ? A tentative turn of the handle confirmed her breathless hope. The door opened outwards, revealing a dark narrow staircase stretching below. As she gently closed the door behind her, she was forced to pause on the top step, until her eyes habituated to the gloom, alleviated only by a long narrow window, which afforded little light. Cautiously now, she descended the bare wooden stairs, holding firmly on to the handrail, which ran down one side.

At the bottom, another door greeted her and she listened for several seconds to the rhythmic pulsing of her heart, before she opened it. She found herself then in another long corridor, as dim and narrow as the stairwell, but punctuated by numerous doors, leading, she presumed, to the kitchens and servants' quarters. Now she could hear rumbles of voices coming from beyond and expected at any moment to be discovered. But amazingly, she crept unmolested along the corridor towards the stout door at the end, under which a long thin slice of daylight beckoned.

The handle was rusty and, for a terrible second, she thought the door was locked, but with a fierce tug it yielded. Expecting an avalanche of light, she was greeted instead by the muted greenish gloom of an archway of trees, which led from the doorway along a paved pathway. Used to the wide open spaces of Tora, she moved along it gingerly, brushing aside insects and trailing branches as she went. Fortunately, she emerged on to the side lawn of the house and luck stayed with her. Nobody was about.

Lifting the skirt of her dress, she now ran until she emerged round the corner of the mansion and faced the scene over which her window looked. She stopped then, dismayed, as she could see no sign of the woman at first, but she had been looking for someone walking. In fact, the nanny had taken a seat on a bench, with Alex now playing on the grass in front of her. She started forward hurriedly with the relief of spotting them, before she became aware that any number of eyes could be watching her from the multitude of windows which overlooked the gardens. She had to appear as if she was out for a leisurely stroll, she realized immediately, forcing herself to slow down. It was agony! At any moment, she expected the woman to scoop Alex into her arms and march off with him — or for someone to come rushing from the house to arrest her progress.

She continued unimpeded, however, her heart seeming to race faster with each slow step. Suddenly, aware her cheeks were wet and stinging in the light wind, she forced herself to stop, ostensibly to admire the trailing white blossom on a thick shrub, but, in reality, to ensure her composure. If she appeared like a wild woman out of nowhere, the nanny would surely take off with her charge. At all costs, she had to remain calm, she told herself firmly, before she moved on.

The woman glanced up as she covered the final yards which separated them and

Mhairi-Anne forced a smile of reassurance, while she determinedly avoided looking at the child playing on the grass.

'Good afternoon!'

The woman responded uncertainly to her greeting and Mhairi-Anne swiftly added, 'I'm Mrs Graham. I've just arrived from Tora.'

The woman promptly stood up, in recognition of the fact that she knew Mhairi-Anne to be a guest in the house. Her expression relaxed somewhat. 'Pleased to meet you m'lady!' she replied, bobbing a curtsy. 'I'm Mrs Davidson — Alex's nanny. I take it you're Mr James's fiancée. I heard you were here, but . . . ' Her voice tailed off awkwardly, and her rugged face coloured, as she realized it would not be appropriate to mention the fact that Mhairi-Anne was a great deal younger than anyone had expected.

Disconcerted by the woman's deference and discomfiture, Mhairi-Anne, nevertheless, tried to put her at her ease. 'Please sit down. I didn't mean to disturb you, but . . . ' Her eyes finally straying to Alex, words failed her.

Fortunately, Mrs Davidson's eyes followed hers, so that she did not dwell on Mhairi-Anne's face at this point, when all the anguish of the many months apart fought with incredulous joy at seeing her child again. As she stooped to touch one of his little hands and he looked up at her enquiringly, an aching sadness trembled over her smile. The baby who had been stolen from her in the Perthshire glen had vanished forever and the sublime pleasure of these moments was laced liberally with the painful realization that she probably would never have recognized him in any other context. His head now had a glossy cap of blue-black hair, similar to his father's, and in losing the chubbiness of infancy, his resemblance to Alexander was now strikingly apparent.

'He's a proper little charmer, isn't he?' remarked Mrs Davidson fondly. 'All the ladies would pay a pretty price for those eyelashes of his and he's so good-natured, he can already wind us all around his little finger.'

As the woman prattled on, Mhairi-Anne resisted the powerful urge to take her child into her arms and, as a solitary tear fell unseen on to the grass, she stood up, carefully averting her face until she was certain of her composure. Luckily, the woman was so proudly preoccupied in demonstrating the achievements of her charge, she was oblivious to her emotional struggle.

'Show the nice lady how well you can walk, Sandy,' she instructed, extending her hand to allow the child to lever himself upwards, while she tossed a jingling rattle for him to fetch like a playful puppy.

As Alex waddled quickly after his plaything, Mhairi-Anne remarked, 'You called him *Sandy*?'

'A pet name the family have started using,' explained Mrs Davidson. 'Apparently his father was called that as a child, as well.'

Mhairi-Anne nodded, nibbling her lower lip at this new piece of intelligence, which seemed to underline the fact that he was no longer her child.

'I'll put on his sun hat, I think,' said Mrs Davidson, as the child returned with his toy and she ran a practised hand over his warm head. 'Heavens! I must have left it inside,' she exclaimed, having rummaged unsuccessfully through the big cloth bag, which sat behind her on the bench. Glancing up at the sun beaming down on them from a wide patch of utterly clear sky, she concluded, 'I'll need to take him back indoors, I suppose.'

Mhairi-Anne leapt on the opportunity. 'I'll look after him, if you want to fetch his bonnet.'

Mrs Davidson's kindly face wrinkled her surprise at such an offer, as she regarded Mhairi-Anne as one of 'them', who were not expected to do favours for the likes of her. But the kitchen had been a hubbub of gossip earlier that afternoon, following the arrival of the party from Tora and, although she usually tried to set herself above the gossip of the servants' hall, by ignoring their chitchat, she remembered that somebody had said the young lady was some kind of teacher as well as an artist. Perhaps, she was as unusual as they all seemed to think. Certainly, she was a beauty, as one voice had claimed, and considering that Mr James was of an age with the Laird himself, she could understand the apparent interest in her.

'It will be no trouble,' Mhairi-Anne assured her, settling herself down on the bench seat, in an attempt to overcome her apparent reticence. 'I'm used to children.'

'Well, I'll only be five minutes, or so,' murmured Mrs Davidson, glancing once more at Alex, who was again seated on his comfortably padded bottom, engrossed in exploring the array of little toys, which surrounded him, before she finally made off at a brisk trot.

Alone at last with her child, Mhairi-Anne could not believe her luck and she longed to revel in these moments, by sprawling on the grass beside him. Mindful of the watching windows behind her, however, she remained on the bench and, instead, encouraged him to bring his toys to her. Alex obliged and promptly stood quite happily, with one hand clutching the skirt of her gown for support, while the other rattled and banged his toys in her lap. Her back to the windows, she could thus fondle his little face unseen and kiss the tips of the fingers he raised near her lips. But most wondrous of all, perhaps, she could murmur what was in her heart, in the bittersweet knowledge that he could not possibly comprehend any outpourings or repeat such forbidden sentiments.

Fortunately, she was silent when the shadow fell over them, but so preoccupied had she been with Alex, she had no audible warning of its approach. Startled by the sudden umbrella of gloom, her movements froze, while her eyes discerned the unmistakable outline of a man. She turned slowly to see Alexander standing impassively behind her.

He looks older, she thought immediately, although this appeared more due to the grimness of his expression than any deterioration in his looks. His hair was still as black as ever; his skin still tanned, and although his shoulders appeared broader, as if he had gained a little weight, it suited him. His eyes, however, held nothing of the devilish gleam she remembered so well from Tora and his lips were set in a taut line, with no grinning flash of strong white teeth. It seemed that he had come straight from the stables, as he was dressed in riding apparel and still carried a crop in one hand.

There were no smiles of greeting — no words — as he walked slowly round in front of the bench. Yet the air was charged by the eyes which inexorably held hers, until Alex, spotting his father, drew his attention with an excited series of monosyllables. 'Pa . . . Pa . . . Pa . . . Pa . . . Pa . . . '

Dropping the crop on the bench seat, Alexander knelt and smiled widely at the child, who bounded into his waiting arms and as he scooped him upwards, she rose quickly, too, eyes fleeing longingly to the house, as she did not wish to witness this display of closeness between father and son. As if anticipating her flight, however, he detained her. 'Where's Mrs Davidson?'

'She went back indoors to fetch his sun hat,' she explained, nodding towards the house, while she wished fervently that the woman would promptly appear, to terminate this excruciating meeting.

'So, she left you to exercise your charms on my son?'

The unmistakable sarcasm of his tone spun her head round. Hostility, she could handle, she thought, summoning a poisonous smile, as the memory of his costly deception, with all its dire implications, washed over her. The sight of Alex bouncing delightedly in his arms, however, disarmed her tongue. A surge of anguish then threatening to overwhelm her, she turned from him hurriedly.

'Running away again?'

The taunt angered her afresh and she halted, turning slowly again towards him. 'What do you want of me?'

His eyes narrowed inscrutably. 'I hear you're engaged to my uncle.'

'So?'

'If my memory serves me correctly, you were supposed to be done with him.'

The last thing she wanted was to have any debate about her fictitious engagement, but she resented the fact that he seemed to think she owed him an explanation. 'We all said a lot on Tora, which we evidently did not mean,' she responded tartly, gazing deliberately at the child, who was now struggling to get down on the grass again.

Alexander stooped and sat Alex beside his toys once more, before he approached her, hands now stuffed into the pockets of his black riding breeches.

'I wonder what my uncle might do, if he learned about you and me,' he muttered tersely. 'As I recall, you were rather anxious to keep it from him. Left the way open for a fond reunion, didn't it?'

Her eyes flashed up at him angrily. 'That sounds like a threat — but you're too late, I'm afraid. Our 'fond reunion', as you put it, included telling him the truth about us.'

Surprised, he nevertheless concealed it well in a ruthless grin. 'So, he now knows of my philandering and he's forgiven you! Perhaps, he'll even leave Tora to you.'

'On the contrary,' she retorted coldly, 'he's delighted by your reproductive powers. The fact that your philandering managed to produce a son was a real coup. Now he not only has one heir, he has two.'

'And so, you take your revenge!'

'Revenge?'

'You're going to marry him. Doubtless, you will have deduced I do not fancy you as my aunt.'

'Revenge has nothing to do with it. You flatter yourself.'

'Do I?' The question hung in the air, while their eyes held and the venom between them seemed suddenly to be consumed by a surge of contrary feelings, which flared unbidden. In a high-necked muslin gown, she was as bewitching as ever, he thought, the pale lilac colour highlighting the transluscent quality of

129

her skin and the golden lights in her hair.

Fighting a sudden swelling urge to crush her in his arms, he muttered tersely, 'This is getting us nowhere, is it?' His hands jammed firmly into his pockets, he suggested in a more conciliatory tone, 'I suppose we should talk reasonably — while we have the chance.' He gestured at the adjacent bench with his head. 'Let's sit. It will appear more natural from the windows.'

A glance back towards the house confirmed that there was still no sign of Mrs Davidson, but she must be back any minute, she thought. She waited, nevertheless, until he had dropped down on one end of the bench in front of where Alex played, before she, too, sat at the other extremity, as far away from him as possible and with his riding crop between them.

At first, they both sat mute now, as if entranced by the child playing in front of them — happily oblivious to the terrible tension in his audience. Eventually, however, Alexander sat forward, elbows digging into his knees, as he massaged his lower jaw. 'It happened once,' he said suddenly, his tone low as he gazed still at his son. 'At the time, I bitterly regretted it and it was before I became involved with you.' He glanced sideways at her. 'So, you see, on Tora I did not say anything I did not mean. I was ashamed of myself and did not wish to confirm the impression that I was a callous rake.'

'I would never have become involved with you, had I known about Victoria,' she responded, although — again acutely aware of the strength of his physical appeal — she recognized that this was probably a lie. In all likelihood, she would have forgiven him, as he had overlooked her affair with James. And, if he had been honest with her, Victoria might never have deceived her, as she did. 'Did you ask her to marry you then?' Her tone was sharpened by the bitterness of what that deceit had cost her, and Victoria's remembered taunt, when they had confronted each other in the Perth hotel.

'Yes,' he admitted. 'But it was no more than a gesture.' He sighed deeply. 'When I learned she had borne a child — well . . . ' His voice tailed to a halt, as Alex laughed and gurgled up at him and he stretched out one hand, so that the child readily clambered to his feet to play drums on his knees. He grasped the little hands that were pummelling him and pressed both to his lips, before he backed him on to his bottom again.

Caught off-guard, when he turned towards her, Mhairi-Anne's eyes were moist, but he

131

had no time to puzzle over her expression, as, in the distance, he caught sight of his mother and Mrs Davidson hurrying towards them.

'Don't look now,' he muttered irritably, 'but the troops are about to arrive and you still haven't answered my question. Why . . . why did you go back to him?'

She might have answered truthfully that she had nowhere else to go, but tears were too near to admit to such vulnerability. 'You're married now — expecting a second child, so I'm told. It's really none of your business.'

Had her tone been harsh, pride would have compelled him to leave it there, but he sensed, albeit unconsciously, a frustration equal to his own and he muttered fiercely through his teeth, 'Isn't it? We'll see about that!'

Suddenly, the fire in his expression was curtained by a mask of control and he stood up with a wide grin to greet his mother, who arrived amidst flutters of agitated lace. Mhairi-Anne rose also and looked round to see Mrs Davidson trailing red-faced in her wake and realized Lady McNair was annoyed, although it was hard to discern this in her general demeanour.

'I'm so very sorry, Mhairi-Anne,' she declared, smiling graciously as ever. 'Mrs

Davidson should have known better than to leave Sandy with any of our guests.' The sweet tone belied the sharp reprimand evident in the words and Mhairi-Anne immediately spoke up for the woman, who had evidently had a more thorough dressing-down in private.

'It was not Mrs Davidson's fault,' she assured her. 'I insisted, and it was a pleasure. I'm very fond of children.'

Behind Lady McNair, Mrs Davidson shot her a grateful glance, before she proceeded to put on Alex's bonnet, while Alexander commented, 'I wish you would stop calling him Sandy, Mama!'

'It's a sign of affection, as you well know, Alexander,' responded his mother tolerantly.

'"A rose by any other name would smell as sweet!"' he quipped sarcastically, before picking up Alex, who was already trying to discard his bonnet, and holding the delighted child high above his head, so that he giggled joyously, while his legs and arms flailed the air.

Aware of Lady McNair's watchful eyes upon her, Mhairi-Anne looked back at the house evasively. 'I really must go and unpack.'

'I'll have one of the servants do that,' her host immediately suggested.

'No . . . thanks . . . I'll manage,' she

133

assured her, preparing to move away.

'I'll walk back with you. You should come, too, Alexander. Victoria has taken to her bed, I'm afraid.' In response to Alexander's immediate frown, she added quickly, 'Absolutely no cause for alarm, darling. Dr Morgan has already seen her and he assured me everything is fine, but she may need some cheering up. She's going to miss the ball, as he's advised rest over the next few days.'

Lady McNair walked between them, as they returned to the house, secretly glad of this opportunity to have them together — all to herself — but the experience did nothing to diminish her inward disquiet. The tension between them seemed palpable, she thought — or was it her imagination playing tricks on her again? In any case, she was obliged to engineer a constant train of small talk to punctuate the silence, which neither of them sought voluntarily to break and she was relieved when they reached the top of the main staircase, where Mhairi-Anne left them to go back to her room in the east wing.

'You really should have warned me about her,' Lady McNair said immediately to her son, as soon as they were out of earshot.

Determined to be obtuse, Alexander responded, 'Why should I have done that?'

Outside her chamber, she stopped in front

of him. 'You've never been as blinkered as your father can be, Alexander, so please don't treat me like a fool.'

He looked down on her, his face resolutely inscrutable. 'I don't know what you want me to say.'

'She's a beautiful young woman!' she said crossly. 'Don't try to tell me you never noticed that fact on Tora.'

He ran one hand carelessly through his hair and gazed irritably at the ceiling, before he responded, 'There has always been an understanding between her and James.'

'But you never thought to mention this to either your father or me on your return.'

'Eric was dying on my return, Mama!'

Her agitation disintegrated before his eyes and he put one arm around her, hating the necessity to lie in this brutal fashion. 'I must go and see Victoria, now,' he murmured gently. 'You're getting yourself whipped up into a lather over nothing.' He kissed her cheek lightly. 'I'll see you at dinner.'

Lady McNair watched him stride on along the corridor, tapping his riding crop with apparent nonchalance against his thigh, while unshed tears stung behind her eyes for reasons she did not dare to examine. He had done nothing to alleviate the cold poultice of fear, which had settled around her heart.

Later, seated on the edge of the bed, Alexander faced another uncomfortable round of questions from Victoria.

'Have you seen her?' she asked nervously, the agony of not knowing outweighing her desire to avoid mentioning her name.

'In the garden,' he responded, before briefly explaining the context.

'Mrs Davidson left her with Alex,' she echoed involuntarily, while Alexander frowned at the strange expression on her face.

'Don't you start to make a fuss about it! Poor Mrs Davidson's already had a lashing from Mother, which was quite unnecessary.' He stood up, shrugging off his jacket and tossing it on to a chair, before adding casually, 'The way Mother came seething to the rescue, you'd have thought he was about to be kidnapped.'

Her eyes darted toward him in alarm, but he was sitting taking off his boots, clearly oblivious to the ironic potential in his comment.

'Your mother was quite annoyed at us I think, when she saw her,' she continued cautiously.

'My mother attends too many sewing circles!' came the disparaging retort, as he yanked off one long boot and it clattered noisily to the floor.

There was a long pause, before she murmured, 'Is she still as beautiful?'

He glanced up to see her looking across at him. 'What do you want me to say?' he muttered helplessly. 'She's grown a beard and two heads?'

She laughed softly, but her tone remained serious. 'You were in love with her.'

Another boot clattered to the floor and he stood up, opening his shirt to reveal the dark hair of his chest.

'That was two years ago. She's engaged to my uncle and I'm married to you. You're going to have our second child, for God's sake! You must think I'm insane, asking a question like that.'

She stretched out one hand to him and he was obliged to resume his seat on her bed.

'It wasn't a question,' she admonished lightly, before kissing his fingers, while her free hand ran possessively over the lean contours of his chest. 'Merely an observation!' He arrested the straying hand and pressed it to his lips. 'You're supposed to be resting — not seducing me — or letting your fevered imagination work overtime.'

'I wish you would seduce me.'

He leaned over and kissed her lightly on

the lips. 'I think I'll report you to Dr Morgan, you hussy!'

She laughed and blushed, realizing she had strayed from her role. But he was rising, in any case, to shrug off his shirt. 'I'm going for a wash.'

In their adjoining bathroom, he closed the door quietly behind him, before he leaned back against the wall, legs spread, breathing deeply, as if he had just gained his release from a jail. He had always hated pretence. Before his fateful visit to Tora, he had prided himself on saying exactly what he thought. Nowadays, however, his life seemed to consist of a merry-go-round of lies, half-truths and inventions, in order to avoid hurting people. *All the world's a stage, and all the men and women merely players.* Yet if he were play-acting, so, conceivably, was Mhairi-Anne — this thought bringing the rudiments of a self-deprecating smile to his face. So much for the unselfishness of love, he mused — rat that he was. But there was no pretence of gallantry in the way he felt about her. At least he could be honest about that. He wanted her to be miserably obsessed with him, not happily in love with James. The possibility that she might share his wretchedness was the only idea which seemed to make the situation more tolerable. But even if this were the case, there was nothing he could do about it. He pushed himself off the wall and glanced at the closed door, which separated him from his pregnant wife. Nothing . . . nothing . . . nothing, he reiterated, thumping his fist softly on the wall. If he could not give Victoria his love, she deserved, at the very least, his fidelity — albeit that in his heart and mind he already knew that he had never ever been faithful to her.

9

Meanwhile, Mhairi-Anne was heading along the corridor to her own room, when James's door opened and he beckoned to her.

'Come in — Calum's here.'

She saw Calum seated on a sofa by the window and she smiled wanly. 'You saw everything?'

'Aye, you got some time with the bairn.'

Mhairi-Anne sat down on the edge of an adjacent chair, nodding briefly, before she murmured, 'I wouldn't have known him.'

James cleared his throat unnecessarily, as he often did when at a temporary loss for words. Calum gazed out of the window, saying nothing.

Eventually, James resumed, 'We were just talking about the news concerning Victoria.'

Mhairi-Anne glanced across at him. 'Another complication!' She looked down at her hands, where her 'engagement' ring glittered up at her mockingly. 'I think Lady McNair imagines I'm a scheming fortune-hunter and Alexander's not pleased, as he clearly does not relish welcoming me into the family.'

'Doesn't he? He's got a nerve, considering

what he got up to under my nose!'

Calum looked at him sharply. 'The 'engagement' was a bad idea, James. It hasn't worked and it's bound to rake open old wounds.'

'It's got her here, hasn't it?' retorted James stubbornly.

'Aye, I suppose there's that,' responded Calum, 'but don't go rubbin' Alexander's nose in it or he might just tell you where you can stuff that island of yours. Remember, he's got Strathcairn now.'

'You know that's the last thing I'd want,' conceded James. 'Damn it, I've always liked the boy, despite all that's happened. We can clear up the matter of the engagement easily enough, when the time is right.'

'I fear the time will never be right for any of this,' intervened Mhairi-Anne apprehensively. 'Apart from the fact that Victoria's pregnant, it's clear they all dote on Alex.' She paused, then her tone became pensive. 'I can't bear to imagine how they'll react if I try to take him back.'

James shrugged. 'You're right about there never being a good moment, but it's guaranteed that things will only get more difficult as time passes. This might just be the best opportunity we'll ever have, with another child on the way as compensation.'

'You make it sound as if we're dealing in objects, James.'

'I don't mean to,' he replied, 'but in families like this, with a lot of money, prestige and power at stake, children — particularly boys — are the lifeblood. I was one of them — remember.'

'But surely that means I have no chance of reclaiming him.'

'I was thinking about how Victoria might feel with her own child on the scene, while Alex always takes precedence.'

'I'm not sure I understand what you mean.'

'I don't want to alarm you,' continued James, taking a cue from Calum's warning glance, 'but, well, after what she did, we have to recognize that she's . . . er . . . unpredictable.'

'You mean she might harm him?' queried Mhairi-Anne, her face paling.

'Och, I'm sure she'd never do that!' Calum interrupted soothingly. 'It's just that — it occurred to us — she might not be as fond o' him, when she has her own bairn and Alex has served his purpose, so to speak?'

Thoughts began reeling in Mhairi-Anne's head. It had always been of some comfort to her that Victoria loved Alex like her own. He might so easily have been hers! But in stealing him, she had already crossed the barrier to

142

criminality. Mhairi-Anne would never forget that dreadful, shocking day in Perth, when she had discovered she had lived with a woman she really did not know. Having taken him so callously in the first place, was it inconceivable that she might, at some future time, decide to 'dispose' of Alex in favour of her own child?

'I . . . I must speak to her!' she muttered suddenly, rising from her chair.

Calum rose to put a consoling hand on her shoulder. 'Now don't you go panickin' 'cause of anythin' we've said. After all, it's only speculation.'

She shook her head. 'I can't take that risk. I'm responsible for this mess. I could have stopped her and I didn't. Money — position — respectability — I put all that first.'

'Aye, for no personal gain. You're too hard on yourself, lassie.' He signalled surreptitiously to James to say something.

'Calum's right!' he rejoined guiltily. 'No need for panic. There's plenty of time to put things right and the question is now, how can we arrange that you meet her privately?'

'Everyone will be at dinner this evening, surely. I could make an excuse and leave.'

'Yes!' agreed James, before looking at Calum, who shrugged.

'Seems as good an idea, as any. But what

are you goin' to say to her?'

'I want my son back — simple as that,' replied Mhairi-Anne, a new determination in her voice. 'You're right about this new child changing everything. Alex was a means to an end, but he could become an impediment, when her own child arrives on the scene. If she won't tell Alexander, then I will.' She paused, as she moved towards the door, where she turned again towards them. 'By the way, I told Alexander that you know about him and me,' she said softly, looking at James.

James, his hackles rising as he imagined Alexander's reaction, retorted tersely, 'I dare say he thinks I'm an old fool for having you back.'

'The engagement was your idea, James — not hers,' intervened Calum.

'Aye, well, he can think what he likes,' muttered James morosely. 'When all's said and done, he's got a bigger shock coming than I did.'

Calum sat down again, to look out of the window pensively, after Mhairi-Anne left to go to her own room, without another word. James's desperation for Alexander to know the truth irked him, as his motives were obviously coloured by some lingering resentment and, given Victoria's previous unprincipled behaviour, he shared their fears for Alex's future, but . . .

'What's wrong with your face?' asked James, brusquely interrupting his thoughts. 'I know that look!'

'My bunion's givin' me fits!'

James's eyebrows rose mockingly. 'Does that mean you'll not be up dancing tomorrow night?'

'It means we're in for some stormy weather by my reckonin', but I've a feelin' it'll be indoors, for once.'

10

Mhairi-Anne dressed with particular care for dinner that evening. She badly needed the confidence of knowing she looked her best when she faced Victoria, and she was annoyed by the feeling that, despite Lady McNair's faultless behaviour towards her, she strongly disapproved of her. The fact that Alexander, too, would be in the party and spurred her efforts was a consideration she did not dwell upon. He was married and she was acutely aware that she should not care what he thought.

Although she made many of her own clothes when on the island, for special occasions she had long used a dressmaker, who lived in a little village near Perth and whom Elizabeth McNair had come to know as a young seamstress, before she had married James and taken up residence on Tora. Over the years, Mrs Baxter had developed a reputation for fine needlework with many of the big houses in the Perthshire district and she had kept Elizabeth's wardrobe replenished with gowns befitting her station in life. Mhairi-Anne's first bought dress had come from her and for the occasion of the Strathcairn ball, she had ordered two new gowns, which they had picked up that morning — one of which she wore for dinner that evening. As Mrs Baxter knew all of her measurements and was particularly gifted in making up gowns to clients' specifications, without the usual round of fittings required by other dressmakers, Mhairi-Anne was well pleased with the results.

In a diaphanous creation of soft rose pink, she scrutinized her reflection in the long gilt-framed mirror in her room. She had never liked the huge leg-o'-mutton sleeves and tightly corseted waists of recent years and she was pleased that only vestigial puffs marked the shoulders of this gown, while the broad yoke and high neck were softened by delicate strips of lace with rich rayon borders and shimmering satin ribbon. The bodice bloused gently over the waistline of the straight skirt, which had layers of ruffles to emphasize the fullness of the back. She wore her hair up in a style reminiscent of the topknot, although unlike many women of the day, who looked like they had grown knobs on their heads, her hair was so long and thick that she had to weave it into a crown of curls, which she secured with hair-pins and two curved pink combs. Diamond and ruby ear-rings, loaned to her by James, as they matched her engagement ring, completed the effect.

When James appeared with Calum to escort her down, both men were visibly impressed. James proudly offered her his arm, his eyes shining his approval, while Calum said simply, 'You look a picture, lassie!'

Lady Rowena was resplendent in a classically simple beige gown, which relied on the quality of the fabric for its flowing line. She stood with Sir David and Isobel in the drawing-room, where the guests had been advised they would gather. Sir David came forward immediately to beam at Mhairi-Anne, while he shook James's hand and said, 'You're a very luck chap, Brother!' Mhairi-Anne was then introduced to Eric's wife, whom she had not met earlier, while Lady McNair stood by, her eyes hooded, as she surreptitiously compared the two younger women. While Isobel was a lady to her backbone, her sense of the style and colours which suited her, often left a great deal to be desired and Rowena presently decided that she must make renewed efforts in future to influence her daughter-in-law's taste. The pale cream of her gown only emphasized the sallowness of her complexion and, while the fluffy and frilly look was all the rage, the over-large sleeve caps emphasized the short-ness of her neck and the overdone layers of frills, ruffles and lace gave the impression of an agitated meringue. Dissatisfied as Rowena was by the comparison, she was nevertheless relieved that Isobel showed no sign of making any frightening discovery in Mhairi-Anne's face, although this, she con-cluded, was not surprising, as Isobel had poor eyesight and they had only recently learned that she was colour-blind. Besides, she had taken it upon herself to warn her daughter-in-law about the surprising nature of James's fiancée, so that there would be no embarrass-ing moments of shock.

'Does Alexander know we're supposed to be dining at eight-thirty?' asked Sir David of his wife, when the grandmother clock on the wall chimed the half-hour and they had all sipped their sherry glasses dry.

Lady McNair nodded. 'You know punctu-ality has never been his strong point and with Victoria being indisposed ... ' At that moment the door opened, however. 'Ah, here he is now.'

Dressed in formal attire, like all of the men, Alexander's concessions to individuality were reflected in a rich ruby-coloured satin waistcoat and white bow tie, which empha-sized his dark good looks, while a strand of his black hair, as usual, hung rebelliously over his forehead, as if he had forgotten to check in the mirror. As James was nearest the door, he immediately faced his uncle — both men meeting for the first time since Alexander's wedding and since their mutual duplicity with Mhairi-Anne had become known to each.

'Nice to see you again, m'boy!' said James with pious politeness, as they shook hands, the moment lengthening due to the sobriety of the looks they exchanged.

'You're looking well, Uncle,' Alexander replied, determined not to be the first to look away, although their handshake had been brief. Considering James's long deception of him, he was not about to appear ashamed of his relationship with Mhairi-Anne, while James, for his part, was equally inclined to show this handsome whippersnapper that he had no right to assume the high moral ground.

Calum, however, interrupted their optical locking of horns, by walking between them to greet Alexander. In the background, Mhairi-Anne hovered, chatting to Isobel, and made no attempt to come forward, Lady McNair noted, before her husband ushered the entire party through the great hallway to the dining-room.

In the subdued glow of candlelight,

provided by silver candelabra, which adorned the table and sideboard, the meal proceeded, served by a small army of servants, who flitted from one shoulder to the next with all the silent efficiency of a well-oiled machine. Cream of celery soup, delicious lemon trout from the River Cairn and avocado mousse were followed by an immense joint of pork loin, teamed with a wide array of fresh vegetables from the estate gardens. Lady McNair was pleased that the party from Tora all thought to compliment her on the prowess of her cook.

Alexander, who was well aware that he had failed to greet Mhairi-Anne in the drawing-room, for the very good reason he had not trusted himself to behave appropriately after one glance at her stunning appearance, was gradually able to relax under the influence of the wine, which flowed freely, and to take full note of her striking elegance from surreptitious glances across the table to where she sat between Isobel and James. Indeed, such was his relief at finding he could cope with the proximity of the engaged couple without betraying himself, he became the life and soul of the dinner party. While his mother noted he was drinking rather more than usual, she was, nevertheless, pleased to see him contribute to the conversation with all the confidence, charm and ease, which his role on the estate had nurtured. Despite himself, James was impressed by his knowledge, his father basked in his reflected glory; and laughter regularly rippled around the room at his wit.

Mhairi-Anne, for her part, was able to contribute particularly to a discussion which arose on the different techniques involved in painting with oils or water-colours and the merits of each. Apparently, Rowena, Isobel and Victoria were all receiving weekly instruction on water-colour painting from a visiting tutor.

'You must let me see some of your work,' suggested Mhairi-Anne politely.

Isobel and Lady McNair exchanged knowing glances. 'I'm afraid we're not at the stage of an exhibition,' remarked Isobel, with a short laugh.

'Oh, I don't know, my dear,' said Rowena fondly. 'Mr Buchanan hailed your creation last week as highly original.'

'But I could hardly take credit for it! A red sky at night may well be the shepherd's delight, but it was scarcely appropriate on a dull Tuesday morning.'

'Isobel has a problem with colours,' confided Lady McNair. 'But it means she produces some remarkable paintings. Mine and Victoria's look dreadfully ordinary, by comparison?'

'I didn't know Victoria was interested in painting,' remarked Mhairi-Anne, reminding herself that she would very shortly have to leave the table, and realizing it was going to be more awkward than she had thought, now that the men were embroiled in a separate discussion about the difficulties encountered in a new island project, which involved the building of a pier and harbour facilities at Port nam Magan. James had promised that he would help her to make her exit, but she knew how easily he could be diverted, when it came to discussing Tora.

'There's no natural timber source on the island, of course,' he was saying, 'but we've discovered a good quarry for the stone we need in the rocky outcrops near Mount Tora.'

'Problem is transportin' it across the island,' remarked Calum. 'So, it's all takin' longer than we'd hoped, but we're gettin' there.'

'I can see you building a railway next,' laughed Sir David.

'Don't think I haven't considered it,' retorted James. 'All we'd need is a small line.'

'Aye, an' steel an' more timber an' the manpower to build it,' scoffed Calum. 'We can turn a hand to a lot of things, James, but

153

I think we've more chance of buildin' our distillery.'

'Distillery?' echoed Alexander.

'Aye, the island council has come up wi' the idea of developin' an island brand o' whisky that we can export.'

'A Tora malt,' mused Alexander. 'I certainly tasted a few powerful concoctions on my rounds,' he concluded with a wry grin.

'That's the point,' chuckled Calum. 'We've already got some expertise, when it comes to alcohol production.'

'And we can grow more barley,' added James. 'We've got ample supplies of good natural spring water. Did you ever see the falls at Mount Tora, Alexander?'

As Alexander shook his head, his father commented, 'I'll take my hat off to you, James, if that island ever turns a profit.'

'Well, maybe not in my time, but the next generation could do it.' He glanced across at Alexander, who, having finished his main course, laid his cutlery on his plate and sat back without comment. He had never told his father about the codicil in James's will, which would obviate any sale of the island, and he had no intention of doing so, having learned that life had too many surprises in store to worry about what might never be.

'You realize Alexander's likely to have his

hands full with this place,' remarked Sir David carefully, still firmly of the opinion that the island should be offloaded, as soon as it came to his son.

'Oh, I don't know about that,' returned James. 'He's got his head screwed on the right way and knows you don't have to keep a hand on every pile of money. He managed a long enough honeymoon, at any rate!'

'I was here!' retorted Sir David.

Alexander sat forward, deciding this turn of conversation had gone on long enough. 'I wish you two would stop talking, as if I were elsewhere,' he admonished lightly. 'In case it's escaped your notice, I'll not be taking orders from the hereafter. You're both going to have to trust me.'

'Trust?' echoed James, glancing at him sharply.

'It works both ways, Uncle,' replied Alexander, meeting James's eyes squarely.

'Aye,' agreed Calum. 'None of us can take it with us, when we go — an' there's always the next generation comin' through to take the reins.' He looked meaningfully at James, who finally remembered he had promised to help Mhairi-Anne regarding the 'next generation'.

He turned in time to hear Mhairi-Anne saying, 'I'm afraid I have the most awful headache coming on.' She had concluded that she would need to effect her exit unaided, but James was timely with his support, albeit rather unconvincing.

'You're looking a trifle pale, m'dear,' he murmured.

Mhairi-Anne smiled weakly, her cheeks, in fact, burning, a fact which Isobel unwittingly noticed, despite the fact that she was colour blind.

'You look as if you might have a temperature.'

'You're probably more tired out after all the travelling than you imagined,' remarked Lady McNair, remembering that Mhairi-Anne had been out in the garden that afternoon, when she could have been resting.

'Why don't you retire?' suggested James. 'Do you want me to come up with you?'

Mhairi-Anne rose immediately. 'No . . . of course not. Enjoy the rest of your meal. Please . . . excuse me, everyone.' She moved swiftly from the room, aware that Alexander's eyes were following her, while she heard Sir David mumbling, 'Too bad . . . too bad . . . lovely girl.'

It was all she could do not to break into a run, as she crossed the great hallway. Dessert had still to be served and they would probably have after dinner drinks, but she reckoned she could probably only count on having fifteen minutes, before Alexander might conceivably return to check on his wife. Thankfully, she had already discovered where their quarters were situated, through casual questioning of a young servant, who had appeared to draw her bath. Thus, she hurried along the corridor of the west wing, *en route*, passing her painting of Tora harbour, before she slowed. The door was the last on the left, according to the girl, but she hesitated outside, imagining she heard voices within. Everyone was at dinner and she had no time to delay, she told herself, however. Consequently, she tapped the door lightly and, without waiting for a response, went in.

To her embarrassment, the first person she saw was Mrs Davidson, who had evidently brought Alex to see his 'mother'. The child was on the bed beside Victoria and all eyes turned towards her in astonishment, as if she were a ghost.

'I'm so sorry . . . I knocked . . . but . . . I wanted to see how you were feeling, Victoria.'

Mrs Davidson recovered first. 'I'll take Alex back to the nursery, if you wish, madam.'

'Yes . . . yes . . . please do that,' Victoria faltered, her eyes large with apprehension, an impression intensified by the thick dark hair which hung loose over her shoulders.

Alex, however, evidently did not wish to leave his 'mother' and clung to her in protest. 'Mama-mama . . . '

Mhairi-Anne steeled herself, as Victoria gently disengaged his little hands from her hair. 'Be a good boy,' she whispered, kissing his cheek, before Mrs Davidson lifted him from the bed.

Alex continued to cry and Mhairi-Anne longed to comfort him, but she knew that she dared not lose focus on the task ahead. Consequently, as Mrs Davidson, carrying her struggling passenger, passed her with a deferential nod, she resisted the temptation to intervene and fixed her gaze on Victoria.

'You'd better sit down, I suppose,' Victoria said, with evident reluctance, as soon as the door closed.

Mhairi-Anne shook her head, but moved closer to the bed. 'I'm not intending to stay.'

Victoria regarded her truculently. 'Why did you come here then? Alexander should be back at any moment. What do you want?'

'My child — I want him back!'

A nervous smile encompassed Victoria's face. 'That's impossible! You had your chance.'

'Did I?'

'It's too late now.'

'You're going to have your own child — I want mine back.'

Briefly, Victoria's head nodded. 'So that's it — now you think you'll ruin everything for me. You're jealous!'

Mhairi-Anne's eyes narrowed on her. 'Yes, I am,' she admitted candidly. 'But I think any normal woman would be jealous, if she heard her child call another woman 'Mama'.'

'So you would ruin his life because of it! He has everything he could ever want here.'

'You played that card the last time, Victoria, and it worked,' retorted Mhairi-Anne. 'But I was homeless and virtually penniless then. Now I have a life — something to offer — and I've realized I can't allow this farce to go on.' She might have added that she feared for her child's safety now — as she never had before — but there was no point in raising that issue. Victoria would insist that she loved Alex, of course, and Mhairi-Anne had no doubt that, at the moment, she would mean it. In any case, she had no time to prolong this debate, unnecessarily. 'I'll be here until Sunday afternoon. You have until then, let's say midday, to own up,' she ended determinedly.

'If you say anything, I can deny it. They won't believe you.'

'I think Alexander will. I'll be able to tell

him all about your house in the glen.'

Victoria moistened her lips, her defiance momentarily giving way to desperation.

'How can I own up?' she cried harshly, her voice rising hysterically. 'How? How?'

'Tell the truth! It's the best time you'll ever have, since you're carrying his child. I could have told Alexander this afternoon, but I didn't — or I could have taken Alex and walked out of here. That way, you would have faced a *fait accompli*, as I did, but I'm giving you a chance I never had. You can put any gloss you like on it, but tell him.'

Victoria gazed at her, her eyes hardening as she looked up and down the length of her shimmering gown. 'This is why you became engaged to James, isn't it? You stand there looking like a lady, but you disgust me! I wonder how he'll feel, when he realizes how he's been used and abused.'

A grim smile played around Mhairi-Anne's lips, while her eyes glittered dangerously in the soft glow of the gas lamps adjacent to the bed. 'Before I left Tora, I tried to be honest with you, because I thought you were my friend. But since I told you about my relationship with James, I've always disgusted you, haven't I? That's why you did what you did — why you thought you'd get away with it. Who would help a creature like me? In your eyes, I don't deserve a child, do I?'

'That's beside the point! If Alexander finds out, so will James. I wonder where your home will be then, when he learns he's harbouring a slut.'

Mhairi-Anne stiffened at the blatancy of the insult and took slow pleasure in revealing how mistaken she was. 'Both James and Calum know everything and are only too happy to help me. Fortunately, they're not as narrow-minded as you are and know me better than you ever did.'

The colour visibly drained from Victoria's face. 'They . . . they know . . . ?'

'Everything!'

Victoria, her head tilting forward at this news, looked wildly at the bedcovers, as if searching impotently for an answer, while her hair tumbled around her face, curtaining the desolation of her expression.

Mhairi-Anne turned away, knowing she had delivered a killing blow, but there was no triumph in the moment. Nothing yet had really been achieved; too many people were going to be hurt; so much could still go wrong. Until she had her child wrapped in her arms on Tora, the nightmare would not be over.

At the door, she was halted, as Victoria's

voice rose again — this time high and despairing.

'Please . . . please . . . don't make me do this!'

Mhairi-Anne looked at the door handle and did not turn. There could be no room in her heart for pity. 'You have until noon on Sunday.'

She yanked the door open, wanting now only to be back in her own room. To her horror, however, she almost collided with Alexander's mother. Caught apparently eavesdropping, Lady McNair stepped back involuntarily into the corridor, a blush rising in a pink tide over her face. Mhairi-Anne had no idea how long she had been there and, at that moment, did not care. Her embarrassment was no less acute — caught as she was in a lie — as well as in breach of all the rules of etiquette, which dictated that she had no business visiting a 'sick room', without prior notice and permission.

Lady McNair recovered her voice first.

'I . . . I thought you had a headache!' she said, her tone accusing, as she struggled to re-exert the iron façade of composure and politeness, which normally characterized her.

'I . . . I decided I'd . . . like to see Victoria, before I retired,' Mhairi-Anne faltered.

'The doctor said she was to have no

visitors,' the older woman countered, the lie lending authority to the unmistakable reprimand.

'I'm sorry,' Mhairi-Anne murmured. 'I should have asked. It was an impulse — I haven't seen her in so long.'

Their eyes met squarely for the first time. 'Your headache's better then?'

The polite enquiry merely underscored the fact that lying was getting Mhairi-Anne nowhere, as her earlier excuse, of course, highlighted the calculated nature of the visit. She decided swiftly not to degrade herself further by compounding the story. 'Please accept my sincere apologies,' she murmured quietly, before moving away along the corridor, with as much dignity as she could muster.

Lady McNair stared after the elegant retreating figure, her knuckles whitening on the door handle.

Victoria was sitting up in bed, arms holding her bent knees in an upright foetal position and when her mother-in-law entered, she turned wretched eyes upon her. The game was up, she thought miserably. There was no point in pretending any further.

'What's wrong? What's happened?' demanded Rowena anxiously, as she approached the bed. 'I've just had the most embarrassing encounter of my life with that woman from Tora.'

'I . . . I . . . wouldn't know where to begin,' Victoria muttered, rubbing the lower half of her face, so that her eyes appeared to swell with a wildness, which frightened Rowena.

'I heard . . . well . . . I don't know, but it sounded very like a threat. You have until noon on Sunday — something like that.'

Victoria glanced up at her, eyes filling with tears, while her mouth trembled. 'I . . . I did a terrible thing. You'll hate me.'

Rowena sat down on the edge of the bed, all her instincts suddenly telling her that calmness must be the keynote. All day she had suspected some dreadful secret. Ironically, now she was being proved right, her fear was being replaced by a steely determination. Her family was under threat. It was not for the first time: she had dealt with situations before and this would surely be no different.

She laid a cool hand over one of Victoria's and her voice was firm, but encouraging. 'Listen to me! Isobel has gone to bed and, judging by the flow of brandy downstairs, Alexander is likely to be there with the others until midnight. We have time to talk, but you must tell me the truth — everything about that woman.' She paused, as she handed Victoria a tiny embroidered handkerchief.

'Then I'll know how to help you.'

'Help me?' echoed Victoria, dabbing at her eyes and nose. 'I don't think you'll want anything to do with me, once you know.'

Lady McNair squeezed the hand she still held. 'Nonsense! You're my daughter, now. Nothing you've done can ever change that. Besides, I've a feeling I'm not going to be nearly as shocked as you might imagine. I suppose all of this must have started on Tora . . . ?'

11

When Alexander arose before seven the
following morning, he was relieved not to
have the thumping headache he deserved in
light of his alcohol consumption the night
before and, having washed, shaved and
dressed, he went to check on Victoria. She
was still sleeping as she had been, when he
had crept past her bed around midnight,
and he made no attempt to waken her
now. Even asleep, she looked fragile,
with dark circles shadowing her eyes and
the lids appeared swollen, as if she had
been crying — possibly because she was to
miss this damned ball, he concluded. Still,
he wanted to ensure the doctor saw her
again today so he went in search of his
mother.

She was in the nursery, Robbie told him,
when he failed to locate her in her room.

'At this hour?' he exclaimed.

Mrs Robertson smiled. 'She's a doting
granny, if ever I saw one.'

When he entered the nursery, which was
located on the third floor of the house, Alex
was playing on the rug in the middle of the

room, while Lady McNair, looking uncustomarily dishevelled, sat watching him pensively. Alexander noticed she was still in her dressing-gown and appeared to have come here straight from her bed. She glanced up and smiled faintly as he came in.

'Are you feeling all right?' he asked, as he went down on his knees beside his child, to kiss his dark head.

'A little tired — that's all,' responded his mother, self-consciously patting her hair, which was as yet undone.

'Why on earth are you up here then? With the ball tonight I thought you would be enjoying a long lie-in.'

'I couldn't sleep,' she confessed. 'All the excitement of today, I suppose.'

'I'm beginning to think this ball was a bad idea,' he responded, drawing Alex upwards, so that he stamped his feet delightedly on the floor.

'He's ready to dance anyway,' remarked his mother.

'A war dance by the look of it,' grinned Alexander, before adding more soberly, 'but it's been far too much work and worry for you and I'm concerned about Victoria.'

'Why? How is she this morning?'

'Still asleep. But I don't like the look of her. In fact, that's why I wanted to see you. Is Dr

167

Morgan coming again today?'

'Yes, he promised to call in, but she's fine, Alexander. I spoke to her last night and she's just disappointed and depressed about missing the ball.'

'She looked as if she's been crying . . . '

'Yes, well, she did have a little weep, but that's to be expected in her condition.'

'I suppose you're right,' he responded, beginning to tickle his son so that his gurgling laughter resounded in the nursery.

'I can't imagine this house without him nowadays,' murmured Rowena, something in her tone causing Alexander to glance up at her.

'You're in a morbid mood this morning, Mother!'

'While you seem altogether more cheerful!'

He shrugged, before burying his face in Alex's tummy, while the child squealed joyously and yanked on his hair.

He was, indeed, in a much more positive state of mind — due, he thought, to his immense relief — not only in surviving unscathed the meeting he had so dreaded, but in rediscovering the simple pleasure of looking at her and being in her company. Contrary to his dire expectations, too, so far he had been spared the vicious spasms of jealousy, which had regularly beset him, whenever he had thought of Mhairi-Anne and James together. Strangely, the actual reality had proved much more benign than the malignant concoctions of his imagination. Whatever the reason for their engagement, he now felt convinced that it was not fired by the kind of chemistry which had flared between them on Tora — and lingered still, awaiting only the right moment to be rekindled. Or the wrong moment, he thought next, reminding himself that, despite the rampant infidelities in his mind, he was resolved to faithfulness.

'I should get dressed,' said Lady McNair, rising from her chair, while Alexander rolled on to his back to hold a giggling Alex high in the air. 'Thank Heaven, he hasn't had his breakfast yet.'

'But it's right here!' Mrs Davidson's voice intervened from the doorway, where she stood carrying Alex's breakfast on a tray.

'Right! Time I had mine, too,' said Alexander, bringing his son zooming back to earth, before he deposited him safely in his high chair.

He and Rowena left the nursery with Alex bouncing 'Bye-Byes' to them.

'You should go back to bed,' suggested Alexander, as he proceeded ahead of her down the narrow stair from the nursery. 'I can have some breakfast sent up to you, if you want.'

'I'm not really very hungry.'

At the bottom, he turned to take her hand, as she descended the last couple of steps, simultaneously scrutinizing her face. 'There's something wrong, isn't there?'

She looked up at him, evidently taking her time before responding. 'I have to make up my mind about something and it's not easy.'

'You're being very mysterious.'

'It runs in the family!'

'You're not still on about that business of yesterday?'

'Why should I be? You assured me that I was making mountains out of molehills, didn't you?'

He nodded slowly. 'So what's this all about then?'

'Absolutely nothing!' Her eyes suddenly flashed angrily up at him. 'Now it's your turn to feel stupid and foolish and trivial!' With that she stalked away leaving her bemused son staring helplessly after her.

Downstairs in the dining-room, he found that his father had started breakfast alone.

'Mother is in a most peculiar mood this morning,' Alexander remarked, as he heaped food on to his plate from the chafing dishes on the sideboard. 'She looks exhausted.'

'I'm not surprised. I thought I was sleeping beside a dervish. Eventually I went next door, but I heard her up and down all night.' He paused, before turning to a new topic. 'By the way, I mentioned to James last night that you might take him and Mhairi-Anne riding over the estate this afternoon. I understand Calum never sits on a horse, if he can help it, but it would take two of them out of the way of all the commotion, which will be going on around the house. I'll need to stay here, to make sure your mother doesn't have a heart attack before this evening.'

Alexander casually signalled his agreement.

'Damned attractive woman, don't you think?' grinned Sir David, with a salacious gleam in his eyes. 'You know, the more I see of my brother, I think he's a bit of a dark horse.'

Alexander glanced up from his plate. 'You haven't been making remarks like that to Mother, by any chance?'

Sir David assumed a look of injured innocence. 'What do you take me for?' he scoffed, before whispering conspiratorially, 'I think your mother's age is the main problem.'

'She's several years younger than you, Papa, or had you forgotten?' Alexander hissed back, mindful of the servant standing to attention by the door.

'But men don't *change*, m'boy. We just learn to suffer.'

'Your sensitivity, as always, knows no bounds,' quipped Alexander, sarcastically.

★ ★ ★

No one else appeared in the dining-room before Alexander departed for the stables — having first checked that Victoria was still asleep. He had an early appointment with his game-keeper, who appeared to think that poaching was becoming a problem on the estate and he was glad of the excuse to absent himself from the house, where all hell was set to break loose.

Weeks of intensive preparatory work were now to culminate in a climax of readiness for the ball that evening and there was no time to lose. Extra servants drafted in to cope with the occasion and the 200 guests who would descend upon Strathcairn, had already arrived in the kitchen to be given orders by Mrs Robertson; others had begun to lift carpets and rearrange furniture in the drawing-room, to ensure maximum space and seating. Burly men were put to work in the great entrance hall, removing and storing furniture, to allow maximum space for the dancing to take place. The floors began to gleam afresh with wax, while flower arrangements, incorporating every hue and variety, gradually began to take shape at strategic points. Outside, laden transport arrived, bringing all the food and catering equipment, as well as musical instruments for the orchestra, while a team of experts prepared the fireworks for the customary midnight display in the gardens.

Having taken lunch of home-baked bread, milk and cheese with one of the tenant farmers and his family, Alexander returned to the stables at two o'clock, as arranged with his father, to conduct James and Mhairi-Anne on their tour of the estate. His father was already there with them and had evidently helped with the selection of mounts, although Alexander immediately warned James that he would need to be careful with the beast presently being saddled for him.

'He threw one of the grooms last week, Uncle. For some reason we've yet to discover, he appears to have developed a temperamental streak.'

'Brownie?' queried his father. 'I didn't hear about that.'

'I'm not too old to handle a bit of spirit!' scoffed James, rubbing his hand down the horse's nose. 'That's a beauty, you've got there,' he added, eyeing the magnificent black stallion, which Alexander rode.

Alexander nodded, before his eyes strayed to where Mhairi-Anne was being assisted into the saddle, in the same attractive green velvet riding attire she had worn, when they had attended the procession on Tora. Later that day, Seorus Dhu had died and she had vanished. It seemed now like a lifetime ago, yet his feelings about her had not altered one iota, while his circumstances had changed irrevocably.

'Enjoy yourselves!' called Sir David, waving as James finally swung himself into the saddle and they set off — Alexander in the lead, as they trotted across the stable yard, followed by Mhairi-Anne with James in the rear. Alexander had just moved on to the woodland path, when he heard a commotion behind him. He turned in time to see Brownie rearing up to paw the air with his hoofs, while James was catapulted backwards out of the saddle.

'Jesus!' he exclaimed, immediately turning back, with Mhairi-Anne at his tail.

As Alexander's father had not yet left the stable yard, however, he was beside his brother first and it was becoming evident as Alexander and Mhairi-Anne dismounted, that little damage appeared to have been done — except to James's pride.

'Where is that beast?' James was blustering, even while he was still seated on his rear in the stable yard. 'And don't you dare say I told you so!' he warned Alexander, as he came forward. 'I've never met a horse yet that I can't master and your Brownie's not going to get away with that.'

While Alexander advised one of the grooms to fetch the horse, who was now munching calmly on the grass at the edge of the yard, James made an unsuccessful attempt to get up.

'Damn and blast! I think I've done my ankle in.'

'Let's have a look,' suggested his brother. 'Can't see much for your boot, but I don't want to take that off until we get you indoors.'

'Indoors? Just help me up, I say!'

It took both Alexander and his father to lift James and it became abundantly clear even to him, that he was going nowhere but indoors, as his foot could not bear his own weight.

'We'll need to get you back to the house, James,' Sir David said, while Alexander instructed the groom, who still stood by with Brownie, to stable the horse and get some kind of transport ready. 'The last I heard Dr Morgan had still to see Victoria. With any luck, we'll get back in time for him to have a look at you, too.'

'Let's hope it's not broken,' said Mhairi-Anne anxiously.

'I don't think it is. He seems to be able to bend it,' said Sir David. 'Probably given it a bad twist though. Don't think there will be much dancing for him tonight.'

'I'm not unconscious, in case you hadn't noticed,' said James crossly.

'No danger of that, Uncle!' retorted Alexander, grimacing under his weight. 'Let's see if we can sit you down on that wall over there.'

When the groom emerged with a cart drawn by one of the mares, the two men helped James into the back of it.

'Not exactly first-class travel, James, but it'll get us there,' said his brother, climbing in beside him. 'Now you two can get on,' he ended, turning casually to Mhairi-Anne and Alexander.

'No, I'll come back to the house, too,' said Mhairi-Anne immediately.

'What nonsense — eh James?' retorted Sir David. 'All dressed up to go riding! We can't have that. Off you go and enjoy yourself!'

'Really . . . I — '

'On you go,' James said stiffly, although he could cheerfully have throttled his magnanimous brother. But he knew that to insist upon her return with him would appear childish and possibly suspicious. Neverthe-less, he subjected Alexander to a penetrating stare, before the cart set off, leaving Mhairi-Anne gazing helplessly after them.

For some time they rode without exchang-ing a single word through leafy woodland paths, meadows bursting with carpets of wild flowers, fields where cattle and sheep grazed and finally open moorland, where Alexander moved from a canter into a gallop, allowing the superb stallion his head, so that he had reached the brow of a hill, dismounted and tethered him to a bush, some time before Mhairi-Anne arrived. She cantered into a slow trot, before bringing her brown mare to a halt some yards away from him, without dismounting.

'You can see much of Strathcairn from here,' he said, pointing and naming various landmarks.

'I had no idea it was so vast,' she responded. 'Is that a loch in the distance?'

'A small one — the river runs into it.' He glanced up at her. 'You should give the mare a rest. She's sweating.' He moved towards her and held up his arms. When she hesitated and continued looking down at him dubiously, he said mockingly, 'I'm married, remember?'

After she let go of the reins and slid down, he held her only for the briefest of moments, before he put his hands into his pockets, and grinned. 'There now! James would be proud of me.'

She could not help smiling with him, but he turned away swiftly to stare at a distant range of hills and they lapsed into a moody silence again, punctuated only by the soft moans of a light wind and the swooping cries of birds. 'It's not as nice as yesterday,' she remarked eventually, lost for something to say and eyeing some brooding dark clouds in the sky. 'Will it rain, do you think?'

He glanced upwards. 'They're passing over. Too bad, we might have claimed we were caught in a storm and stayed out all night in a shepherd's hut.'

'Then I wouldn't be able to wear my ball gown,' she responded lightly.

He paused for a moment, before saying, 'You looked beautiful last night.'

'The setting helped,' she murmured, as his eyes brooded upon her.

'I like this setting,' he revealed softly. 'Sometimes I come up here to think.'

She looked away evasively over the landscape. 'The moorland's peaceful — quiet except for the wind and the birds — a little like Tora in a way.'

'Yes.' There was a long silence, before he

added, 'I've never been able to forget, have you?'

She looked down at her gloved hands — mute — while her heart screamed.

Suddenly, he kicked at a clump of grass. 'Come on! It's time we went back. We'll follow the river.'

Having helped her back into the saddle, he swung himself easily on to the stallion and they rode hard until they reached the river, where he led the way at a leisurely pace along a woodland path, which bordered one of the tributaries. At first, Mhairi-Anne found it pleasant: the tributary was narrow and shallow, as it burbled over its rocky course — little more than a stream at this stage. Gradually it widened, however, as it was joined by other tributaries and the water gushing past them became deep and broad.

'This is where most of the good fishing is done,' Alexander called from the front. When she did not reply, he glanced back to see that her face had become as pale as the churning foam and her eyes had the frozen stare of a frightened animal. 'Are you all right?'

Fortunately, the path was broad enough for him to dismount and he tethered the stallion, before hurrying back to her.

'Help me down!' she said immediately,

giving him little warning before she slithered into his arms.

'What's wrong? You're shaking!'

'The river . . . ' Her lips trembled to a halt, as she clung to him wordlessly.

Gradually, her heartbeat slowed and the shaking ceased. 'I feel such a fool. I . . . I had a stupid accident, you see.'

'On Tora?'

'It was before I went back there. I . . . I almost drowned in a river. I'm sorry for being such an idiot, but I had the terrible feeling I was going to fall . . . '

'You should have told me. We didn't need to come this way.'

'I didn't anticipate for one moment that I'd feel like that. I haven't been near a river since, but I suppose it brought everything back to me.'

'Had that anything to do with why you went back to Tora?'

'Partly — I was ill for a time afterwards.'

'Evidently the sea doesn't affect you like that?'

'I was brought up with the sea. Rivers are strangers.' She smiled faintly, his arms still holding her — both suddenly aware of their proximity. Gently, she pressed against him with one hand and his arms dropped.

'We can walk back through the woods, if you like?'

There were too many overhanging branches to ride, but the horses were quite comfortable, walking behind them on the rein, along the woodland path, which was broad enough to accommodate them abreast.

'Where did you go when you left Tora?' he asked suddenly.

'I travelled — all over,' she responded evasively, wishing she could tell him the truth now, while the trees whispered protectively around them, barring the outside world. 'That reminds me — I owe you twenty guineas,' she murmured, recalling the purse she had taken from his room, to ensure her disappearance from his life.

'My emergency fund,' he recalled, thinking how dearly this sum had cost him. But Victoria must already have been pregnant at that point, he thought next. His fate had been sealed on a freak summer day, when he had seduced her on a deserted beach, while the seagulls cried indifferently overhead. 'You can call it an engagement present,' he added, the bitterness of his thoughts spilling into his words. 'I hope Uncle James is sitting now, wondering what we're doing.'

'That's childish!' she retorted.

'Yes, I suppose it is.'

'What about Victoria? Does she trust you?'

'Where you're concerned — no. But where

you're concerned, I don't trust myself.' He stopped in front of her, so that the stallion snorted in protest and he drew a reassuring hand gently down his nose, before he turned to her. 'You never answered my question yesterday: why did you go back to him?'

'James has been good to me.'

'You don't love him!'

'As you love Victoria?'

'I don't deserve Victoria.'

You don't know her, she thought bitterly. But, perhaps, he soon would. Then what would he think of her own part in it, she wondered? She had allowed him to step into a marriage trap. At the time, she had told herself it was all for the good of her child, but, essentially, she had also concluded that Alexander was not worth saving, due to his philandering duplicity. Soon he might hate her for it. For what appeared now to be a solitary mistake, he had been given a life sentence with a woman he evidently did not love. The fact that Mhairi-Anne presently felt all too ready to forgive him seemed far too little, far too late.

As she looked up at him, unable to bear the thought that soon he might despise her, she surrendered to an impulsive longing. 'Hold me,' she whispered suddenly. 'Just hold me.' Her head pressed to his chest, his arms surrounded her and they stood like that, tasting a thin slice of a forbidden Heaven for several minutes. He might so easily have kissed her, he thought later. But it was as if they were both held in the thrall of their circumstances — unable to move backward or forward. Eventually, she lifted her head.

'It's time to go.'

* * *

Meanwhile, at the house, Lady McNair managed to contain her outrage, while Dr Morgan pronounced no bones broken and wrapped a stiff bandage around James's ankle. Back in their quarters, however, she turned on her husband with a fury he could not comprehend.

'How could you do this, David? It was clearly you, not James, who encouraged them to go off riding on their own? Poor Victoria lying ill and you send Alexander off to keep another woman amused!'

Slumped in an armchair, while he was subjected to this onslaught, Sir David looked up at his pacing wife in bemusement. 'I'm beginning to worry about you, Rowena,' he muttered wearily. 'You make it sound as if I've sent them off to a hotel bedroom somewhere!'

'Don't be vulgar! You're far too fond of reducing conversation to the gutter.'

'It's your imagination that's evidently working overtime — not mine! Alexander's a married man — she's engaged to James! Where's the harm in it? God knows, we've both done our fair share of flirting over the years.'

'You've been a witness to any flirting I've done!' she retorted. 'You might have had something to say, if I'd gone off riding in the woods with some young buck?'

'Considering you've never been fond of horses, I dare say I might have raised an eyebrow, m'dear! But Alexander practically lives in the saddle these days and I must say she sat well on that mare. You'd think she'd been born to it.'

'The crux of the matter does not revolve around horsemanship!' she replied, her tone exasperated. 'Victoria is depressed enough about missing the ball, without Alexander neglecting her for another woman.'

'Well, I never thought of it that way. I'll apologize to Victoria, if you like — say it was all my fault.'

'You'll do no such thing! That would only blow the whole thing up out of all proportion.'

'Like you're doing!' he muttered under his breath.

'What was that remark?'

'Tell me what I should be doing then?'

'Perhaps, you could chain yourself up next door, until we go downstairs to greet our guests. That way you might just avoid giving me any more to worry about.'

Sir David rose obligingly. 'I think that might just be the best idea you've had all day.' As he moved towards the adjoining door, he glanced out of the window. 'Worry's over, my dear! Seems like we'll not have to send out a search party.'

Lady McNair looked down to see Alexander and Mhairi-Anne walking back to the house, evidently saying little, or nothing, to each other. 'So, they're back,' she said, relief evident in her voice.

Her husband shook his head at her. 'I'll be glad when this blessed ball is over. I'd never have allowed it, if I'd known it would have this effect on you.'

'It's not the ball, David,' she responded, her voice suddenly weary, as she lowered herself on to the edge of her bed.

'What is it then?' he asked, moving to her side and placing an arm around her shoulders.

'I think I'm beginning to feel old,' she murmured eventually — a truth of sorts.

Guiltily recalling his careless conversation

with his son that morning, remorse coloured his words. 'You're still as beautiful as ever to me,' he responded, before adding with a rueful grin, 'most of the time!'

'Words are easy to say.'

'Not when you mean them. Maybe I don't say it enough, but — well — I still love you and that's a fact.'

She touched his face appreciatively. 'We've been lucky, David. I know that.'

Having kissed her lips gently, he rose from the bed. 'There now! You're smiling again. '*Age cannot wither her, nor custom stale her infinite variety*'!'

She pressed his hands. 'I'm sorry for being such a dreadful grouch! You know I love you, too, darling.'

He patted her cheek reassuringly. 'I'll leave you to beautify yourself. It's time I had my bath.'

As the adjoining door closed softly behind him, she lay back on her bed, wishing she could lie in her bath, as blissfully ignorant as he was. She had always kept secrets from him, but they were always *little* secrets: the *real* price of a gown; the *real* cost of a jewel; the *actual* men she found attractive. She had never kept a secret so huge it could ruin their family, and she longed to confide in him. But in doing so, she feared that she might precipitate the very ruination she sought to avoid. He was a man of action and decision — not a diplomat and a thinker. While he was reliable, courageous and clever, in many ways, he was also volatile, amazingly insensitive at times, and blinkered in his judgements. Telling him would be to invite the proverbial bull to the tea party, after he had smashed numerous china shops. She had to do this alone. Tonight there was the ball; tomorrow she would find out what Mhairi-Anne Graham was really like, and their conversation would have nothing to do with horses.

12

When the musicians started to play and carriages began to roll up the drive of Strathcairn shortly before seven o'clock, at the entrance to the great hall, the family assembled in all their finery to greet their guests. As a traditional feature of the ball was that the male contingent appear in Highland dress, Alexander and his father wore matching Prince Charlie jackets and the colourful red and green Royal Stewart kilts, which reflected a link to Lady McNair's family. The women were attired in gowns which cost considerably more than the 'small fortune', at which Sir David had scowled. In an elegant silk and satin gown of bois-de-rose, trimmed with rosebuds to emphasize the scooped neckline and lace-trimmed chiffon loops to create the illusion of capped sleeves, Lady McNair was magnificent and she was pleased to see that Isobel, in a gown of lavender chiffon and lace, was looking as well as she ever could.

'How is Victoria feeling now?' Lady McNair asked Alexander, who was on her left in the line.

'Absolutely fine!' he responded, repeating exactly the phrase his wife had used, even as a frown creased his forehead.

'You don't look very certain,' whispered his mother, before graciously extending her hand to another couple, who had just been announced.

Alexander had time to reflect, as he waited for the couple to pass. Isobel had evidently prepared the way for him, by revealing where he had been all afternoon, so that it came as no shock. But he had expected lots of questions and the need for reassurance, which had not materialized. On the contrary, she had actually appeared in a strangely buoyant mood — joking with him, when he had difficulty securing his sporran — and kissing him all too seductively, when he had bent over her bed to take his leave. He had been relieved, of course, not to be grilled about his afternoon excursion, but her lack of interest hardly seemed natural. But, perhaps, this was his ego talking.

'Well?' prompted his mother, as the couple dispersed into the growing crowd and the door bell sounded again. 'Did you tell her where you had been?'

'Why wouldn't I tell her?'

'I know it wasn't your fault, Alexander, but it was rather thoughtless to go off like that

. . . Marjory — how are you? So nice to see you again.'

Alexander restrained himself until Marjory and her noxious husband had passed. 'I understand you've already pilloried Father for this, so can we let it drop?'

'Certainly!' Lady McNair responded through her teeth, with the fixed smile of a ventriloquist, as she extended her hand once more, while her son smothered a laugh at her side.

Mhairi-Anne, Calum and James came down the stairs to join the other guests some thirty minutes later. James — leg encased in a thick bandage concealed by knee-high socks — hobbled manfully on a stout walking stick, still bemoaning the need to appear in a kilt. Sir David had wanted them to participate in the formal greetings, but Mhairi-Anne had been glad of the excuse of James's accident to decline, as she did not wish to collaborate in any further broadcasting of her role as James's 'fiancée'. Unlike Victoria, he had been huffy and annoyed when she had visited his room on her return, to find out how he was faring.

'The less you see of him alone, the better I like it,' he had muttered, when she chided him gently for his attitude. 'All he can do is hurt you again. He's married now, remember.'

'I'm scarcely likely to forget, James!' she had retorted, wondering whether he was jealous or genuinely concerned.

'Maybe not for much longer,' Calum had observed, from his favourite window seat.

'What's that?' James had looked at him enquiringly.

'The question is, will he stay married when he discovers the truth?'

'Of course he will — she's pregnant. He can hardly kick her out on to the street.'

Calum had shrugged, before taking several thoughtful puffs on his pipe. 'Aye, but he might want to, I'm thinking.'

Mhairi-Anne had made no further comment. She did not wish to dwell on the possible repercussions of her ultimatum. Alex had to be her prime focus and she had to remember that Victoria had brought all of this on herself.

'There's James and the others!' Sir David said to his wife, waving as he saw them come downstairs. 'He seems to be managing on that stick I gave him.'

Lady McNair looked up, her eyes focusing on Mhairi-Anne, not her brother-in-law. Her gown was not nearly as elaborate as hers or Isobel's, but it was a wonderful aquamarine colour, which, she noted, was already arresting eyes, as it suited her to perfection. The simple lines, which included a gored skirt with a central double pleat to add fullness to the back, highlighted the slim elegance of her figure and the low neckline was tastefully inset with a transparent chiffon yoke, with small frilly sleeves, highlighted by tiny bows on her shoulders. Her hair, arranged on the crown of her head, was decorated by one fluffy feather of the same hue — a dashing touch, which added panache.

'How striking she looks!' breathed Isobel, leaning past Alexander, as she whispered to her mother-in-law.

'Doesn't she!' agreed Lady NcNair. 'She certainly knows how to dress.'

'You say that as if it were her only accomplishment, Mother,' muttered Alexander tersely, uncomfortably sandwiched between them. He noted her appearance with a sick yearning in the pit of his stomach.

'As you failed so miserably to tell me anything about her, you can hardly blame me for my ignorance, darling,' retorted Lady McNair, still smiling graciously around her mingling guests.

The great hall was now ablaze with the colours of myriad tartans and a bedazzling array of extravagant dresses, many adorned with ribbons, bows and sashes, in the matching tartan of their partners.

'I think it's about time we began the

dancing, David,' she continued, turning to her husband. But before they could move to signal to the conductor to strike up the inaugural Military Two-Step, another figure arrested her attention. 'Good heavens! Are my eyes deceiving me?'

They all turned in the direction of her astonished gaze to see Victoria sweeping down the stairs towards them, dressed in the rich topaz-coloured ball gown, which had been made for her.

As planned, she made an entrance which drew many admiring eyes, and her confidence soared. She had been right to take her courage in both hands and brave her enemies, she thought. Over the long afternoon, when she had fretted and fumed over Alexander's absence, it had gradually dawned on her that the core purpose of her feigned indisposition had already been thwarted by Mhairi-Anne daring to visit her room and that she might be losing ground to her now, for no good reason. Mhairi-Anne must think she was beaten. In revealing her secret to her mother-in-law, however, Victoria had not only experienced tremendous relief in sharing her burden, she had secured an ally, who had agreed Mhairi-Anne must be stopped and felt sure there were ways of persuading her to see reason. Victoria regretted, of course, that she had damaged her own high reputation with Lady McNair, so carefully nurtured over the months she had known her, but, if all went well, she felt certain she could regain her approbation in future. What a blessing her pregnancy had proved to be! Her mother-in-law had evidently recognized, without any need to be convinced, that, regardless of what she had done, her marriage had been legitimized and there was no way back. So, far from being beaten, she now harboured the precious hope that Mhairi-Anne might finally be put in her place, once and for all. Surely, when she saw that Lady McNair was also against her, she would recognize the futility of creating a scandal. And, surely, she had decided, it could only help her mother-in-law and undermine her rival's confidence, if, instead of skulking in her room, she appeared tonight to show that she was firmly part of this family — as Mhairi-Anne could never be.

On the other side of the hallway, where James had managed to claim a seat, Calum, who still stood alongside Mhairi-Anne, also spotted her.

'Now, there's an unexpected vision!'

Mhairi-Anne's eyes followed his. 'What a miraculous recovery!' she whispered incredulously.

James, who could see nothing above the sea

of people in front of him, nudged her arm enquiringly.

'Victoria has joined us after all.'

'Has she, by God? That girl is full of surprises.'

'She's got more guts than I'd ever have thought,' opined Calum.

'Or brass neck!' retorted James. 'You told her we both knew, didn't you?' he queried, looking up at Mhairi-Anne.

She nodded, as she watched Victoria being received with some excitement into the bosom of her family. When Alexander kissed her, she turned back to James. 'She has nothing to lose now. Hiding away didn't work. She's probably out to show me how strong she is and I've a nasty feeling that she has told Lady McNair.'

'What makes you think that?'

Mhairi-Anne explained for the first time how she had encountered Alexander's mother on Friday evening, before ending, 'Something has given her fresh confidence.'

'But that's good, is it not, if one of them knows?'

'Not if she supports her. Who knows the lies she has told?'

'Doesn't change a thing!' declared James. 'The truth's still the truth.'

Isobel, meanwhile, was exclaiming, 'How

wonderful that you're with us!'

'You're absolutely sure Dr Morgan gave you the all clear?' Alexander queried.

'Absolutely!' beamed Victoria. 'He thinks the pains the other day were nothing more than a little indigestion.'

'Thinks?' echoed Lady McNair.

'I'm fine! Honestly! Dr Morgan concluded it would be more stressful for me to lie upstairs.'

'He never said a word of this to me.'

'Because I wanted so much to surprise you all.'

'You certainly did that!' declared Sir David. 'A beautiful surprise at that.'

'Yes, you're looking wonderful,' agreed Alexander, trying to inject enthusiasm into his voice, which was denied by his guilty heart.

'Wonderful,' echoed Lady McNair, rapidly deducing now that there had probably never been anything wrong with her daughter-in-law in the first place, although she doubted that Victoria would ever admit it.

Just as she was set to find out tomorrow what Mhairi-Anne Graham was really like, it occurred to her now that she was also rediscovering her daughter-in-law and, unfortunately, she did not like what she was learning. Since listening to Victoria's story on

Friday night — despite her colourful version of Mhairi-Anne's immoral history and her son's foolish promiscuity on Tora, which had seemed to make Victoria's claim of Alex at least understandable — Rowena had increasingly wrestled with her conscience and the uncomfortable knowledge that this wide-eyed girl had, nevertheless, trapped Alexander with an unforgivable lie and that she was, in essence, a criminal. When she had become suspicious of Alex's parentage, because of the resemblance she had spotted in Mhairi-Anne, she had feared, at most, that the two women had somehow come to an arrangement between them, which would reflect the diabolical nature of this creature from Tora. Most shocking, therefore, had been the discovery that Victoria had actually stolen the child from his cradle. Now, in appearing so brazenly in front of the woman she had wronged, it seemed she was displaying a kind of courage, or effrontery, that was more despicable than it was admirable. Of course, she had an ally now. Rightly or wrongly, Rowena had assured her of help and this, no doubt, had boosted her spirits. It struck Lady McNair presently, however, as Victoria and Alexander joined her and David in leading off the first dance to the applause of the whole assembly, that, if they managed to escape the dreaful scandal looming so perilously over them, she might take pleasure, at some future moment, in enlightening Victoria about the motivation behind her support, which had everything to do with saving her family from disastrous notoriety and little to do with protecting her. She had said that Victoria would always be her daughter and she had meant it, at the time. But just as she feared Mhairi-Anne Graham and all the havoc she might wreak, the seeds of revulsion were growing in her against this girl who had wormed her way so deceitfully into her family.

As the night wore on, the great hall resounded with increasingly raucous laughter and gaiety, while the reels of the dancers became ever more explosive and daring. In the dining-room, the army of servants repeatedly replenished the immense array of dishes, which comprised the buffet, and empty cases of champagne, wine and spirits mounted in the kitchen cellar. Lady McNair was glad she had insisted that the large double doors in the dining- and drawing-rooms should be removed for the event, in order to avoid damage, as it allowed the revellers to cavort freely from one area to another. As it was a mild, clear night, the heat of many bodies quickly led to the French doors in both rooms being opened, so that, in growing numbers, the dancers spilled, like colourful bubbles, on to the terraces and lawns, where some couples promptly vanished into the seductive darkness.

At eleven o'clock, a lull was imposed, when the perspiring musicians declared an interval and, having fulfilled countless obligations to dance with an interminable number of young women propelled in front of him like prize blooms by matriarchal minders, whose main aim that evening was to secure for their daughters, the everlasting kudos of a dance with the handsome heir to Strathcairn, Alexander was inwardly furious that he had not once had an opportunity to dance with, or speak to Mhairi-Anne. Despite James being anchored by his twisted ankle, she had not been short of partners, he had noticed, all evidently eager to make the acquaintance of this intriguing stranger, who had sprung up in their midst, and he had been quizzed several times about her identity. His father had managed to secure a dance with her and — to his annoyance — at one point was seen taking evident pleasure in wheeling her before a range of his whiskered shooting set, for inspection, like a flightless pheasant. There was no sign of her in the drawing-room, where Victoria had finally been persuaded to sit and rest and, as she, Isobel and his mother began to hold court with a coven from their sewing circle, he slipped away.

Longing for anonymity and weary of the need to smile inanely, or offer a constant stream of meaningless comments, he milled through the crowds in the great hall — his mood of frustration burgeoning into an urge for recklessness, with every glass of champagne, which he downed *en route*. In the dining-room, he saw his father, James and Calum and a team of the old guard ensconced in a corner with plates of food. Having passed them unnoticed, he wandered on to the spacious terrace, where he nodded to a number of couples, before he finally spotted her, seated alone in the shadows on the low stone wall on one side, evidently deep in thought. Occasionally, she plucked leaves from one of the bushes behind her, only to discard them at her feet. He restrained his desire to join her, in favour of another more daring impulse, which rapidly assumed the guise of irresistible temptation.

His dark-grey eyes gleamed dangerously, as he calculatingly measured the odds of success, with a glance around the terrace. There were too many people about, he would have to await an opportunity and, in the meantime, she might move. It was juvenile, foolish and risky, he concluded, but, even as he did so, he backed into the room and turned to lay another empty glass on a passing tray, then strode past his father and the others with only the barest of glances to ensure they were still embroiled in conversation.

In the great hall, he then edged his way along one wall, smiling and nodding at familiar faces in the sea of people, until his back found the closed door which led through a corridor to other rooms on this floor of the house. With one hand behind him, he felt for the handle and turned it — a silent curse rising in his head for an instant, when he thought his mother had ordered it locked. But suddenly it creaked fractionally ajar and he steadied himself, to await the right moment. None of the family was about and that was all he needed to worry about. Surely, no one else would follow, if they saw him slip through.

In one movement, he backed against the door and rotated to close it behind him. Grinning then at the immediate pleasing discovery of the key lodged in the lock on the other side, he turned it at once, before dropping the key into his sporran — at last a use for it, he thought irreverently. From this side of the door, the muted clamour of the crowded hall crept after him along the darkened corridor, where gas lamps were low. Alone, at last, he felt a surge of irrational satisfaction. Even as half of his brain chided him for the madness possessing him, the other half was glorying in a dangerous sense of freedom he had denied for too long.

The library was in total darkness, alleviated only by moonlight spilling in through the long French windows, and the dusty smell of countless volumes of unread books filled his nostrils. It was a room seldom used in the house, except by Alexander and his father, who, although never having discussed it, by means of genetic telepathy, had separately acquired the habit of using it as a locus of escape. He needed no light, therefore, to thread his way through familiar tables, chairs and desks to the window, which he opened carefully on to the hard, stone steps, that looped down to the gardens. More importantly, however, from the second stair there was a well-trodden, but secluded dirt track through the shrubbery, leading to the adjacent dining-room terrace.

Mhairi-Anne, meanwhile, had found little relief in thought from the apprehension which had built steadily in her, since Alexander's wife had made her unexpected appearance at the ball. Perhaps it was her imagination, but she felt that Victoria's every movement, every look, every smile and every word had somehow been designed and staged for her eyes especially. It was as if she was repeatedly saying to her, 'Go home! You don't belong!' Despite the fact that she knew from the many admiring glances she had attracted — as well as the strangers who had sought her out to dance — that she looked like she was one of the McNairs' affluent circle, she had increasingly felt at odds with everything and everyone around her. This, in itself, was of no importance, she had told herself firmly, but it was as if the yawning gap she perceived between her and 'them' underscored the magnitude of the task she faced in reclaiming her son.

This feeling of alienation had not been helped, of course, by her repeated, fraudulent introduction, as James McNair's fiancée — the lie constantly reminding her that she had no legitimate social status among these people and that her real goal, when known, would assuredly result in her being cast into a diabolical pit of notoriety. She sighed in the shadowed nook of the terrace, as she heard the music resume and concluded she could not go on hiding. Eager couples were now streaming in from the gardens and as another group vanished through the French doors, she made to follow them.

The iron feel of an arm grabbing her waist gave birth to a tiny yelp of surprise, which might easily have become a scream, but for the hand which clamped firmly over her mouth. Hauled backwards into the shrubbery behind her, she struggled instinctively, until a familiar voice whispered mockingly against her ear, 'Don't move and keep quiet — or we're done for!'

She heard the voices and laughter of another group of guests moving across the terrace, while his warm breath fanned her ear lobe. Her body having fallen backwards against him, her head was cradled in his neck and she sat, as if on his lap, while he crouched on his knees, holding her tightly against him from behind.

He released the pressure of his hand on her mouth as the voices receded on the terrace, and she immediately hissed at him, 'You're mad! Utterly crazy!'

'I know, but isn't this fun?'

'Let me up!'

'Now that would be madness!' he whispered, as more activity sounded on the terrace. 'You don't want to be caught climbing walls in that outfit, do you?'

'You're drunk!'

'Just a fraction, but I know how to get us

out of this. Keep your head down and follow me.' He released her and she turned to glare into his grinning face.

'You're enjoying this, you fool!'

'Best time, I've had all night! Sorry about the gown, but it's dry. You'll dust off! Come on!'

Crouching low, as he was, she followed him through the shrubbery until they reached the stone stairs to the library window, where he hesitated to check that there was no one positioned in the garden, to see them emerge.

'All clear!' he whispered, catching her hand and pulling her up with him through the French door, which he had conveniently left ajar.

The dark solitude of the library enclosing them, she glanced up at him warily, in between fits of shaking her gown, to get rid of dead leaves which had stuck to her.

'Now what?'

Having brushed similar debris off his kilt with his hands, he leaned back against the side of a desk, legs indolently spread, arms folded loosely in front of him. 'Well, it would be a pity after all the risks I took to get you here, not to stay a while.'

Flattered, in spite of her better judgement, a faint smile played with her lips, although she said soberly, 'We'll be missed.'

He shrugged. 'So long as they don't find us.'

'And what do you propose we do with this time?' she asked, glancing around the room, as her eyes acclimatized to the darkness. 'Read some Shakespeare, perhaps?'

'*Romeo and Juliet* might be apt.'

'We're a little old to play the star-crossed lovers,' she retorted. 'And we're too old for childish games like this.'

'Do you never want to turn the clcok back?'

'Who doesn't?'

'This reminds me of that time on Tora, when we were closeted in your studio.'

'There was a little more light, as I recall. I was beginning your portrait.'

'Did you ever finish it?'

'No!' she lied.

'Lose interest?'

'I couldn't remember what you looked like.'

He laughed softly. 'Liar!'

'Come to think of it, we could read *Hamlet*. You might do a fair interpretation of a man who couldn't make up his mind.'

'Ah, but I don't have any dilemma about murder. I've decided James can live, as I know you don't love him. My conflict centres on passion, I'm afraid, between a forbidden

Gertrude and an ideal Ophelia.'

'And I suppose I'm cast as Gertrude!' she scoffed lightly. 'You forget, a mother can't be six months younger than her son.'

'But you *are* forbidden and you think I'm childish,' he mused with a grin. 'I could try to bring out your maternal instinct.'

The unwitting irony in his comment quenched the smile on her face. 'But it's rather late for your ideal Ophelia to be sent to a nunnery, isn't it?'

He nodded, his face sobering, as he looked at her intently. 'Yes, I'm afraid it is.'

As their mood darkened, their eyes held in the darkness and she felt the magnetic pull of the attraction between them — so powerful, she looked away uncomfortably. 'I hope your plans for this kidnapping included an escape route.'

'This is my escape! But don't worry. You can go back through the garden, while I can return the way I came. Listen . . . a slow waltz, at last!'

The muted strains of Chopin drifted to her ears.

He stood up to his full height, as he raised his hands. 'One dance before we go back to our cages?'

She did not respond, as he gathered her against him, one hand spreading on her back, the other gradually tightening on the fingers of her right hand. Initially, she kept her head firmly bowed towards his chest, fearful of the mood which was overtaking them. He spoke softly over her head, his breath fanning her hair and sending delicious shivers down her spine.

'I believe the recognized form of deportment for this dance, requires your left hand on my right shoulder,' he teased.

When she did not comply, the hand on her back pressed hard into her spine, so that her head rocked back and she found their faces now inches apart. As her hand lifted to rest lightly on his shoulder, he buried his lips in her hair and for the rest of the waltz, they were lost in poignant reminders of the familiar feel and smell of the intimacy they had shared and which neither had ever forgotten.

The music of the waltz had died and another reel had begun before they halted their slow rotation.

'I wish I could have more champagne,' he murmured, 'so the world would stay away.'

She opened her mouth to respond, but his lips grazed hers, tantalizingly brushing over their softness, while the tip of his tongue left a tingling trail of sensation.

It was fate, not his enfeebled conscience,

however, which intervened. As the clocks in the house chimed midnight, the darkness outside exploded, while a cacophony of bangs, crackles and hisses erupted in the gardens. The window, behind which they stood, was suddenly illuminated by flashes of light.

'The firework display,' he muttered.

'We'll be seen.'

'On the contrary, it seems we've been granted a convenient time to go,' he revealed reluctantly, as they moved apart.

He kissed the palm of the hand he still held, before he opened the French door and conducted a cursory check of the immediate vicinity.

'There's no one near here right now, but you'll have to hurry. Just follow the stairs into the garden and join the crowds,' he advised. 'I'd better go the other way.' With a final lingering look and a squeeze of her fingers, he allowed her to slip away. Now he had to engineer his own re-entry into the world.

Having turned the key in the lock of the door, which led on to the great hall, he crossed the fingers on one hand, before yanking the door open confidently. A furtive appearance would not do! His acting skills were not tested at this point, however, as he found the place deserted — everyone having pressed outside to see the display. He followed quickly, able to join the onlookers, unseen at the rear, before gradually threading his way forward, until he spotted Victoria, Isobel and his mother at the front of the throng. Satisfied, he remained where he was until the display was over, when the women turned and promptly saw him.

'There you are,' said Victoria, immediately linking her arm through his, her eyes searching his face. 'We thought you'd missed it. I couldn't find you anywhere.'

'Call of nature,' he muttered. 'What did you think of the display?'

'It was spectacular, wasn't it?' enthused Isobel.

'The colours were amazing!' said Victoria.

'Talking of colour,' intervened his mother, 'what have you done to your shirt, Alexander?'

Glancing down, he saw a dark smudge of dirt, evidently acquired in the shrubbery. 'I imagine one of our young ladies forgot to take a bath,' he muttered, with a careless shrug.

Isobel and Victoria giggled, while Lady McNair's eyes narrowed, as he looked away evasively. 'There's Papa and the others.'

They stopped, as Sir David came forward with James, Calum and Mhairi-Anne bringing up the rear.

'Quite a show, eh?' remarked Sir David, as they all proceeded together back into the house, where they formed a loose circle in the great hall. It was the first time they had been together all evening and Victoria's heart hammered, as she faced the full contingent from Tora.

'Nice to see you looking so well, Victoria,' remarked James, the sobriety of his eyes belying his smile.

'And you!' she returned, her eyes swivelling jerkily over all of them. 'I'm so glad you could come.'

'I'll be expecting a full turnout to church in the morning, by the way,' intervened Lady McNair. 'It's not often we have the chance to fill the front pews, and the minister is expecting us.' She touched Mhairi-Anne's arm lightly. 'Afterwards, I must take you to see my special rose garden behind the church, my dear. You might want to take some cuttings back to Tora.'

Mhairi-Anne nodded and smiled politely, before Lady McNair added, 'By the way, you seem to have lost that attractive feather you were wearing?'

Mhairi-Anne's hand rose abruptly to her hair, while her face flushed guiltily.

'I don't believe we've had a dance all evening, Mhairi-Anne,' Alexander suddenly declared, his intervention as timely as the drum roll which heralded the renewal of dancing. He kissed Victoria's cheek, before he took Mhairi-Anne's hand to join the growing formation of couples in the centre of the hall.

'Your mother has eyes like a hawk,' she whispered through her teeth.

'So I've discovered. She spotted that my shirt is no longer pristine.'

'What if she finds that feather in the library?'

'She won't. I found it after you left. It's in my sporran!' He winked devilishly, before bowing to begin the reel.

At the side of the hall, Lady McNair and Victoria watched with fixed smiles, the older woman presently suspecting that she had missed something. Victoria's thoughts, however, were on another vein.

'Do you really think she'll back down?' she asked quietly, her confidence wilting, as she saw how well their steps matched on the floor.

'If she's as intelligent as I think she is . . . but who knows?' She glanced sideways at her daughter-in-law. 'I wonder if I'm such a good judge of character as I've always thought.'

'You'll never know how grateful I am — '

'I think I do,' intervened Lady McNair

abruptly. 'But if you'll excuse me, I want to tell the conductor when to announce the last dance. I'm suddenly feeling rather tired.'

Victoria looked after her mother-in-law, a frown knitting between her brows. There was no mistaking the coolness in Lady McNair's attitude; she had never spoken so dismissively to her before. And it was all the fault of that slut, she thought bitterly, her brown eyes darkening with renewed venom.

'Victoria, are you all right?' Startled from the darkness of her thoughts, she manufactured a smile for Isobel, who had appeared at her side.

'Yes, of course, I'm fine.'

'You were looking so . . . strange for a moment.'

'Was I? I expect my eyes are still dazzled by the firework display. But here's Alexander . . .' She promptly linked her arm through his. 'I think you've been borrowed by enough women for one night.'

Irritated by the shackle on his arm, he, nevertheless, smiled down at her before he said, 'You wouldn't begrudge your sister-in-law a dance, surely?'

With Isobel's face instantly lighting up at the prospect, Victoria reluctantly let him go with a feigned laugh. 'I'll make you pay for this desertion later.'

As the night lengthened into the early hours of a clear, starlit morning, carriages started to arrive to transport inebriated guests home, and the cacophony of laughter, music, movement and voices began to fragment into disparate waves of drunken hilarity and emotional farewells to friends and neighbours, who would probably be seen again within a week. Thankful to spot the signs, Rowena promptly signalled to the conductor, as arranged, that he could now bring the event to a close. The ball then ended traditionally, with Sir David and Lady McNair taking centre stage, while their guests linked hands in a circle around them and all voices rose to a raucous rendering of Robert Burns's bittersweet song of parting and separation:

Should auld acquaintance be forgot,
And never brought to mind?
Should auld acquaintance be forgot,
And days o'lang syne?

Proudly, Sir David insisted on Alexander and Victoria joining them in the centre, while tears coursed quietly down his wife's face, at the haunting, ironic sadness of lyrics she had never contemplated before. In light of the disaster looming ominously over them, which promised grief and division and war, she wondered if they would remember this occasion as the last time they were all able to be together harmoniously.

By contrast, the moist eyes of Sir David were due to exuberance! Fate had been cruel in robbing them of his elder son, but tonight he felt invincible. The evening marked a wonderful rebirth of their family, he thought happily — no wonder Rowena was emotional. They had one strapping grandson, another grandchild on the way, a son who had surpassed all his expectations and his brother back in the fold, with his startling new fiancée. Life, as far as he was concerned, could not have been much sweeter.

13

The following morning, the contingent who went to church was no larger than usual, although the composition of the group varied. Alexander was not present, as he had been called out early to the stables, where a mare had gone into premature labour with a foal sired by his black stallion. Victoria — feeling genuinely squeamish — had been only too glad to absent herself as well, since her husband would not be there, and James was left behind, steeping his ankle in a large bowl of water, as it had apparently swollen so badly overnight, he could not get on any of his footwear.

Calum, however, accompanied Mhairi-Anne, who was particularly delighted to find that, in addition to Sir David, Lady Rowena and Isobel, Mrs Davidson was in the party, who walked the short distance to the little church on the estate, with Alex in his perambulator. It was a bumpy ride for the youngster, as the lane leading to the church gates was unsurfaced, but he happily gurgled and laughed his way there, to the delight of Sir David — evidently another devotee.

Inside the church, however, the child's high spirits meant that he lasted only a portion of the service, as he made repeated uninvited contributions to the sermon. Mhairi-Anne watched him being carried out, bouncing in Mrs Davidson's arms, with a mixture of pride and grief, as she did not know when she might see him again.

An hour later, they all emerged, blinking sleepily in the dappled sunlight, beneath the tree-shrouded entrance. The Reverend Blunkett, unlike William Morrison, who had kept his congregation rigidly alert, by terrifying them on to the edges of the pews, had honed his soporific powers to a fine art. All over the church, bursts of snoring had broken out, like a choir without a conductor — all ending abruptly with little snorts, courtesy of nudges from their neighbours, if they chanced to be in a wakeful moment. Mhairi-Anne had noted with a little smile, that Sir David's ribs would be black and blue by the end of the service. She felt tired herself after the late night, but apprehension had kept her alert. Both she and Calum suspected that Lady McNair's invitation to see her special rose garden after church was a guise for something more significant and Mhairi-Anne was not looking forward to a likely confrontation with this formidable woman.

This impression was confirmed, when Isobel suggested she join them and was gently urged to return to the house, with the plea that she keep an eye on the clearing up process. Thus, she went off with Sir David and Calum, who were happily heading back to bed, while Mhairi-Anne reluctantly followed Lady McNair round the side of the church and into the little cemetery beyond, adjacent to which was the garden she had created.

They walked first down one of the paths lined with gravestones, marking the resting places of many of the people who had worked on the estate over the years. Lady McNair pointed out in front of the far wall, a row of more elaborate tombstones, where ancestors of the family had been interred.

'Of course, we'll all come here in the end,' she said quietly. 'That's why I wanted to create a garden — where the living might sit a while and remember.'

At the back of the cemetery, they passed through an iron gate into the rose garden itself. Higher walls surrounded it on all sides, adding seclusion to its serenity and several benches were placed at strategic points.

'Most of the roses are not in bloom this early in the year, of course,' remarked Lady McNair, 'but the weather's been unusually fine and I noticed a few buds appearing last Sunday. I've named quite a few specimens after ladies in the family and I intend to have one myself, when my time comes. It's nice to think that something living will go on, with one's name, don't you think?'

Mhairi-Anne nodded. 'Immortality of a kind.'

'In July, the colours are blinding and I always wish I could bottle the perfume.'

'I've a feeling they would be too fragile to survive on Tora, but I'd like to try some cuttings, if you can arrange it.' She bent over a bud, which was just beginning to show the rich ruby of its petals, while the older woman observed her closely.

She was wearing a simple morning or afternoon gown of warp-printed taffeta, which featured a tiny pink floral design against a background colour of green, complimenting the startling jade of her eyes. The outfit was teamed with a plain straw-brimmed bonnet, with a single small pink flower.

'I love that ruby colour, don't you?' remarked Mhairi-Anne, glancing up from the rose when Lady McNair did not respond, and finding the woman's intent gaze upon her.

'It's easy to understand why my son was attracted to you on Tora.'

The softness of her voice had never altered and, for a moment, Mhairi-Anne was startled by the subtlety of her approach and froze over the rose bush, before, slowly, she stood erect. 'You've been speaking to Victoria?'

'She confirmed on Friday night that you're Alex's mother. I had suspected some of it myself. The child is very like his father, of course, but you'll remember my little dizzy turn when we met. I was shocked to discover my grandson has your eyes.'

'You're an unusually observant woman.'

'In these circumstances, I'm not sure whether I'm cursed or blessed. I half-expected others to notice, but as they haven't, it seems fate has decreed that I should intervene.'

'On Victoria's behalf?'

'Naturally — she's my daughter-in-law.'

'Who happens to have claimed my son as her own.'

'He's also Alexander's son and my grandson. We're devoted to him.'

Mhairi-Anne steeled herself. 'I, too, was devoted to him, before he was stolen from me. Perhaps, you'll understand, then, why I want him returned.'

Lady McNair stared back at her defiantly for several seconds, before — unexpectedly — the proud head suddenly drooped fractionally, like a wilting flower, and she raised a hand to rub her forehead, as if it ached.

'I've learned so much this weekend,' she murmured slowly. 'But, I don't feel I *understand* any of it. I look at Victoria . . . you . . . my son . . . James . . . and I can scarcely believe . . . ' Her voice shook to a halt, her eyes searching Mhairi-Anne's face, as if she might find there the answers she sought.

Suddenly aware that the woman's mask of control had slipped and that she was deeply upset, Mhairi-Anne responded, 'I'm sorry — very sorry — this must all have been a dreadful shock to you.' Last night, she had appeared like the invincible queen of the McNairs; today, with smudges of dark shadows beneath her eyes, as if she had not slept, and wrinkles evident in the cruel light of day, she seemed much more like the grandmother that she was — and there was no doubting her distress. Mhairi-Anne was rather taken aback, but just as Lady McNair's upbringing made it difficult for her to comprehend the nature of this woman from Tora, Mhairi-Anne had little experience of aloof women of her sort, bred in a different age and a totally different society.

They resumed their walk along the garden

path, before Lady McNair continued, her voice again calm. 'I brought you here today, with the intention of telling you why it's impossible for you to have Alex and I fancied that, in the process, I would enjoy telling you exactly what I think of you.' She glanced at Mhairi-Anne, with a fleeting, self-deprecating smile. 'The problem is that none of my conclusions seem to fit the picture you present.'

'I know you can never approve of me, Lady McNair,' Mhairi-Anne replied. 'But does that matter now? Alexander married Victoria.'

'Yes, it matters. Whether I like it or not, you're the mother of my grandson.'

'I'm sure Victoria gave you a colourful report on me,' she murmured sarcastically.

'Sadly, one of the results of this memorable weekend is that I can no longer trust my daughter-in-law,' she murmured, glancing at her companion. 'I confess, I had no idea she was capable of what she has done, but then again . . . looking at you . . . ' Her voice tailed to a halt.

Mhairi-Anne stopped walking and gazed directly at her. 'I'm not certain what you want me to tell you, Lady McNair, but the fact is that I fell in love with your son when he came to Tora. Unfortunately, I was then in a relationship with James.'

'A relationship of which Alexander knew nothing!' intervened the older woman abruptly.

'At first, no, but I told him about it before I became involved with him and when I decided it was over between James and me.'

'He knew of this?' echoed Lady McNair incredulously.

'Yes, of course, you must find that very hard to believe. I was surprised myself at first, that he still wanted me — '

'Wanted!' echoed the older woman, contempt in her voice.

'I believe he loved me,' Mhairi-Anne replied evenly. 'Perhaps he realized that many people can have more than one relationship in life. Widows often remarry.'

'According to my information, you seem to have gone from being a widow to a mistress — twice over. It's hardly the same thing. Three times over, in fact, if we now count the current disgrace of your engagement to my brother-in-law. You seem determined to have a McNair at any price — including my grandson!' Her face coloured angrily with these words and, stung by her evident distaste, Mhairi-Anne experienced a similar rise in temper.

'Just to set the record straight,' she responded, her voice deceptively low, 'I've made several serious mistakes in life, but these have never included trying to ensnare any man for his money. And if you imagine that you can silence me by buying my child, you're very much mistaken!'

'I had hoped to silence you with reason,' replied the older woman, on a more conciliatory note, surprised by the vehemence she had aroused. 'I apologize if I have insulted you, but how else am I to understand any of this?'

They walked on in awkward silence, before Mhairi-Anne said quietly, 'I said earlier that you would never approve of me, Lady McNair, and I doubt if understanding is possible either.'

'Now you insult me!' retorted the older woman sharply. 'True, I've led a privileged and sheltered life, but I'm not a prude and I resent the implication.'

Mhairi-Anne glanced round at her, pausing for several pensive seconds, before she said quietly, 'What is it you want to know?'

During the ensuing half-hour, Mhairi-Anne discovered that Rowena McNair essentially wanted to know everything and while she began hesitantly at first, with the story of her disastrous marriage, she very soon discovered that the woman was a good listener, who was able to inspire trust, prompt her when she fell silent, and evidently capable of a level of understanding, with which she had not credited her. Encouraged by this, it dawned on her that, despite what she had said, she wanted her understanding. She was the mother of the man she loved and, although Mhairi-Anne could have no place in his future, legitimizing her place in his past, she realized, was significant in light of her claim of Alex. Victoria had clearly painted her as a worthless trollop, bent on Alexander's ruination. It became evident to her companion, however, from her story, that Mhairi-Anne had left Tora to avoid this prospect and had never had any intention of contacting him again, but for Victoria's abduction of her child.

For Rowena, it was an enlightening mental journey, not only into the mind of her companion, but into the behaviour of her son and his wife. She had often thought that Alexander had never been the same man, since his sojourn on the island, and, at last, she understood why. Sadly, she realized, too, that he was probably still in love with this woman — as she was with him.

'I can understand why you returned to Tora,' she said eventually, 'but to become engaged to James . . . ?'

Seeing no reason now to continue with this uncomfortable lie, Mhairi-Anne was relieved to explain the real reasons behind this ruse.

'I had a feeling my brother-in-law might have a hand in this,' Lady McNair responded, frowning as she sat down on one of the benches in the garden. 'He talked you into this, didn't he?'

Mhairi-Anne sat down beside her. 'He feels Alexander should know the truth.'

'Perhaps, if he'd had more regard for the truth at the outset, none of this would have happened.'

'He didn't want his brother to know about me.'

Rowena's eyebrows rose derisively. 'Heavens — David and I both knew he was never faithful to poor Elizabeth.'

It was Mhairi-Anne's turn to be shocked. 'I always thought he idolized her.'

The older woman shrugged. 'Perhaps, he did, but that didn't stop him coming regularly to the mainland, where — inevitably — we heard about his exploits.' Her eyes suddenly twinkled with amusement at the continuing astonishment evident in Mhairi-Anne's expression. 'I see that, regardless of your flouting of the marriage contract, you value fidelity. At any rate, it's likely he was faithful to you, as we stopped hearing such stories after Elizabeth's death. We thought he was a reformed character!'

As their eyes met simultaneously they both started to laugh — merriment which continued disproportionately, until tears flowed on to their cheeks in a cleansing release of the tension between them. While they both extracted handkerchiefs to dab at their eyes, Rowena exclaimed, 'I think I'm a trifle hysterical!'

'Me, too!' echoed Mhairi-Anne.

'My ancestors will be twirling in their graves,' whispered Rowena, suddenly conscious of where they were, but this comment only engendered further outbreaks of uncontrollable mirth.

They did not speak again until they had both calmed — their laughter leaving strangely in its wake, a contrary reflective sadness.

'I think I might have liked you,' Rowena confessed pensively, after staring soberly into space for several moments, 'if you were not set to start a war in my family.'

Mhairi-Anne glanced round at her. 'That's not my intention.'

'No . . . ' agreed the older woman, rising rather stiffly to her feet. 'Let's walk again. These benches play havoc with my back.'

They had resumed their course round the garden paths, before Rowena continued, 'The point I should have made about James is that

227

it's not surprising he's encouraged you in this. David always said that his wild behaviour in years gone by was down to his frustration at not having children. Given his previous relationship with you, he probably sees Alex as the child he never had.'

'But it's not just about James,' Mhairi-Anne insisted. 'For a while, I did think it was too late and he did encourage me at first — but now I believe, too, that it's got to be done.' She paused before carefully adding the point, which had effectively clinched her decision. 'Victoria will have her own child in a few months.'

'Yes, but that's the main complicating factor, from our point of view. If Alexander finds out about this, I've no doubt his marriage will be in ruins. Divorce, of course, would cause a scandal if she weren't pregnant, but, as things are, it's not even an option.' She sighed deeply. 'He's trapped, I'm afraid, and he may well blame you and James.'

'James did not know in time to stop the marriage,' Mhairi-Anne pointed out.

'No, but Alexander is never more unpredictable than when he is hurt and I'm afraid he might see his uncle as your accomplice, if he wants to hurl blame.'

'I never imagined it would be easy,'

Mhairi-Anne replied, 'but I have to think of the future. At this stage, Alex is still young enough to make the change without being damaged by it.'

'You're seriously mistaken, my dear, if you think Alexander will relinquish the child without a war. He's utterly devoted to him. Even if he recognizes that his own promiscuous behaviour allowed Victoria to act as she did, and even if he appreciates the dire position she put you in, he will defend that child's legitimate place here until his last breath. And my husband will support him in this — which could then mean he'll also come into serious conflict with James. I'm afraid you're set on opening a dreadful can of worms, my dear, with dire consequences for all of us, including you and Alex.'

Mhairi-Anne remained silent and Rowena added after a few moments, 'I'm inclined to think that you've not thought all this through. Before we spoke today, I imagined I would enjoy telling you all of this — but I was wrong. It's a desperate situation and I feel deeply for you, but I honestly cannot see you profiting from any disclosure. As things are, you can come here to see him — I could even write to you with any news — but if we all end up in a bitter fight, who knows what will happen?' She paused before adding soberly,

'My husband took some time to accept Alex as his grandson and heir, but, unfortunately, I can see him now being even worse than Alexander, if he learns of this. Unfortunately, he has an unscrupulous streak when it comes to protecting his interests. If it came to a battle in court — '

'Court? Surely no one would want that kind of scandal.'

'No, obviously not, but what I'm trying very badly to say, my dear, is that you would need to take things that far, if you remain set on this course, and it could mean years and years of heartache for all of us.'

Mhairi-Anne sat down on another bench, her legs suddenly weak beneath her and a nauseous feeling rising in her stomach.

'Are you all right?' Rowena asked gently, having dropped on to the bench beside her. 'I'm sorry for being so brutal, but I had to make you see. Alex will have all the care and attention you could ever wish for him here and soon he'll have a brother or sister for company.'

Mhairi-Anne nodded, but, unwittingly, Rowena had raised the issue, which had strengthened her resolve to reclaim her child. 'That's the kind of thinking which caused this mess in the first place,' she murmured. 'I thought he would have everything that I could never give him, but I'm afraid things have changed.'

'How? We all love him to distraction, I assure you.'

'I never considered the possibility of Victoria having her own child and I'm afraid I have very good reason not to trust your daughter-in-law.'

Rowena's expression darkened. 'I'm not sure I understand your meaning.'

'I think you do. You implied that her behaviour had shocked you. When I found that my child had vanished, 'shock' barely describes my feelings. I trusted her implicitly, but no more. With her own child on the scene, Alex will not only be redundant, he'll be in the way, as far as she's concerned.'

'But we would never allow her . . . '

Mhairi-Anne smiled weakly. 'Of course you wouldn't, but the point is you can't possibly guarantee she'll continue to love him — nor his safety twenty-four hours a day.'

'I'm sure you're wrong in this. Victoria wouldn't harm a hair of his head . . . I . . . ' Her voice tailed to a halt, as Mhairi-Anne continued to gaze evenly at her and it occurred to Rowena that, despite her assurances, she did not have the conviction to deny this argument. Victoria had stolen the child to secure her ends; what more might she do, to secure the future of her own child?

Mhairi-Anne shrugged. 'Besides, it's not only about his safety, it's about how she may feel towards him. You know better than I do how much may be at stake, when it comes to inheriting all of this.' She spread one hand expressively. 'I don't want my son growing up, wondering why his 'mother' does not care for him.'

She stood up, renewed strength in her posture, while Rowena, too, arose on a deep sigh, as she recognized she had failed in her mission and, oddly, felt now a perverse sense of relief that she was to be spared living with such a terrible burden of secrecy.

However, she chose the moment to issue a different plea. 'I can see your mind is made up,' she murmured earnestly, 'but do one thing for me.'

Mhairi-Anne gazed at her enquiringly.

'Wait until Victoria's child is born. That's not too much to ask.'

As they began to walk slowly along the path towards the iron gate, Mhairi-Anne responded uncertainly, 'What will that achieve?'

'The child she's carrying is my grandchild, too.'

'She's not really ill, though, is she?'

'No, but in a situation like this, who knows

what might happen?'

As they reached the entrance to the rose garden, Rowena stopped and urged persuasively, 'I realize she seems to have had no conscience about you, but give her this time to prepare herself. I'll try to help her and I give you my word that it will be done after her child is born.'

After a long moment, Mhairi-Anne nodded slowly. 'I suppose I owe you that, although I owe her nothing.'

As Rowena opened the iron gate and they passed through, she remarked, 'James will be furious, of course. Patience never was one of his virtues.'

'Yes,' agreed Mhairi-Anne. 'But it's my decision, isn't it?'

14

Mhairi-Anne found James seated alone in his room, where she had left him prior to going to church and, having closed the door behind her, she braced herself. She fully expected him to be furious at her agreeing to delay, but when she had finished relaying what had happened, ironically, he was smug.

'I knew she'd talk you into putting it off. I knew it!' he declared complacently, while she struggled to comprehend the note of triumph in his tone. 'Fortunately, I took precautions.'

'Precautions?' she echoed, a puzzled frown slicing between her brows.

He stood up — the decisiveness of the movement drawing her eyes to his feet, which were encased in brogues. 'The ankle's fine now,' he muttered, a trifle sheepishly.

Her eyes fled back to his face. 'What have you done?'

'I went to see my brother, when he got back from church,' he revealed, his expression now defiant. 'I told him the whole story. The truth had to come out.'

At that moment, the door behind Mhairi-Anne opened and Calum came in — initially unaware of the drama he was interrupting. 'So you're on your feet. Ankle better?' As he walked forward in front of Mhairi-Anne, he glanced round and was stopped instantly by the gravity of her expression. 'What's up? What happened with Lady McNair?'

Her eyes pivoted slowly towards him, her mouth moving soundlessly, before dry words emerged. 'I agreed to wait until Victoria had her baby.'

'I see,' murmured Calum, glancing from one to the other.

'But it's too late,' she added, her eyes meeting Calum's for a brief moment, before he spun accusingly on James.

'I knew you were up to something. I knew I shouldn't have left you!'

'Well, it's done now,' James retorted belligerently. 'If everything goes wrong, she'll not have to blame herself and you can both take it out on me.'

'Very magnanimous!' muttered Calum sarcastically. 'But you had no business takin' that on yourself — an' well you know it.'

James was shaking his head dismissively, when they all became aware of a growing noise rumbling down the corridor. The sound of rapid footsteps was punctuated by a series of thuds and bangs as doors were thrust carelessly open. Their eyes were all turned apprehensively towards the door to James's room, when it too burst open to reveal Alexander. For a moment, he stood breathing heavily, as if he had been running, his eyes brooding on the group before him, his hands grasping each side of the door frame, as if to restrain himself.

When he moved, a nasty smile stretched his mouth, while his eyes remained darkly unforgiving.

'All three of you together!' he declared. 'That will save me time.'

James opened his mouth to utter some platitude, but Alexander was not done. 'I want all of you packed and out of this house within the hour.'

'For God's sake!' James exploded. 'Is this how we're to be rewarded for telling the truth?'

'Rewarded?' hissed Alexander contemptuously. 'You come here plotting to take my son and you expect gratitude!' He turned suddenly on Mhairi-Anne, like a hunter spotting his prey. 'If you were a man, I think I'd kill you!'

As Mhairi-Anne paled at the fury in his face, Calum stepped forward. 'It was your wife who took the bairn — not her.'

'She was not *my wife* then!' retorted Alexander, turning his glare back to Mhairi-Anne. 'And *she* did nothing . . . nothing!'

'It wasn't like that — it wasn't as simple as that!' Her voice was steady, despite the trembling of her limbs.

'Indeed?' he sneered. 'Seems simple enough to me. You might have told me — and you didn't! Apart from that insignificant little detail,' he continued, the freezing sarcasm of his tone matched by the icy disdain in his eyes, 'your silence speaks volumes about your lack of motherly concern.'

'You were out of the country for months on end,' interjected James.

His eyes slid contemptuously away from her to his uncle. 'I was married in this house — remember — you were there! There was plenty of time.'

'Neither James nor Calum knew anything then about what had happened,' Mhairi-Anne intervened, drawing his gaze once more.

'No — so my father tells me — but they've known for long enough to get embroiled in your scheming. Is it money, you're after? Too bad — you're not really engaged to him, I hear. Too old for you — huh? Or, doesn't he want my leftovers?'

'Why — you . . . ' James charged the few paces toward him, but Calum, anticipating this reaction, darted between them.

'Let's not make this any worse than it is,' he ordered tersely, before pushing James back and raising his arms placatingly. 'A brawl will get us nowhere.'

Alexander shrugged off Calum's restraining hand and moved back towards the door. 'Don't worry — I'm going, and so are you. You have an hour.' In the doorway, he paused only long enough to issue another contemptuous warning. 'And by the way, Uncle, you should give some serious thought to leaving Tora to someone else.' With that he strode away along the corridor again — the door left gaping like an astonished mouth in his wake.

Mhairi-Anne subsided into an adjacent chair, fingers pressed to her quivering lips, while Calum dropped on to the edge of the bed. James, by contrast, could not keep still and began to pace the room in a maelstrom of impotent rage.

'David won't stand for this!' he muttered furiously. 'He's not in charge yet — not by a long shot. Ordering us out of my brother's house — by God! He's gone too far this time.' As his pacing suddenly assumed the purposeful direction of the door, Calum sprang up and barred his way.

'Wait a moment! Just stop an' think for once, will you? You've stuck your nose in once today and look where it's got us. Now you're set on comin' between father and son. Give them time to get their wind back, for Christ's sake! We were leavin' anyway this afternoon. There's no need to make an issue of it.'

Before James could respond, Mhairi-Anne suddenly rose to her feet. 'I must see Alex before we go.'

Both men turned towards her as she made to pass them. 'Hold on, lass! Hold on!' pleaded Calum.

She halted, but her agitation was evident and Calum pressed her shoulders in a calming gesture. 'They'll not let you near him,' he murmured quietly. 'Not now.'

She looked in bewilderment from him to James, whose rage was rapidly evaporating in face of her distress.

'But they must . . . ' She darted past them, shrugging aside Calum's hands.

'We'd better get packed,' Calum muttered grimly, as she vanished into the corridor.

In her room, Mhairi-Anne hurriedly threw all her belongings into the chest in which they had arrived, her agitation mounting with every flurry of movement. Having abandoned all care in the process, she was struggling to close the lid with the stout leather straps, when there was a knock on her door.

'Come in — come in!' she called impatiently, assuming it was one of the servants, sent to assist their removal. When she glanced up, however, she saw Lady

McNair closing the door quietly behind her.

Still on her knees on the floor, her movements stilled and she leaned on the chest in front of her, as she looked up at the older woman.

'I was too late,' she murmured unnecessarily.

'So I gather,' responded Lady McNair resignedly. 'Leave that! I'll have one of the servants do it.'

Mhairi-Anne pushed herself up to her feet, her idle hands now clasped tightly in front of her. 'I must see Alex before we go.'

Lady McNair approached her slowly. 'My husband and Alexander are with him right now. I'm afraid there will be a terrible scene, if you attempt to see him.'

As Mhairi-Anne digested this silently, her expression was, nevertheless, eloquent of the strain of controlling the protests within her. Rowena placed a calming hand on her shoulder. 'It's been a dreadful shock for both of them and the way James unloaded all of this has not helped. They imagine you're set to take the child this very day and I couldn't reason with them.'

Mhairi-Anne backed slowly away from her, her hands clasping and unclasping in front of her. 'All . . . all I want to do . . . is see him. That's not too much to ask.' She stopped as one of her legs struck a chair behind her and she dropped into it, her body rocking forward, as if she were in physical pain. She knew Lady McNair was right: it was the wrong time. But they might never let her see him. It was like that day in Perth, all over again.

As she watched Mhairi-Anne struggling to compose herself, Rowena subsided on to the edge of the bed. This should have been a moment of inward triumph, she thought, to see this alien woman broken and afraid of the power of the McNairs. But having lost one of her own sons, she could empathize all too easily with the agony etched on Mhairi-Anne's features and, regardless of her desire to keep her grandson at Strathcairn, she could feel nothing but pity in her heart. 'Once they get over the shock of all this, I'll speak to them,' she resumed persuasively. 'Whether they like it or not, they . . . we all . . . will have to recognize that you are Alex's mother and we will have to work something out.'

'But you were right,' Mhairi-Anne muttered stiffly, her jaws tensed against the trembling which threatened to engulf her. 'There'll be a war. Alexander hates me now — hates all of us.'

'I'm not his favourite person at the moment, either,' Rowena responded drily.

'When they learned I had discovered this and had actually been trying to dissuade you from telling them, my husband was speechless with rage, and Alexander looked at me as if . . . as if I was Judas, incarnate.' She stopped, as her voice quivered with the burning memory of her son's incredulous eyes, before she added quietly, 'I was afraid, I suppose, and I wasn't right. Terrible . . . terrible as this is, even now I can see that trying to perpetuate this lie would have been another mistake. Their anger is fuelled — at least, in part — by the length of time it has gone on, and the idea that we all knew . . . ' She paused before adding hastily, 'Not that James was right either! He should have let you tell Alexander first. The fact that his father told him and he was the very last to know is obviously salt to the wound. Apart from everything else, he must feel like an utter fool.'

Mhairi-Anne gazed down at her hands through a mist of unshed tears, while her agitation slowly dissipated and a chilling cloud of resignation drifted over her. Much as she might blame Victoria for starting all of this, her own stupidity and apathy in dealing with what she had done was now glaringly obvious. Alexander had every reason to despise her. Victoria had acted out of love — twisted, deceitful and selfish, as that might be. Mhairi-Anne had failed to act to save all she held dear and, ironically, it was no comfort now to remember how much that inaction had cost her. Cruelly, she had punished herself in the erroneous belief she was doing the right thing, when she might have followed the dictates of her heart so much more easily.

She looked up once more at Rowena. 'I'll go as you ask, but I intend to take legal advice.'

'He'll fight you all the way.'

'Yes, but I sat back before and did nothing and look where it's got me. He does not even credit that I love Alex.'

At that moment, there was a light tap on the door and Calum called out, 'Can I come in, Mhairi-Anne?'

She rose and opened the door. 'I'm ready,' she said, her apparent composure bringing relief to Calum's expression.

He nodded. 'I'll tell James.'

Lady McNair followed Calum into the corridor, before she turned towards her once more in the doorway. 'Thank you for this.'

Mhairi-Anne swallowed on the lump in her throat. 'I owe you all some time, I suppose.'

Rowena nodded. 'I'll get the servants to help with the luggage.'

Downstairs in the great hall, servants still scurried about, clearing away the debris of the ball and restoring the area to its previous order. Their presence provided a convenient excuse not to linger before they all moved outside. The Strathcairn carriage had already been ordered and was awaiting to take them on the first stage of their journey. The tension between Rowena and James was palpable, as he turned stiffly to his sister-in-law, before he finally embarked.

'You can tell my brother that I'm deeply disappointed that he's allowed us to be treated in this way.'

'None of us is taking any pleasure in this,' responded Rowena.

'As for that hot-headed son of yours — '

'James!' The barked reprimand from Calum, already inside the carriage beside Mhairi-Anne, sliced between them. 'Let's away with some dignity, for God's sake!' he added urgently.

It was the sight of Mhairi-Anne's pale determined face, staring resolutely ahead, however, which drew him inside without further ado.

As the coach clattered noisily away, Rowena stood watching, the regal poise of her slim figure marred only by a betraying tremor of her chin. High above, unseen at one of the nursery windows, other eyes watched, too.

'Well, that's that!' said Sir David grimly, as

he and Alexander turned away from the window. 'I hate to see James go like that, but if he's teamed up with that woman — what else can he expect?'

'I'm going for a ride,' said Alexander tersely.

'But you need to speak to Victoria — see what she's got to say for herself. I still can't believe she deceived us all like that. And we'd better contact Phillip Donaldson,' he urged, referring to the family's solicitor. 'We're going to be needing legal advice.'

'Later! I need to clear my head.'

'Pity you didn't clear your head before you got involved with two women at the same time!' retorted his father, anger rising to the surface, now the 'enemy' was gone. 'Good God, Alexander! I sowed some wild oats in my day, but you have to take the prize for downright debauchery!'

'I don't need this!' Alexander hissed, aware that his son lay sleeping in the room next door and that Mrs Davidson possibly had her ear to the keyhole. He paused in the doorway, to glance back at his father, whose wrath, he knew, was born out of love for his grandson and fear of losing him. 'For what it's worth, I'm sorry — sorry for everything.'

On the stair he met his mother and, although her duplicity still rankled, he had already realized that none of this was his parents' fault and he stopped, when she did.

'Where are you going?'

'For some air.'

'Victoria knows what's happened. I spoke to her earlier. She'll be expecting you.'

'I've had to wait long enough for the truth. She can wait till I'm good and ready to speak to her.'

His mother nodded, but held his arm lightly when he made to pass. 'I know you must be devastated, Alexander,' she said softly. 'But you'll need to remember there's another baby to consider.'

His smile chilled her. 'Yes — of course! And this time, I can be absolutely sure she's the mother.'

★   ★   ★

The dappled sunlight of the morning had given way to an unrelenting blanket of leaden clouds, which reflected his mood, as he galloped off from the stables that afternoon. With only a light breeze, fine rain inevitably descended in a steamy drizzle, that quickly and quietly drenched the parched meadows over which he rode and the hard ground softened, so that flurries of divots rose in a thick spray behind the horse's hoofs. By the time he reached the summit of the hill, which he had visited with Mhairi-Anne the day before, he was soaked through and it was like a different place. The landscape was carpeted in quilts of rolling mist, which merged with the sky and, having dismounted, he stroked the stallion's nose, as he looked out on the wet grey world surrounding them in a curious natural prison. Only then did he choose to think and examine the feelings which awaited him.

Strangely, he discovered very quickly that the expected well of anger and outrage against Victoria did not exist. He had lived so long with the gnawing guilt that he could not love her as he believed she deserved, foremost among his emotions now was a surprising sense of release. Although her deceit meant he was legally bound to her — in his heart, he was free, as he had never really been since that freak summer day on Tora. They were even, it seemed. In her treachery, she had exacted a heavy price for his debauchery, including the fact that their charade of a marriage would necessarily have to continue. But the gate was open on his prison of pretence and any anger he felt about her lies and trickery was liberally laced with perverse threads of satisfaction that she had unwittingly relieved him of all obligation beyond

247

practical, mercenary concerns. He would love their child, but he had no need to love her.

While he could welcome the prospect of justified indifference to Victoria, however, his outrage at Mhairi-Anne's betrayal, as he saw it, consumed him. The fact that she had been able to deduce his infidelity and had failed to act to save him from being tricked into marriage was, perhaps, understandable on its own, but he could not begin to understand — far less forgive — her abandoning all claim to their son, until it suited her. What kind of cold-hearted creature was she, he wondered irately, that she could ignore his abduction and return to her life on Tora? Having never known the limitations of poverty, nor the helplessness of the powerless, and never having fully credited the privileges into which he had been born, he could not imagine the agonizing nature of the choice Mhairi-Anne had faced, in sublimating her love of her son in favour of his birthright. He had been prepared to over-ride all considerations to claim him; to be disinherited, if need be, and her silent acceptance seemed like an utterly unforgivable offence against Alex and his devotion to their child. Through everything, he had never stopped loving her, but no more, he thought now. Even when the freshness of his anger dissipated, that love would surely remain crushed. Then his heart really would be free, he concluded bitterly.

Meanwhile, back at the mansion house, Victoria could not bear to wait quietly any longer, as her mother-in-law had advised, and she went to her room.

'Where can he be?' she exploded, when Lady McNair opened her door. 'It's almost five o'clock. I'm going out of my mind. You don't think he's gone after them, do you?'

'No, of course not,' responded Rowena. 'Why would he do that after asking them to leave? Come in and sit down. I'm just explaining to Isobel all that's been going on.'

'Oh . . . ' Reluctantly now, Victoria followed the older woman into her bed chamber, where she was obliged to face her sister-in-law for the first time since her deception had become known.

It was an embarrassing experience for both of them. Isobel, she found, could hardly bear to look at her, when she sat down opposite her in one of the many comfortable armchairs, and Victoria was sick with the knowledge of all the affection she had lost on account of that slut from Tora. Fortunately, Isobel, very soon after her arrival, politely made excuses and departed, and she was left alone with her mother-in-law, who was perched on a chair in front of her writing bureau, intent, it seemed, on tidying its surface.

Victoria's head was throbbing and she leaned her head back to gaze up at the ceiling with a sigh, which drew Rowena's attention.

'Are you feeling all right?'

'Isobel despises me, too, now, it seems.'

'None of us despises you,' Rowena corrected mildly. 'She's very fond of Alexander and Alex and is simply worried, as we all are, where this will lead.'

'Perhaps, everyone should remember that if it weren't for me, Alex probably wouldn't even be here,' Victoria responded tartly.

Lady McNair glanced up sharply, the huffy expression in her daughter-in-law's face irritating her as much as her words. 'I'm not sure how you've jumped to that conclusion.'

'You can't tell me you'd have welcomed James's mistress into this house as Alexander's wife-to-be. And she'd never have given the child up voluntarily.'

Rowena's eyes narrowed on her. 'So you knew she loved Alex, but you took him all the same.'

Victoria sat up straight, realizing she was revealing too much. 'The point is that you surely would not have approved of them marrying, would you?' she resumed, in a more conciliatory tone. 'And how could Alex have come here otherwise? That's why I did it — so that he could have the life he's due, as Alexander's son.'

'Is it?' queried the older woman, unable to suppress the scepticism in her voice. 'I thought it was because you were in love with my son.'

'Were? You say that as if it's all over. I still love Alexander. I'll always love him — whether he hates me for this, or not.'

'In that case then, the point is that you should not have attempted to play God, by assuming you knew what was best for him, Alex or us.'

Victoria stared at her, tight-lipped, before she rose suddenly. 'I think I'll go back to my room.'

Rowena, too, stood up, realizing she had said too much and that with so much at stake there was nothing to be gained by making an enemy of her daughter-in-law. 'We are all in need of a good night's sleep, I think. In the morning, things will seem better. I'm sure Alexander will be back at any moment. He always takes off like this, when something upsets him.'

Despite her words to Victoria, however, Rowena was as worried about Alexander as she was and when the clock struck seven in her bedroom, she looked out on to the bleak gloom of early nightfall and her heart leapt with relief, when she saw him approaching the house. It was some time before she heard the first sounds of his footsteps in the corridor and she opened her door immediately. As she approached him, her mouth gaped at the sight of him, but she resolved to remain calm and even managed a tiny smile, as she greeted him.

'You look as if you've been swimming in the loch.'

He shrugged, before raising a hand to brush back dripping tendrils of hair from his face. 'It's wet, but still muggy.'

'I'm just going to see Robbie about dinner. Will eight suit you?'

'I've already spoken to Robbie. I'm going to have something in my room and have an early night. I was up at dawn with the mare, remember?' He paused, before adding, 'By the way, I've told Robbie to get my old room ready.'

Rowena stared at him, for a moment dumbfounded by the nonchalant way he was communicating the fact that his marriage was over. As he made to move on, however, she muttered hastily, 'You haven't even spoken to her yet! And what about the servants?'

'What about them?'

'Don't be obtuse, Alexander! You know

252

very well what I mean.'

'I think the servants might have a lot more to talk about in the future than my sleeping arrangements. Besides, in her condition, Victoria will be much more comfortable without me thrashing about.' As he moved away from her, he called over his shoulder, 'Tell Papa we'll talk in the morning.'

Victoria had assumed a vigil in a chair by the fireside in their bedroom and, having decided, too, that she had no wish to face a family dinner, she had got ready for bed, her hair brushed loose over her shoulders, the way she knew Alexander liked it. She started from the chair, however, as soon as the door opened and gasped at the sight of him.

'Good Heavens! I've been worried sick. You're drenched!'

The sobriety of the look he cast her froze all the other 'normal' utterances she might have made and she sank back into her chair, as he advanced into the room. 'I'm going for a bath.'

'We have to talk,' she muttered, unable to look up at him, afraid to see again the freezing indifference of his eyes.

'Do we? There's no explanation you can give which will change anything. We're married and we'll stay married, if that's what's worrying you.'

She looked up, the flicker of hope in her eyes promptly extinguished when he added, 'But I'll be sleeping in my old room from now on.'

Fear and pride gave way instantly to desperation and she shot to her feet once more, to grasp his arm — heedless of his sodden jacket and the fact that it was now soaking through her nightgown.

'Don't do this, Alexander! We can be happy again. We were happy in Capri, remember?'

He gripped her wrist, gently trying to free himself. 'Don't make me say things that will hurt you,' he murmured.

The hint of pity in his expression was worse than contempt, but she clung on to him. 'You can sleep next door, as you've been doing anyway. What's the difference? You don't need to humiliate me.'

'Humiliation has nothing to do with it. It's over. I won't pretend any more.'

'You weren't pretending when you made love to me. I have a child in my womb to prove it.'

'That's why I'm moving.'

'You're afraid you'll still want me!' she declared, triumphantly.

He jerked her wrist and pulled back to free himself. 'If I've learned anything from this mess, it's the difference between making love and being in love.'

'You're afraid!' she taunted defiantly, as he turned his back on her and walked toward the bathroom door.

His fingers on the handle, he glanced back at her. 'You're right! I am afraid. All the more so because you stand there — pregnant with my child — and I realize I've never really known you. Apologies for what you did would have been pointless, I suppose, but I expected them, nevertheless. But you're not even sorry, are you?'

'Of course, I'm sorry I've hurt you, but you wouldn't have Alex, but for me.'

For the first time, she saw an anger in his face. 'I could lose him because of you, if his new *mother* decides to be difficult!' As he jerked open the door to the bathroom, she hurried across the room.

'You won't lose him! No judge in his right mind would give custody to a woman like that.' She lifted her hands, as if to touch him again, but he brushed past her.

'I've changed my mind. I'll have a bath in my old room.'

'Coward!' she screeched after him, as he strode to the door into the corridor. 'You're still in love with that whore, aren't you? That's what this is all about?'

He turned briefly. 'Not any more! You've

seen to that as well.'

As he vanished into the corridor, her voice followed him. 'Liar! Liar!'

For a moment, she stared after him, the wildness in her eyes gradually dying into a curious smile. Was it possible, she wondered, that he had seen through that tart at last? If she was trying to take his precious Alex, that might be the end of the ghost that had always been between them. And he had promised they would stay married! Once their own child was born, surely he would see reason. He was too young to live without a woman's love and the fact that he had moved out was proof that he did not trust himself.

As she sat back down in the chair by the fire, a new calmness enveloped her. If she was clever, she concluded, the future might not be as black as she had feared.

15

During ensuing weeks, a cloak of normality settled over life at Strathcairn, courtesy of the well-established routines, which had always coloured their lives. After the initial awkwardness of meetings with Victoria passed, everyone, it seemed, was only too glad to fall back on behavioural and attitudinal patterns, which afforded superficial harmony. While Alexander and his father consulted their solicitor and held secret meetings about the possibilities ahead, they resumed their working lives, which meant that Alexander, at least, was usually absent from the house for most of the day. Meanwhile, Rowena, Isobel and Victoria continued their habitual involvement in sewing circles, charity committees and painting class.

It was sometimes as if that traumatic weekend had never happened, Rowena thought, one sunny morning, as the three women sat outdoors in the garden with their easels, trying to capture a view of the River Cairn, under the instruction of their tutor. Victoria was laughing at Isobel's latest unusual concoction of colour and they seemed as close as ever. But 'seemed' was the operative word which undermined everything, Rowena realized, and she wondered if life would ever be 'real' again.

Isobel, she knew, had been deeply shocked by the discovery of Victoria's duplicity and had confessed openly at the time, that she would never trust her again. Equally, David's attitude towards his daughter-in-law appeared little changed, but, in private, he cursed the day his son had ever met her and was astonished by her apparent lack of shame at how she had ensnared him. Alexander, too, behaved impeccably towards her in public, but the division of their private lives was marked daily by the separation of their living quarters within the house. And as for Rowena herself, she lived with a brooding fear of the now apparent discrepancy between Victoria's outwardly innocent facade and the darker, unstable qualities, which she increasingly sensed within her. Rowena had noticed, for example, subtle changes in her attitude towards Alex over these weeks. Visits between them were fewer and shorter and twice, when she had been in their company, she had caught Victoria staring intently at the child, in a way which somehow disturbed her.

The whole house had been tainted by her, concluded Rowena, who was too well acquainted with the ways of servants not to be aware that gossip about the young McNairs had spread through their ranks, like a contagious disease. One day, she tentatively broached the subject with her housekeeper, Robbie, whom she had known all her life.

'Tell me then, what are they saying about Alexander, these days?' she queried, after they had finished discussing the menus for the week.

Mrs Robertson's already florid complexion took on a deeper hue, although she initially prevaricated. 'I don't know what you mean, m'lady.'

'Come, we know each other too well for secrets,' said Rowena disarmingly. 'I must be kept abreast of what's going on under my own roof.'

'Well, m'lady,' resumed Robbie, secretly flattered that she was apparently being drawn into her employer's confidence, 'there're some that's been sayin' how odd it is that he — I mean the young master — has moved back into his old rooms.'

'And why do they think that is?' prompted Rowena.

Robbie shrugged helplessly. 'There're all sorts of ideas about — you know what they're like m'lady — always ready to make a mountain out of a molehill, I say. Mind you

I've told them all that they better keep their mouths shut, as it's all down to Miss Victoria being so far on . . . not Mr Alexander's exploits,' she ended, her voice lowering to a discreet whisper.

'Precisely!' agreed Rowena smoothly. 'I know you'll do your utmost to curb any wild stories, Mrs Robertson, and, of course, remind everyone that idle tongues do nothing to commend people for work on this estate.'

While Robbie left her employer that morning, marvelling anew at the way Lady McNair could deliver a warning without batting an eyelid, Rowena knew very well that any gossip about the family would always be the central entertainment in the servants' hall — likely to continue, regardless of this conversation. Still, it did no harm to remind everyone how highly she rated the family's privacy. She considered it ironic that it was probably preferable that the favoured story focused on the possibility of Alexander having strayed, than the truth about Alex's parentage.

By early July, the roses at Strathcairn were in full bloom, perfuming the warm evening air drifting in through the open windows of the drawing-room, where the family had all assembled after dinner, on Sir David's instructions. He waited, warning everyone with his eyes, to make no enquiries as to the purpose of this gathering, until the last servant had finished dispensing drinks and the door to the room was firmly closed. The veil of normality was about to be lifted by some disturbing news he had to impart.

'I had a call from Phillip Donaldson this morning, after you left,' he began, standing with one elbow supported on the imposing mantelpiece of the fireplace and directing these words particularly at Alexander, who had sat down beside his mother, carefully cradling a glass of brandy, as he lowered himself into the plush settee. 'He's met with James's solicitor, Arthur Bannermann, and I think you all have to know, we might have problems ahead.'

A frown creased Alexander's forehead. 'What kind of problems? The last time I spoke to him, he seemed to think they had no case.'

'Well, that view was based on our presentation of the position. But apparently the gloves are off on the other side. Bannermann has hinted that they're considering bringing charges.'

'Charges?' echoed Rowena, laying down her teacup with a surprised clatter. 'Against whom?'

Sir David glanced at Victoria, who was

sitting on a couch next to Isobel. But while Isobel kept her eyes trained tactfully on the contents of her teacup, Victoria looked up indignantly at him. 'Against me? For what?'

'The problem is all to do with how we came by the child. There are laws against abduction in this country, you know!'

'But Alexander was with me. How can they say the child was abducted, when his father was there?'

'Unless Alexander were to perjure himself, he'd have to admit that you led him to believe you were the mother of the child.'

'But perjury is a criminal offence, isn't it?' interjected Isobel, suddenly alarmed on Alexander's behalf. Since that fateful Sunday after the ball, regardless of her previous closeness to Victoria, her loyalties lay firmly with Alexander, whom she now secretly adored with an affection which bordered on the unhealthy.

'Of course,' said Sir David. 'But in any case it's not an option that would achieve anything because the fact remains that the child was taken without the permission of the mother, with whom he had been living since birth.' He paused, sitting down at last in a chair opposite Alexander, who had sat tight-lipped, while this conversation ranged around him. 'You're not saying much,' observed his father.

'Perhaps we should discuss this alone.'

Isobel made to rise, but Victoria stopped her. 'I've a right to know what will happen to me. We all need to know,' she insisted, a tremor in her voice.

'If you're charged and found guilty?' responded Sir David. 'Probably very little, according to Phillip — given your position, extenuating circumstances which might be raised and, of course, the fact that you'll be a young mother yourself very soon will be in your favour.'

'Well then?' she murmured hopefully, looking at Alexander, who could restrain himself no longer.

'The point is that it puts me in the wrong from the outset!' he muttered tersely. 'And a judge may decide to rectify that position temporarily or otherwise.'

'Precisely,' agreed his father. 'Our whole case hinges on the proposition that the child already lives here and we are more fit, morally and financially, to continue his upbringing.'

'Consequently, the idea that we're degenerates, who've resorted to kidnapping hardly suggests we're the upright citizens we pretend to be,' added Alexander morosely.

'And the scandal would be unthinkable!' muttered Lady McNair between her teeth.

'But surely we could summon a whole

island to testify to the immorality of *her* character,' Victoria erupted, her tone indignant. 'When all is said and done, she'll still be a single woman of very dubious character, even if she is being supported by James McNair.'

'For your information, young lady,' intervened Sir David, subjecting her to one of his glacial stares, 'my brother is well connected in legal circles and it seems this Mhairi-Anne woman is rapidly gaining renown and respectability as an artist of some merit. Furthermore, James has apparently hinted that they may be married by the time any case comes to court.'

As Alexander downed his brandy in one swallow and rose to refill his glass, Lady McNair exclaimed, 'I don't believe it! This is all your brother's doing, I'm sure of it. I can't believe Mhairi-Anne will be countenancing all of this.'

Alexander returned grim-faced to stand with his back leaning against the mantelpiece, as Sir David responded. 'You've certainly changed your mind, Rowena! As I recall, you had her down as the fortune-hunter from hell, when she arrived here.'

'And you were right first time!' rejoined Victoria. 'She clearly has no scruples, whatsoever.'

'Unlike some people!' Alexander muttered under his breath, while he directed a venomous look at his wife.

'This is getting us nowhere,' voiced Rowena worriedly. 'I don't care what any of you say, I don't think Mhairi-Anne will be any keener for all this to go to court than we are. She cares about that child — I'm sure of it — and if we all start throwing dirt at each other, she'll know what a scandal like that could do to Alex's future.'

'She has an odd way of showing it,' Alexander murmured above her.

She looked up at him. 'Perhaps, she has, but if I'm right — there might be an alternative. I didn't want to raise this before, as I was hoping it wouldn't be necessary.'

All eyes turned towards her, as David urged, 'Out with it then! I know you're an authority on the female psyche,' he added sarcastically.

Rowena was hesitant. 'It's not an ideal solution, of course, and I know you won't like it, but if she agrees, we might avoid courts altogether.'

'That would be a miracle!' said Isobel encouragingly. Only she was privy to the idea that her mother-in-law was about to propose, Rowena having sought her opinion secretly some two weeks before.

'More a practical alternative, my dear,' said Rowena, with an answering smile for this support.

'We're all ears, darling!' exclaimed Sir David lightly, impatient with his wife's procrastination.

Rowena braced herself. 'You all know Mrs Davidson announced a couple of weeks ago that she's leaving us in August to go and live with her daughter in America. Well, it occurred to me that, if things proved difficult, we could offer Mhairi-Anne the position.'

The astonished silence, which followed this proposal, was quickly filled by guffaws of derisive laughter from Sir David and a simultaneous gasp of dismay from Victoria, while Alexander merely looked at his mother, his expression incredulous.

'You must have lost your mind, woman!' declared Sir David, still chuckling disparagingly. 'We're trying to figure out how to keep that woman out of our lives and you decide it would be a good idea to open up the house to her.'

'All right, laugh if you want to,' said Rowena irritably, 'but I don't see a better way out. Even if we win a court case — with all the scandal that will entail — the best we can hope for is that we retain custody and that Alex will have to be sent back and forth to

Tora to see her, because at the very least, she's bound to be given access. Alternatively, if we lose, the scandal will be even worse, and the rest does not bear thinking about. This way, she may be content to be near her son, knowing that she is protecting his future!'

'You must be joking!' Victoria asserted, joining briefly in Sir David's laughter, although her heart was beginning to hammer wildly, as she noted Alexander's expression changing to a thoughtful frown. 'You're not saying that you'd actually consider allowing your grandson to be looked after by such a woman?'

'Given that she's his mother, many people would say she's the best person for the job,' countered Rowena with the calm disdain which was her forte. 'Not that I would wish that relationship to become known beyond the family.'

'Of course, I know you're only trying to think of a way to avoid a scandal,' responded Victoria magnanimously, as she realized she must try to avoid antagonizing her mother-in-law. 'But how could we tolerate her living here among us, after . . . after all that's happened.'

'I know it would be . . . er . . . awkward for you, my dear,' returned Lady McNair smoothly, 'and Alexander, of course. But this is a big house and we could, perhaps, team her up with one of the young servants, who could do all the running and act as go-between. Naturally, I understand you'd not be wishing to come into contact with her very often, and it's not as if I'm suggesting she be treated like one of the family, or that we acknowledge her openly as Alex's mother.'

Victoria listened, tight-lipped. It was evident her mother-in-law had thought all of this out very carefully and would consider anything which avoided a scandal to be a victory. But the idea of that woman installed above her in the nursery was appalling . . .

'I can see what you're getting at now, m'dear,' conceded Sir David, intervening on Victoria's thoughts, 'but I can't see her agreeing to such a proposal.'

'Neither can I,' agreed Alexander. 'All these threats about charges being brought and marriage to James may be part of a game to extract as much money out of us as she can, before she backs down. Or, alternatively, as she's always been reviled on Tora, she may now fancy herself in the role of queen of the castle, with her son installed as the heir apparent, if James has decided to make an honest woman out of her.' His tone was icily flippant, but the darkness of his grey eyes reflected an inner rage. 'At any rate, I can't see her swapping these grandiose notions for the role of a servant.'

'Of course, she won't,' rejoined Victoria, glad to latch on to her husband's dissent. 'Even as the island's teacher, she always acted above herself, although I had no idea why at the time.'

'I think you're misjudging her,' argued Rowena determinedly. 'In any case, I thought we could give her the status of a sort of governess. She is a teacher after all.'

'Alex is surely far too young for a governess,' retorted Victoria, with a disparaging laugh.

'Yes, but we can put that down to the modern idea of doting, ambitious parents,' responded Rowena. 'It will provide an explanation for the household servants, at any rate.'

Sir David laughed again — but this time in admiration of his wife's ingenuity. 'You've certainly thought this one through, Rowena! So James's teaching fiancée will return as Alex's governess! I suppose you've also come up with an explanation for the disappearance of James's ring?'

'You're ridiculing me, David, and I don't like it,' she responded sharply.

'No, I'm not! On the contrary, I'm impressed as always by the dexterity of your mind. Really, I am!'

Somewhat mollified, Lady McNair resumed, 'Well, I don't think it will be unreasonable to claim that she's come here in the wake of a broken engagement. Heavens, everybody except you, David, thought it odd enough, in the first instance, that they appeared to be engaged at all.'

'*Touché*, m'dear! But they might think it a little odd that we're taking in the errant beauty and not my broken-hearted brother.'

'You're determined to be silly!' reprimanded Rowena.

'You're both being silly,' interjected Alexander mildly, 'considering she's likely to laugh in our faces.'

'But surely, it's worth trying, Alexander,' urged Isobel, suddenly sitting forward on the couch and entreating her brother-in-law.

The contribution earned her a tolerant smile from Alexander, but a venomous look from Victoria, who insisted stubbornly, 'I don't agree. All we'll be doing is making fools of ourselves and showing them that we think there are weaknesses in our case?'

'That's a good point!' agreed Sir David, momentarily raising a smile to Victoria's face. 'But then again, Phillip Donaldson was saying only this morning that if we can devise any means of delaying court proceedings, it will be in our favour, because the longer the boy is here, the less likely it is that they'll consider uprooting him.'

'So, even if she laughs in our faces, we may be helping our case,' said Alexander.

'I think you're all mad!' interjected Victoria, desperation creeping into her tone, as she realized the argument was being lost.

'You may feel rather differently, if you find yourself standing in a dock on an abduction charge,' responded Alexander sharply, before turning to glance from his father to his mother. 'I don't think for one moment, she'll go for it, but if delay is in our favour, we've nothing to lose. Our case will still be as strong as ever, whether she thinks so or not.'

Nodding thoughtfully, his father remarked, 'How to go about it is the next question, then. Or, have you got that all worked out as well, Rowena?'

'I thought I could write to her. Such a proposal coming from a solicitor is likely to smack of trickery.'

'Yes, the personal touch is more likely to work with a woman,' agreed Isobel.

Realizing that the two had been in cahoots over this, Alexander again smiled at his sister-in-law in a way which made her heart quicken. 'It seems the pair of you have been very busy recently.'

'Yes, haven't they just!' remarked Victoria, her voice verging on a sneer, before she added brokenly, 'Of course, my feelings are of no account in this ridiculous scheme.' She rose clumsily from the couch, tears erupting from her eyes. 'Nobody cares how I'll feel with that woman installed in this house.'

'But if you're right about her, Victoria, she won't agree,' Lady McNair murmured consolingly. 'And besides, how do you imagine we would all feel to see you treated like a criminal? We need to try to avoid that at all costs, don't we, however slim the chances are.'

Victoria gazed down on her, thinking, not for the first time, that her mother-in-law had a brain like a rat-trap. 'I think I'll go to bed,' she murmured wearily, knowing she had been out-manoeuvred on this occasion.

But she would not underestimate Rowena or her sister-in-law again, she resolved viciously, as she meekly allowed herself to be led from the room on Isobel's proffered arm. The stupid young woman, who had turned down Alexander's proposal on Tora, on a point of principle, was long gone, as was the conscience-stricken new bride, who had ruined her happiness then, with thoughts of what she had done to that creature on Tora. If Mhairi-Anne Graham was fool enough to think she could reclaim her son and get her claws back into Alexander again through this backdoor arrangement, then abduction would be like child's play, compared to what was currently coursing through her mind.

16

Although Mhairi-Anne liked Robert Wallace and his wife, Morag, and the new minister had been privy to different versions of her colourful story from numerous islanders, she had never confided in him with regard to the loss of her son. Consequently, he could only guess at the reasons for the brooding sadness which he sensed in her, and which, it seemed, even his encouragement of her reconciliation with God could not assuage. Thus, he was frequently possessed with the urge to send his daughters to visit their schoolmistress on some pretext — a habit which had grown more marked over recent weeks, when he had noted with some disquiet increasing evidence of her deep unhappiness.

Thus, with school having finished for the summer, Mhairi-Anne was on the shore one morning in July at the invitation of Margaret and Heather Wallace, while they played in rock pools, gathered shells for her inspection and collected multi-coloured stones, worn smooth and beautiful by time and tide. A stiff breeze blew off the ocean, crested with foamy white-capped waves, and the sun played hide and seek in the sky with cotton-wool clouds, whipping across the blue. She shouted to one of the girls not to stray too far out on the rocks, when she noted with a practised eye that the tide was turning, as she sat on a hillock of sand, sketching the scene she overlooked. To any casual observer, she might have been a mother, happily watching her children at play, but those who knew Mhairi-Anne recognized, as Robert Wallace did, that since her return from Strathcairn, she had been enveloped in a fog of depression, which was making her look ill. She had lost weight again, the bloom had gone from her cheeks and the normal sparkle in her green eyes had been lost, like the sea deprived of sun.

Although she would never regret having had the opportunity to see her son, the experience had robbed her of all the hard-won emotional stability she had achieved in living with her loss, and with every day that passed, with no word from Arthur Bannermann or Strathcairn, the fear that she would never see him again deepened like a knife pushed further into her heart.

Before returning to Tora, they had paid a visit to James's solicitor in Dundee and asked him to investigate how she could secure rights of access to her child, in the difficult circumstances which prevailed. While he had, at first, seemed hopeful, if they took the matter to court, Mhairi-Anne had expressed her strong desire to avoid such notoriety for her child and, in these circumstances, Bannermann had advised that they would be reliant on negotiations and the benevolence that he might generate with the opposing party. Even if they did ultimately resort to legal proceedings, he had explained, serious weaknesses in her case were the facts that she had failed to take any action following Alex's abduction, that she was a single woman, and that the child was now long settled in a home where he would obviously want for nothing.

'Except his mother's love!' James had pointed out sharply.

'As I understand it, in addition to his father, he has a stepmother, grandparents and a nanny,' Bannermann had responded with the detached candour of one long used to shedding all emotive elements of case, as naturally as a snake might discard its skin.

Thus, Mhairi-Anne had left the dusty office, her hopes precariously buoyed, not so much by confidence in Bannermann's skills, but by her recollection of Rowena McNair's promise to speak to her son and her husband on her behalf. But while the summer heather increasingly spread its vibrant purple carpets all over the hills and moors of Tora and the bracken bloomed to light the slopes with golden yellow suns, this hope faded and withered in her heart. Why would Lady McNair jeopardize her cosy, affluent world by challenging the views of her husband and son? And why would she risk alienating her pregnant daughter-in-law by championing her cause? She had been a fool to pin any hope on such an eventuality, she had already concluded, but the problem now was that the only other avenue lay with Bannermann and court action — the whole idea of which, she abhorred.

She stood up swiftly, her sketch book dropping on the sand, when Heather, the younger of the two Wallace girls, vanished behind a bulging rock on the shore. The child's head promptly reappeared at the call of her name and, although she waved reassuringly, Mhairi-Anne beckoned to her and her sister, who played nearby. The thick white rollers on the ocean beyond now suggested that the tide was fast encroaching on their playground, and she picked up her sketch pad, ready to leave, while the girls bounded over the rocks towards her.

As she turned, however, she spotted Calum coming towards them. 'I thought I'd find you here,' he said. 'Hello there, Margaret

. . . Heather,' he added, as the girls joined them, cheeks whipped to poppies by the wind.

'Hallo, Mr MacRitchie!' they chorused. 'Look what we've got,' added Margaret, while Heather hunkered down proudly behind their cache of stones and shells, which they had secreted at Mhairi-Anne's feet.

'My, you've been busy this mornin'! How are you goin' to get that lot off the beach?'

Mhairi-Anne picked up the basket they had brought. 'Here, girls! It's time to go home now.'

As the sisters carefully loaded the basket with their cargo, Mhairi-Anne turned to Calum. 'There's nothing wrong, is there? Where's James?'

'He's embroiled in a council meeting this mornin', but we thought you'd want to see this.' He produced from his inside jacket pocket a cream-coloured envelope, which she noticed immediately bore the embossed crest of the McNairs. 'It arrived at the castle this mornin',' revealed Calum. 'James thinks it's Lady McNair's handwritin'.'

She took the envelope with a suddenly trembling hand and a nervous laugh escaped her lips. 'I'm frightened to open it,' she murmured, staring at her name.

'Do you want me to see the lassies home

and leave you here to read it?' asked Calum.

'Would you? Yes please, Calum.'

'James said to invite you to lunch, by the way. He's dyin' to know what she says — as I am.'

She nodded. 'I'll see you later then.'

As she waved Calum and the girls away, she settled back down again on the sand, the letter nestling untouched in her lap for some minutes, as she prepared herself to face its contents — whatever they may be. Low as her spirits were, the prospect of another disappointment was terrifying. Was this a conscience-saving polite letter to say she had tried and failed to influence Alexander and her husband, or was it possible she had actually achieved something? A brief prayer hovering on her lips, she prised the envelope open.

17

Not surprisingly, James was totally against the idea posed in Rowena McNair's letter and, over lunch, he endeavoured to convince Mhairi-Anne that she should not even consider such a proposal, far less accept it.

'Don't you see, this proves they're running scared,' he declared, tossing the letter disparagingly on to the table between them.

'I don't undestand,' responded Mhairi-Anne. 'God knows I've reason to be scared — scared I'll never see Alex again. And that's why I'm excited about this. At least it's something, when I thought . . . But I don't see why you're saying they're suddenly scared.'

James glanced at Calum, who said immediately, 'You better tell her.'

As her eyes darted apprehensively between the two men, Calum continued, 'James paid Arthur Bannermann another visit, when he went to the mainland a few weeks back.'

'Why didn't you tell me?' demanded Mhairi-Anne of James.

'It wasn't only him,' admitted Calum, drawing her accusing eyes. 'We were both in on it, but you've been so depressed of late, we didn't want to upset you any more — or raise false hopes.'

'I should be furious with both of you,' she responded, glaring at each in turn, 'but if this letter is the result of it, then — '

'But that's the maddening point!' intervened James. 'It probably is the result of my visit, but we never anticipated this hairbrained scheme would emerge.'

'What exactly did you say — or do?' she asked.

'Calum and I had come to the conclusion that you had been all too soft in your brief to Bannermann and decided we might get somewhere faster, if we issued a few idle threats.'

'Just as a bluff, mind you,' Calum assured soothingly, as her eyes began to widen in alarm.

'Anyway, it occurred to us, and Bannermann agreed incidentally, that it would do no harm to make noises to their solicitor about the possibility of charges being brought against Victoria, even at this late stage.'

'Good heavens!' exclaimed Mhairi-Anne. 'But Lady McNair mentioned nothing like that in her letter.'

'Well, they're not going to admit why they've concocted this scheme, are they, and you can bet every word in that proposal has been hammered out carefully among them.' He paused before adding, 'They didn't mention either that they might have heard we may get married.'

'What?'

'Part of the bluff!' added Calum swiftly. 'Bannermann pointed out again that your single status wasn't helpful and James decided to add to the fantasy. Mind you, I'd be surprised if they swallowed that one, considerin' they've already been subjected to a fake engagement.'

'Fantasy or not,' James muttered, gazing earnestly across the table at her, 'they'll know now that if you chose, you could present a solid case to rival anything they can concoct.'

'And make a laughing stock of Alex's whole family in the process,' retorted Mhairi-Anne drily, 'including you, I dare say, if they decided to make anything of our history.' She paused, before adding thoughtfully, 'And, in the long-term, Alex might end up hating me for it, when he's old enough to understand.'

Morosely, James lifted another piece of cheese from the board and slapped it on to his plate — breaking in half the oatcake, which lay underneath. 'You tend always to think too far ahead of yourself,' he responded tightly. 'Yet, ironically, with regard to this offer of a job, you're not thinking far enough. Understandably, you're desperate to see the boy again, but this letter means they think you've a chance of winning custody, if you took it all the way.'

'Yes, a chance,' she agreed, nodding pensively. 'But at what cost? And I could also lose very easily and Alex would still pay the price for the rest of his life. I know what it's like to live with people sniggering and pointing, James. I don't want that for him.'

'People forget, Mhairi-Anne! Just think — he could grow up here among us, and he'd have everything you'd want for him.'

'Except a father and grandparents.'

'He hasn't got you at the moment!'

'But if I went to Strathcairn, he could have me as well.'

'Not as his mother. She makes that very clear in the letter, doesn't she? Things will continue as they are and you'll be little more than a servant.'

'But I'll be there with him. And if I don't go, how long will it be before I have any chance of seeing him, far less claiming him? In the meantime, Victoria will have her own child and anything might happen.'

'For God's sake, talk to her Calum! Tell her to think — '

'I am *thinking*, James!' she insisted, anger

colouring her tone for the first time. 'I'm thinking out loud and I'm trying to consider all the options. I've not made up my mind yet, but you're seeing it only from one side.'

'She's right in that,' rejoined Calum, staring across the table at James. 'I honestly don't know what to advise because whatever way you look at it, there's no easy right answer.'

'Trust you to sit on the bloody fence now, Calum!' exclaimed James in frustration.

'Aye — an' glad I'll be that I perched here, if she takes your advice and loses out in the long-term. We've stuck our noses in to get her this far, but no more. This has got to be her decision, because she'll have to live with it.'

'I'm beginning to wish I'd kept my mouth tight shut!' muttered James huffily, as Mhairi-Anne rose to her feet. 'Where are you going? You've hardly eaten a thing.'

'I promise, I'll think over everything you've said,' she murmured consolingly, as she lifted Lady McNair's letter from the table.

James looked up at her, a fresh appeal in his eyes. 'I don't want you to go.'

She smiled sadly. 'I'll let you know what I decide.'

As she left the room, the two men silently and unenthusiastically resumed their meal, which had taken on all the appeal of cold porridge. Eventually, James gave up and rose, too, from his chair.

'Her mind's made up, you know,' he muttered, gazing bleakly at Calum.

Calum glanced up at him. 'Aye, I think you're right. But we've done all we can — an' maybe too much.'

★   ★   ★

Three weeks later, in the middle of August, Mhairi-Anne left Tora on the afternoon ferry and her departure, on this occasion, was vastly different from the time she had stolen away under the black cloak of night, with Neil Graham at the helm, in the wake of Seorus Dhu's death. Robert and Morag Wallace, along with their two girls, had turned out to see her off to her new job as a governess, as well as Calum and James, and other pupils from her class. And there were hugs and tears all round. James held on to her a long time, making her promise to write and to return to the island, if her life proved miserable.

Eyes blurred, she waved to all of them, until the ferry moved into the swell beyond the harbour wall and she lost sight of them. Immediately, she sat down on the bench seat behind her, the enormity of the decision she had made, suddenly weakening her knees. She had made up her mind — yes — but she had no idea whether it was the right decision, or she was on the verge of making yet another calamitous mistake. Ultimately, she had realized one night in the isolation of her schoolhouse parlour that she must go for a reason, which had never been raised in her discussions with Calum or James and had nothing to do with common sense or practicalities. Despite her belief that he now despised her, she still loved Alexander McNair and she had recognized that, regardless of any personal sacrifice, in the end, she could never rob him of their son.

18

Dearest James and Calum

I am with my son! You, who have known more of my heartache, than anyone else, will appreciate the joy this means. At this very moment, he's sleeping like an angel and, after two weeks, I still look down on him with happy disbelief, which far outweighs any misgivings I have about the strange new life I lead here.

It all seems unreal and that frightens me a little, as I fear it cannot last. Sometimes, I feel as if I have stumbled into a parody of Brontë's Jane Eyre, in which the governess remains secreted in the attic, while the mad wife romps free downstairs! But, knowing how worried you were by my decision, I must emphasize, I am not unhappy!

Lady McNair has done everything to ensure my comfort. Far from being treated as a servant, she has allocated a young maid, Alice, to work with me and for me. I have the freedom of extensive nursery quarters on the top floor of the house, including my own parlour, a bedroom, next door to Alex, and a water closet complete with bath. In addition, we have a playroom and Alice has a bedroom on the other side of mine, so that she is always on call.

In many ways, I live a private existence. Although I have seen Alexander twice from the window, Lady McNair is the only family member I have spoken to, since my arrival and only she has ever come to the nursery. She didn't say so, but, obviously, I am a pariah, as far as the rest of the family is concerned. However, we both understand why these arrangements are necessary, if this peculiar agreement is to work, as it would hardly be tolerable for me to intrude on Victoria's territory any more than I have. Evidently, the aim is that they can all forget I am here, for the most part.

I think Lady McNair is concerned about the solitary nature of my life, however, and, as compensation perhaps, she has suggested that I use another empty attic room beyond the nursery quarters, as a studio. It has two large skylight windows, which yield ample light, and Alice has recently been set the task of cleaning it for my use. One of Alice's main duties, however, is to act as go-between, as she takes Alex downstairs every morning, afternoon and in the early evening, at fixed times, to be with the family, and a bell is located in her room, so that she can be summoned for any fresh instructions.

In case you imagine that I am like a prisoner in the house, let me assure you that I do go out, usually every afternoon, when Alex is taken downstairs, although, again I take care not to intrude on the life of anyone else. Ironically, although the servants are all housed in quarters at the back of the house, a servants' stair, direct from the attic, leads to an exit near the little church and Lady McNair suggested I might enjoy her rose garden, whenever I wish. It's a heavenly place now the flowers are in full bloom and I'm already doing preliminary sketches of some of the bushes. But you'll be pleased to see my first protrait of Alex, once I complete the painting of it. I've already done numerous trial sketches and chosen one, which I believe you'll like. Perhaps, I'll finish it in time to send it with my next letter.

Alice is to deal with my mail and any other such requirements, I may have. Courtesy of her, I do not need to have any contact with the other servants either. She brings meals to my parlour, where there is a little table for this purpose and it makes sense for us to eat there together, which means I have some adult company, at least. Evidently, she is a bright, trustworthy girl who is aware that there is some mystery governing the odd nature of my isolation from the family, but she has been well schooled in the discretionary aspects of her position. At first, I found her guarded and aloof but I believe we are beginning to like one another. I'm afraid that Lady McNair is mistaken, if she imagines that any two women can remain distant in the enclosed world in which we live and I am starting to receive limited information from my go-between. Last night, she told me that the other servants imagine that I am a heart-broken recluse, since you finished our engagement, James! Clearly, Alice is already sceptical of this idea, although I did not enlighten her. In this environment, I will have to remember, too, that I will have to guard my tongue! This morning she revealed also that it is common knowledge among the other servants that Victoria has her heart set on another son. In my current state of renewed joy in my own child, I can only wish her a safe delivery, despite all the grief she has caused me. Indeed now I am with Alex, I feel much more positive about *this imminent event. He is so utterly adorable, I cannot envisage Victoria could do other than love him and it is possible, I suppose, that motherhood might ultimately cause her to reflect on what she did to me, with a greater degree of remorse and understanding.*

I will write again soon with all my news, as I miss you both.

Love
Mhairi-Anne

Having finished reading over her letter, Mhairi-Anne folded it into an envelope and sealed it carefully, just as the door to the attic parlour opened and Alice came in, bearing a tea tray, heaped with hot scones, raspberry jam and butter.

'They look and smell delicious,' said Mhairi-Anne, clearing away her writing materials from the table in front of her, so that Alice could lay down her burden. 'Can you post this for me?' she asked.

'Of course.' Alice took the envelope and put it in the large pocket of her immaculate white apron, before she joined Mhairi-Anne at the table.

In her early twenties, Alice had already been spotted by Lady McNair, as a girl with potential to rise through the ranks, some time before Rowena realized she had need of a special maid to ensure the arrangement with Mhairi-Anne could work with minimum intrusion on the family. Smart and slim in her appearance, with brown eyes and dark hair worn up in a neat knot, on which her white frilly cap sat perfectly balanced, she was a pretty girl, but not in an ostentatious way, which Lady McNair might have considered unsuitable. This job, Rowena had told her prior to Mhairi-Anne's arrival, required special qualities and would be a particular test of her discretion and initiative, as well as her ability to follow precise instructions unquestioningly. Alice had naturally been flattered to be chosen for such an unusual assignment and, since Mhairi-Anne's arrival, she had had no cause to regret her involvement, although already she somehow felt sorry for this beautiful woman and she was certain that empathy was not part of her remit.

'Be helpful, co-operative and friendly to a degree, Alice,' Lady NcNair had instructed her. 'But always remember where your loyalties lie and that in such a special position, you're being paid not to carry gossip.'

As she and Mhairi-Anne shared the scones she had brought direct from the oven in the kitchen, she remembered her employer's words, but decided that the news she might impart was fact — not tittle-tattle.

'Young Mrs McNair has taken to her bed,' she revealed. 'The doctor's been sent for and so has Mr Alexander.'

Mhairi-Anne digested this revelation with apparent calm. 'I hope it's all over quickly for her.'

'You never had children?'

The question startled Mhairi-Anne and her face flushed, before Alice added swiftly, 'I mean — when you were married.'

'My husband died three months after our wedding,' revealed Mhairi-Anne carefully. 'I suppose it wasn't meant to be.' She stood up, dusting the crumbs from her lips with her napkin. 'I'd better check on Alex.'

When Mhairi-Anne returned to the parlour with Alex bouncing in her arms, Alice was clearing the table.

'Do you think he would like a scone?' she asked. 'It's a pity to take this one back to the kitchen.' She held it aloft in front of Alex, who promptly gave a squeal of appreciation and lunged for it.

Mhairi-Anne laughed. 'I think a little cut up on a plate will suffice.'

'Will I fetch his high chair?'

'No, I'll sit here with him on my lap.'

'Alice! Alice! Where the devil are you?' The unmistakable male voice rose in the attic corridor, as Alice handed Mhairi-Anne the plate.

'Good heavens! It's the master!' exclaimed Alice, her voice perched precariously between a whisper and a screech.

'Quickly! Go and see what he wants,' hissed Mhairi-Anne.

Alice sped into the corridor to be confronted by Alexander.

'I've been pulling that blasted bell for all of five minutes, Alice,' he informed her brusquely.

'But there must be something wrong with it, sir. I mean, sorry, sir! But it never rang up here. We'd have heard it for sure. But I'm very sorry all the same.'

Alexander nodded, reining in his temper. 'I'll have it looked at. I wanted to tell you, my wife won't wish to see Alex tonight. Her confinement has started. In fact, I think it would be better if he remained in the nursery meantime. I don't want him alarmed . . . if there is any . . . er . . . excitement. I'm sure you know what I mean.'

'Of course, sir.'

'Where is he now?'

'In the parlour with Mrs Graham, sir. Do you want to see him?'

Listening, Mhairi-Anne noted the distinct pause, before he said abruptly, 'No — I'll have that bell seen to immediately. I'll ring in the morning with fresh instructions.'

Alice returned to the parlour, as his footsteps receded down the corridor. Mhairi-Anne, head lowered, continued to feed Alex the crumbs of scone from the plate, as if she had not heard the hurtful words that told her he could not even bear to look at her.

'Phew! He was angry, but he's not usually like that. Always so charmin' an' handsome an' — ' She stopped abruptly, realizing her tongue was running away from her brain. 'But you know him yourself, don't you?'

Mhairi-Anne looked her squarely in the eye. 'Yes, of course, I know him.' She paused before wiping Alex's chin. 'I think he's had enough scone for one day.'

Alice took the nearly empty plate, which Mhairi-Anne handed to her and put it on the tray with the others, before she murmured, 'I expect he was angry because he's worried. Bound to be! It's not every day your wife has a baby, is it?'

As if to underline this point, the two women looked at each other in silence, when a thin, distant scream reached their ears.

'No wonder he wants Alex kept up here,' Alice said, her voice a respectful whisper, which seemed somehow appropriate in the circumstances.

It was the beginning of a very long night.

Although very few other such distinct sounds reached the attic floor, Mhairi-Anne hardly slept at all through the hours of darkness, as she was acutely aware that there was activity below. Numerous times, she heard the muffled pad of rapid footsteps and the indistinguishable rumble of voices rose and fell in intermittent waves. All of it brought back vivid memories of the terrifying night she had spent in the house in the Perthshire glen, giving birth to Alex, attended only by a midwife, whom she increasingly feared was not up to the job. Victoria had held her hand through those dark hours — yet all the time she had hated her.

Silence cocooned the house, as the first streaks of dawn light sprayed up into the sky, but Mhairi-Anne rose then to wash and dress, before she sat down by the attic window to watch morning creep quietly over the grounds outside. Mist rose off the river in thick banks, which dispersed like the ghosts of ancient dragons, to snake over the lawns, leaving trails of dew. An aching wave of loneliness swept over her. She had suggested in her letter to James and Calum that she was not a prisoner, but she was a leper, living a

296

separate existence alongside all she loved most and all who hated her most. At that moment, the desire to feel Alexander's arms around her was a physical hunger and, for the first time, she began to appreciate the full enormity of the difficulties which lay ahead.

One look at her son, sitting in his high chair for breakfast that morning, was enough to dispel her lingering gloom, however. Already, he was attempting to say her name — and although there was a cruel irony in the way he tried to shape the words, which came out as 'Ma-man', her delight was free of bitterness.

'The bell's working!' Alice said suddenly, rising from the table, as the first sounds reached their ears. 'I'd better get down.'

Minutes later, she was back with her instructions.

'I've to take Alex down to see his new sister!' she exclaimed excitedly. Only then, did the strangeness of the situation strike her and she looked at Mhairi-Anne, with a helpless shrug. 'I . . . I expect you'll see her, too, some time.' As she lifted Alex from his chair, she added softly, 'I'll clear up the breakfast things, when I get back.'

Mhairi-Anne nodded, summoning a bright smile, as she ensured that Alex's face was free of egg. 'Be a good boy,' she murmured, before kissing his forehead.

As soon as Alice had departed with the child, she went to the window to look out again, but this time, despite the tears which glittered in her eyes, she steeled herself against the emotions which were threatening to engulf her. She had to learn to live like this, she thought determinedly. There was no alternative. After all, she'd had plenty of practice in being an outsider, separated, as it were, by glass — none more so, than during her years as James's mistress on Tora. At least here, she would be spared the contemptuous looks and evil sniggers of those on the other side.

As she turned back to the table, to begin stacking the breakfast dishes on to a tray for Alice, she sighed, nevertheless, as she wondered if there would ever be a time in her life, when the glass would shatter and she would be welcomed inside.

19

'A beautiful granddaughter! I can scarcely believe it,' said Lady McNair, over the dinner-table that evening, although she wished that her outer display of happiness did not resonate with such a hollow feeling inside.

Nothing, these days, could lift entirely the sense of impending doom which seemed to shadow her heart. Every morning, she awoke to a new awareness of the transience of life; every night she went to bed with anxious prayers on her lips, that they might all be spared to live another day. In between times, she was generally able to rationalize her feelings of foreboding. They were simply a product of the terrible stresses and strains of recent months, she had told herself resolutely only that day and surely now she should be pleased that things were settling down. A war over their grandson had been avoided; he was still safely with them in the nursery; they had a new life to celebrate.

'As soon as Victoria is recovered, we'll need to start planning for the christening,' she resumed, determined to be cheerful.

'Have you decided on her name yet, Alexander?' asked Isobel.

'Victoria was so certain we'd have a boy, we never discussed girls' names.'

'My great grandmother was called Gwendoline,' remarked Rowena. 'I've always loved that name, although I never knew her.'

'Gwendoline,' mused Isobel. 'Yes, I like that, too.'

Alexander smiled tolerantly. 'I'll tell her!'

'Is she still asleep?' asked his father.

Alexander nodded. 'Last time I looked in.'

'I think I slept for all of twenty-four hours after you were born, Alexander,' said his mother.

'So did I!' recalled Sir David wryly. 'Although I did nothing, of course, except strut and worry.'

'I expect we'll all sleep soundly tonight,' commented Isobel, noting the shadows under her brother-in-law's eyes. 'In fact, if you'll excuse me, I think I'll have an early night.'

As she suspected, this was all the excuse Alexander needed. 'Me, too! I'm exhausted.'

'You'll look in on Victoria and the baby again, won't you?' queried Rowena as they both rose.

'Of course, if I can get past that virago of a nurse,' said Alexander, dropping his napkin on the table.

Lady McNair smiled. 'I've noticed she's a trifle over-enthusiastic about her guard duties.'

'I certainly wouldn't like to meet her on a dark night,' quipped Sir David, as Alexander and Isobel departed.

Left alone, Sir David eyed his wife speculatively. 'You look worried now the audience is gone. Nothing wrong in the attic, is there?'

'No everything's fine. She's settled in remarkably well, I think.' She paused, before adding pensively, 'I know I shouldn't, but I like her more every time I meet her.'

'No, you shouldn't,' agreed Sir David. 'But I've been thinking myself lately that it's a pity about this business. I suppose she must be genuinely fond of the boy, since she agreed to what we asked. I hate to think of her shut up there, at times.'

'Well, I'm glad you listen to me sometimes,' murmured Rowena, weariness evident in her tone.

'You're tired — but there's something else annoying you, isn't there? The baby's all right, isn't she?'

'Yes, fine.'

'And Victoria?'

She shrugged. 'I expect she was just exhausted, but she seemed terribly disappointed that she had had a girl. I can't understand it really. You know how I'd have loved a daughter.' She paused before adding, 'Sometimes, I think I don't know her at all nowadays.'

'I worry about Alexander. Do you think he'll move back now she's had the child?'

'I doubt it. The adjoining-room already looks like a nursery and Victoria's determined Gwendoline — or whatever we call her — won't go upstairs.'

'Does that mean we're going to need another nanny?'

'Looks like it, although not for a while yet. Nurse Rankin will be here for at least a month, to see she gets on her feet.'

'Alexander certainly won't move back there with that battle-axe around.'

'I can't see him moving back at all,' responded Lady McNair on a sigh.

'But he's too young to live like a monk, Rowena.'

'I know! So was your brother.'

Sir David's snort gave way to a pensive frown. 'Talking of James, I think I'd like to write to him now. Try to patch things up. What do you say?'

'Why not! We could invite him and Calum to the christening.'

Meanwhile, upstairs, Alexander had said goodnight to Isobel and went to see his wife and child. Nurse Rankin shot out of her chair like a jack-in-the-box, as soon as he entered.

'She's still asleep!' the woman hissed immediately, in a whisper which might have sliced iron.

Before Alexander could respond, Victoria opened her eyes and contradicted her. 'No, I'm not.'

'Well, you should be!' declared Nurse Rankin, turning on her patient.

'Give me five minutes with my husband.'

Nurse Rankin folded her arms tightly beneath her ample bosom, causing it to bulge even more aggressively. 'Five minutes then, and not a second longer.'

Alexander, meantime, had taken it upon himself to go into the adjoining room to peep into the cradle, where his daughter lay oblivious to the world — an initiative which instigated a charge across the room, when he was spotted.

'You're determined to wake them both up, I see.'

Alexander subjected her to a melting smile. 'She's beautiful, isn't she?'

'Not when she's crying, she's not,' retorted the nurse, although her voice had lost its cutting edge. 'You have five minutes. She has a bit of a temperature and needs rest. I'll shut this door, so you won't wake up Baby.'

Alexander returned to the room where Victoria lay, head propped up on strategically positioned pillows. She patted the edge of the bed for him to sit, but he drew in a chair.

'How are you feeling? She says your temperature is up.'

'That woman would make anyone's temperature rise,' she muttered disdainfully. 'I don't think I'll be able to stand her a week, far less a month.'

'You sound fighting fit, at any rate.'

'I'm certainly glad it's all over,' she responded, although her voice appeared far from glad and after a pause, she added, 'I was hoping for a boy.'

'She's healthy — that's all that matters.'

'Is it? Not when it comes to the McNair fortune, it isn't.'

'We already have a son.'

She looked away from him, eyes fixed on the ceiling. 'You do!'

'Mother's been asking about names,' he said brightly, determined to change the subject. 'She's already thinking about the christening.'

She looked back at him. 'Always full of plans, isn't she? I expect she's picked out the name, as well.'

'We'll choose the name.'

'But she had some suggestions, surely?'

He sighed briefly. 'She likes Gwendoline.'

'We were set on Charles, if it was a boy. Why not Charlotte?'

He shrugged. 'Charlotte she is then.'

'You don't even care, do you?' she muttered, accusingly.

'Of course, I care!' he hissed back at her.

'If she was a boy, you would.'

He opened his mouth to respond, but instead, stood up. 'My five minutes are up.'

'How is the lady in the attic?' she asked abruptly, her eyes hardening, as she gazed up at him narrowly.

'How would I know?'

'Alice mentioned this morning that you went up there yesterday because the bell wasn't working.'

'I didn't see her.'

'But you wish you had!'

A nasty smile spread over her face and, as he stared back at her, he swallowed twice on the sick feeling of hate, which rose from his stomach to scald his throat.

'Time up!'

He spun away from the bed gratefully as Nurse Rankin's voice rose behind him. 'I'll say goodnight then.'

Beads of perspiration broke out on his forehead, as he strode back along the corridor to his own room. She could still turn the knife of guilt in him, like no other, and all because of that stupid escapade yesterday, he thought, thrusting his door open and banging it angrily behind him. There had been nothing wrong with the bell to Alice's room, but there had been something wrong in his idiotic head. Possessed by one of his irresistible impulses, he had suddenly felt compelled to see her. Why had she accepted their invitation to come here? The question had hammered relentlessly at his brain since her arrival, making a mockery of all his theories that she cared nothing for the child and his resolution to despise her. But as soon as he had set foot on the attic floor, sense had prevailed. His mother had gone to all sorts of trouble to ensure they need have no contact and his wife was about to have a baby. What kind of moron was he, he had suddenly demanded, the compulsion turning then into rage against himself? Alice must have thought he was mad!

His boots kicked into a corner and his tie tossed on to his bed, he now headed purposefully for the brandy bottle. A large measure in his hand, he subsided into an armchair, where he took a long gulp, his intention being to get thoroughly drunk as quickly as possible, But thought intervened — raising images and memories and feelings he could not suppress. After a few minutes of staring blindly into space, he closed his eyes slowly and wept without a sound.

20

Nurse Rankin and baby Charlotte very quickly made their presence felt in the household. With her daily demands for pristine new linen, strict dietary requirements for her and her patient and militaristic cleaning regime, the nurse soon acquired enemies throughout the ranks of servants, while Charlotte's healthy lungs and evident temper soon had her known fondly as 'the little madam'.

Dr Morgan called twice a day to see his patients and happily reassured Alexander and his mother that there was absolutely nothing to worry about in Charlotte's frequent fits of crying, but he became increasingly concerned about Victoria, when her temperature continued to creep up and she began to show signs of a fever.

On the fourth day after the birth, there was a sudden deterioration in her condition. She complained of a severe, unrelenting headache and began to sweat and shiver, despite all attempts to alleviate her symptoms. Rowena became really worried when Nurse Rankin insisted that afternoon that Dr Morgan be summoned again, although he had visited that morning and, on her advice, Lady McNair also sent for Alexander to come home immediately.

In the attic, Alice arrived with their afternoon tea tray, as usual, and communicated news of the rising disquiet.

'They're sayin' in the kitchen that young Mrs McNair's not well.'

Mhairi-Anne frowned, as she lifted a pancake from the plate. 'What's wrong with her?'

Alice shrugged uncertainly. 'I heard the other day, she was runnin' a bit of a temperature, but they were sayin' that it was all down to that Nurse Spankin . . . '

'Nurse Spankin?' echoed Mhairi-Anne doubtfully.

'That's what they call her, on account of her bein' such a bossyboots. Rankin's her real name, I think. Anyway, they say she was insistin' on fires bein' lit, an' bed-warmers an' more blankets — in this warm weather, when nobody needs them.'

'Perhaps, Mrs McNair has a cold,' opined Mhairi-Anne.

Alice nodded, before taking an appreciative bite of her pancake. 'I expect so. The baby's fine, at any rate, although a squealer, according to all accounts.'

Later that evening, Alice took Alex downstairs, as usual, before his bed-time, but returned with him almost immediately, her frown telling Mhairi-Anne at once, that something was amiss.

'It's more than a cold wrong with Mrs McNair, I'm afraid. Lady McNair said we've to keep Alex up here in the meantime, as his mother's ill. An' the young master was nowhere to be seen, although he's usually waitin' in the corridor to collect him.'

'Ma-Man! Ma-Man!'

Mhairi-Anne took Alex, who was bouncing in the maid's arms and calling her name.

'Maybe she's infectious,' continued Alice, her brown eyes large and fearful.

'I expect it's just a precaution,' responded Mhairi-Anne, trying to calm the young maid. 'She'll probably be fine in the morning.'

The following day, however, when Alice came with the breakfast tray at seven o'clock as usual, the news was no better.

'Everybody's in a right state down there. That nurse is not lettin' anybody in the room now, except the family, and they say they've been up all night. It must be bad, they reckon, because the doctor didn't go home either.'

Remembering how Flora and John could exaggerate, Mhairi-Anne tried once more to make light of the situation, but their conversation over breakfast was desultory.

Mhairi-Anne was about to go and fetch Alex from his cot, when they heard footsteps in the corridor of the attic.

'Somebody's coming'!' whispered Alice, springing to her feet, as the door to the parlour suddenly opened.

Alice's mouth gaped, while Mhairi-Anne slowly rose to her feet at the sight of Alexander — haggard and unshaven.

'I'd like to speak to Mrs Graham alone for a moment, Alice,' he said, his voice sounding surprisingly normal, considering his dishevelled appearance.

'Certainly, sir.' She glanced at Mhairi-Anne. 'I'll go and see to master Alex.'

As soon as the door closed quietly behind Alice, he resumed, 'Victoria is seriously ill. Septicaemia — blood-poisoning has set in.'

Mhairi-Anne dropped back down in her chair, her face blanching.

'It's only . . . a matter of time,' he added, his voice cracking.

She looked up at him, her heart seeming to race into her throat. 'What do you want me to do?'

'She's delirious, but she keeps saying your name. I think she wants to see you. Will you come down with me?'

She rose immediately and he went ahead of her into the corridor again, where she called for Alice, who emerged from Alex's bedroom, holding the child in her arms.

'Give Alex his breakfast and look after him, Alice. I'm going with Mr McNair for a time.'

Alice nodded, while Alex — seeming to sense something was amiss — stared soberly at his father, his eyes large and unblinking.

Alexander bent and kissed his child's forehead reassuringly, before he turned away and Mhairi-Anne followed him, although Alex proceeded to wail her name.

They did not speak until they were outside Victoria's room, where he paused in front of the closed door.

'Father and Isobel have gone to try to get some sleep, but mother's there and Dr Morgan and the nurse. I have to warn you, she's not a pretty sight. She was quiet when I left, but it's not easy to look at her.'

She nodded briefly, steeling herself, as he opened the door.

Daylight was still shut out of the room by heavy curtains and the artificial light added to her feeling that she was entering another world. Dr Morgan stood looking grim and helpless on the far side of the bed, while Lady McNair sat in a chair next to him, her head down in an attitude of prayer, replicated by

312

the nurse who sat alongside her. Victoria lay propped up on pillows in the bed, her face a ghastly bluish-grey mask, cruelly at odds with the vital quality of the lustrous dark hair, which cascaded over the pillow and which was the only reminder of the fact that she was not yet twenty-two years of age. Despite the bowls of rose petals which adorned the room, the smell of death was unmistakeable. Alexander grasped Mhairi-Anne's hand to lead her forward.

As they approached the bed, Lady McNair rose to greet them. She touched Mhairi-Anne's arm gently. 'This is good of you.' Then she looked up at her son and shook her head, before she took his fingers and pressed them to her lips. 'It's too late. She's gone.'

He exhaled loudly, as if he had been punched, before he wrapped his arms around his mother, who subsided against his chest.

Mhairi-Anne pressed Rowena's shoulder, as the woman started to weep quietly against her son, while she continued to stare disbelievingly at the immobile form on the bed. Despite all the grief that Victoria had caused her, she was relieved to find nothing but sadness and pity in her heart, but her throat was dry of any words.

From the adjoining room, baby Charlotte's cries spilled incongruously into the scene and, as the nurse rose to attend to her, Mhairi-Anne, feeling suddenly like an intruder, chose this moment to slip quietly away, leaving mother and son still locked in their grief-stricken embrace.

21

Although, in life, Victoria had been at the centre of much conflict, her funeral was marked by the beginnings of reconciliation. James and Calum came from Tora to attend, and the family was reunited by the fresh perspective that only death can achieve, with its devastating finality and speed. Attired in a mourning dress, loaned to her by Lady McNair, Mhairi-Anne, too, sat with Calum in the pew behind the family in the little church on the estate, which was packed to capacity with mourners inside and outside, in the grounds. Victoria had not been well known within the world of the estate, but Alexander's personal popularity drew throngs of people — even from the district beyond — anxious to unload their burden of sympathy on the passing of his young wife — or eager to indulge their voyeuristic curiosity about the effects of death, that great equalizer, on those affluent individuals, with whom they had normally little in common.

After the service in the church, the crowds were dispersed, before the coffin was solemnly borne outside, to the strains of a lament by a lone piper, for another short service of internment over the grave in the cemetery behind, next to Lady McNair's rose garden. Only the family attended this and Mhairi-Anne walked back to the house on Calum's arm, but James accompanied his brother, his wife, Isobel and Alexander for the most harrowing part of the ceremonial ritual.

While the minister presided over the service at the head of the grave, Sir David and Rowena sat at the side on chairs next to Isobel and James, and Alexander stood alone at the foot, as his wife's coffin was lowered gently into the earthy depths by four pallbearers. Garlands of white lilies, dotted with crimson roses soothed the steep edges, but nothing could disguise the nature of the deep, gaping hole in the ground, into which he looked with eyes so determinedly dry, they felt like burning coals.

'Ashes to ashes, dust to dust . . . ' The minister's voice droned on interminably, while Alexander's mind winged back to that freak summer day on Tora: the crashing sounds of the ocean and the screech of seabirds, and the terrifying, mindless rapidity with which he had blighted her young life. No matter what she had done, he thought, he was the worthless wretch, who had started her on this calamitous route to dust.

James sprang suddenly to his feet, as Alexander swayed under the relentless burden of his self-recriminations.

'Steady!' he murmured, grasping his nephew's arm.

The remaining excruciating minutes, as they stood shoulder to shoulder, finally marked their true forgiveness of one another.

★   ★   ★

'We'll be leavin' in a couple of hours,' Calum was meanwhile informing Mhairi-Anne, as they walked slowly along the path from the church.

'I think you'll be expected to stay longer,' she responded, as they had only arrived that morning.

'Aye, but we've explained to Sir David and Alexander, your replacement is comin' to Tora tomorrow an' we've no way of getting in touch with her. We'll need to be there to meet her, or she might turn round and head back for Lewis.' He paused, before adding, 'Besides — in the circumstances, James thought we'd better keep this visit short. We've all made up, but everybody's under a lot of strain. What the house needs now is some peace and quiet.'

'It's all so hard to believe, isn't it?'

'Aye, it is that.'

'I still wonder if she really wanted to see me and what we might have said?'

Calum sighed. 'Probably better the way it happened. You can imagine what you like.'

'We were friends once . . . '

'Aye, but you're still livin' wi' the legacy of what she did.'

'She paid a high price for it.'

'I always think that death has an uncanny way of raising folk to sainthood who were never due that honour in life. Don't persecute yourself with 'if onlys'. How're you managin', anyway?'

'Alex is a delight. I can't tell you what it means to wake up in the mornings and know he's there.'

'But it can't all be easy.'

'The hardest part is . . . I still love him, Calum. But he'll probably hate me all the more after this. Did you notice, he can hardly bear the sight of me?'

'I think he can hardly bear the sight of himself at the moment. He's a lot of healin' to do.'

As they reached the house, they stopped, and Mhairi-Anne turned to him. 'I probably won't get the chance, Calum, but will you tell James I miss him? I know I disappointed him coming here.'

318

'I'll tell him, but don't worry about him. He loves Tora more than anythin' or anybody, an' maybe he's lucky in that because he'll never lose it. The land has a kind of immortality, that you and I can only glimpse in the passin'.'

22

September was almost at an end and autumn was painting the leaves yellow, orange and brown, when Mhairi-Anne looked out of the attic parlour window one bright afternoon, after Alex had been taken downstairs, and decided to go for a walk in Lady McNair's rose garden, before the blooms entirely vanished. She had not been near the garden since Victoria's funeral, as she knew she would need to pass the grave, which she suspected would attract visitors for some time. However, she could turn back, if necessary, she thought, as she descended the long narrow servants' stair and stole outside into the crisp sunshine, which masqueraded as summer.

It was colder than she had expected and she was glad she had thought to bring her red woollen shawl, which she gathered over her shoulders, as she walked smartly down the path towards the church. A hat might have been a good idea, too, she mused, as the breeze lifted the tendrils of her hair, which had escaped its plait, and rustled ominously through the dying leaves on the trees around the church, as she hurried beneath their waving shadows on to the path beside the church, where she paused to check first that the cemetery beyond was deserted.

Still covered with wreaths, Victoria's grave was easy to spot, and she walked more slowly now, over to the path, which ran parallel to the row of elaborate tombstones, marking the resting places of long dead ancestors of the McNairs, before she reached the island of withering flowers, next to the black marble headstone over the more recent grave of Alexander's brother, Eric. No doubt, in due course, a tombstone would be erected for Alexander's wife, she thought, but, for the moment, there was only a wooden cross with VICTORIA inscribed on it and the mass of decaying blooms, which were already being ravaged by the breeze. Everything was dying, it seemed, and a fresh sadness hung in a pall over the spot. She remembered the first time she had met Victoria on Tora, when she had fled to the island in the wake of her father's suicide — so young, so seemingly vulnerable — and so eager to be friends. Her desperate love of Alexander and her hatred of her had changed all that, but they had all been to blame, in different ways, she concluded. If only . . . was the relentless lament of life.

She picked up the stray petal of a sugar

pink rose and held it briefly beneath her nostrils, before she walked thoughtfully on to the iron gate into the walled rose garden. As she lifted the latch and the gate swung open, it was only then that she saw Alexander sitting on one of the benches, evidently deep in thought. He looked up, as the gate yawned noisily on its hinges and saw her. There was no going back or forward, until he stood up and beckoned to her. She walked forward then, her heart beginning to knock against her ribs, while he put his hands in his pockets and waited.

He looked leaner and older, she thought and there was a weariness about his broad shoulders, which plucked at her emotions. Unsmiling and uncertain, they looked at one another for a long moment in silence, as if testing the possibilities of this chance meeting, before he said, 'Let's walk.'

'I thought you would be with Alex,' she murmured tentatively, as they made their way slowly along one of the paths.

'I saw him this morning. Anyway, I've been coming here a lot in the afternoons — hoping we might meet. I heard that my mother had allocated you this space.' She glanced up at him hopefully, but he was looking at a white rose bush where a few stalwart blooms held on to their beauty. 'I'm never far away,' she murmured, wondering why he had not sent for her, if he had something to say.

'Despite my mother's gallant attempts to keep the reins on gossip, I'm afraid your being here is still a subject for speculation. If I showed any interest in you, the tongues would be wagging before we had finished our conversation.' He paused, before adding, 'I owe Victoria respect in death — all the more so because I never loved her in life.'

She glanced up at him again, but it was as if he were hardly aware of her presence. 'We might be seen here.'

'Unlikely! My mother's the only regular visitor and she knows I intend to speak to you.'

She swallowed on the fear rising in her throat. Was he going to ask her to leave now there was no risk of charges being brought against Victoria? She clasped her shawl around her shoulders, her knuckles whitening, as she braced herself for the axe to fall.

'I'm going away for a time,' he revealed.

She gathered the shawl tighter under her chin, the action suddenly drawing his attention.

'Are you cold?'

His coolness was chilling her, but she shook her head jerkily. He was going to take Alex abroad again and she was to be sent packing. Why hadn't she listened to James?

They had reached one of the far corners of the garden and he stopped, turning towards her for the first time, but before he could utter the crushing words, all pride deserted her.

'Please don't take Alex! I couldn't bear to be parted from him again.'

The outburst of anguish evidently surprised him and he frowned at her, before he said slowly, 'But you'll bear being parted from me?'

'I've no claim on you.'

He smiled weakly. 'If only that were true, I might have been happily married.'

'I thought you despised me.'

'I certainly tried very hard.'

'You could hardly bear to look at me!' she accused, breathlessly.

He shrugged. 'I don't think I was aware of that, but it's sometimes hard to look at what we cannot have.'

He turned away suddenly and they began to walk again along the path adjacent to the back wall of the garden.

'I'm selfish — always have been,' he resumed, in a matter-of-fact tone. 'But, at the moment, I feel lost somehow — in a state of limbo. I can't go forward as I might wish and there's no going back. My mother thinks I need time to find myself — whatever that means — or so she says. She's probably afraid — as I am — that if I stay here at the moment, I'll make a mess of things again. And my father can manage without me for a time, the way things operate nowadays.'

Speech was now impossible for her. She looked away at the withering splashes of colours in the garden, blinking desperately on the glaze of tears forming in her eyes, as she wondered how she could appeal to him.

'I want to ask a favour of you.'

Head down, she did not dare look up.

'But you may not be interested.'

As she continued to take an inordinate interest in the ground, he added, 'Probably you won't be interested, as I know Alex will take up a lot of your time.'

Her head whirled immediately. 'You're . . . you're not taking him?'

He stopped, evidently bemused by the solitary tear which trickled down her face. 'I'm not handling this very well. I thought we'd established that I'm going away, but Alex will stay here with you.'

She smiled, causing further tears to cascade over her lashes. 'I thought you were taking him . . . '

His hands rose to hover, trembling, inches from her face, before he jerked them away and muttered tersely, 'Stop crying, for God's sake! Let me get through this with some dignity.'

He walked away ahead of her and she hurried to catch up, as she hastily rubbed her shawl over her face. 'Please, say what you want. I'm fine now.'

He stopped again, eyes narrowing on her, before he murmured, 'I wanted to ask if you'll look after Charlotte, as well.'

She was stunned. 'Victoria wouldn't have wanted that, would she?'

'Not if she'd lived,' he conceded. 'But — who knows — I might be deluding myself, but I like to imagine that, if she'd had time, in the end, she would have tried to make peace with you. I want Charlotte to be brought up with her brother and I don't want them scarred by our mistakes. So, will you look after Alex and her for me?'

A smile bloomed on her face. She wanted to laugh and jump and kiss him. But instead she said simply, 'Of course I will.'

'She's a screamer, I'm afraid. But beautiful . . . like her mother.'

'Alex needs some competition.'

He nodded. 'That's settled then.'

'Will you go abroad?'

'Abroad? No, I'm going back to Tora.

Seems an appropriate place to try to pick up the pieces.'

Despite his earlier annoyance, her eyes filled again. 'James and Calum will be . . . pleased.'

He looked at her, a glimmer of his old, dazzling smile tugging at his mouth, before he took her hand and raised her fingers briefly to his lips. 'Wait for me.'

We do hope that you have enjoyed reading this large print book.

Did you know that all of our titles are available for purchase?

We publish a wide range of high quality large print books including:
Romances, Mysteries, Classics
General Fiction
Non Fiction and Westerns

Special interest titles available in large print are:
The Little Oxford Dictionary
Music Book
Song Book
Hymn Book
Service Book

Also available from us courtesy of Oxford University Press:
Young Readers' Dictionary
(large print edition)
Young Readers' Thesaurus
(large print edition)

For further information or a free brochure, please contact us at:
Ulverscroft Large Print Books Ltd.,
The Green, Bradgate Road, Anstey,
Leicester, LE7 7FU, England.
Tel: (00 44) **0116 236 4325**
Fax: (00 44) **0116 234 0205**

Other titles published by
The House of Ulverscroft:

THE WITCHING WOMAN

Sarah Vern

Alexander McNair, son of the Laird of Strathcairn, cares little for his prospective inheritance of Tora, a Scottish island; and he is not pleased when his luxurious lifestyle is interrupted by an enforced visit . . . However, his attitude alters when he meets two women who dramatically affect his life. He becomes obsessed with an alluring young widow, Mhairi-Anne Graham. Nevertheless, he recklessly seduces the vulnerable Victoria Liversidge . . . On returning home, Alexander is unable to forget Mhairi-Anne. He is dismayed to discover that Victoria has a claim on him, and that, consequently, his family will be scandalized.

BRINGER OF CLOUDS AND RAIN

Wendy Hayden Sadler

Bringer of Clouds and Rain is a Chinese euphemism for 'Lady of the Night'. But why has the man she loves branded Maxine in this way? Having been betrayed by her fiancé, Jonathan, Maxine is whisked off to a holiday in Hong Kong with the mysterious Adam Warwick. Together, they discover Hong Kong . . . and each other. But Maxine becomes jealous as the secretive Adam spends time with the beautiful Eleanor. When Jonathan reappears, in an attempt to win back Maxine's affections, there follows a maelstrom of misunderstandings, culminating in the ultimate insult — Bringer of Clouds and Rain.